Mudlarks

&

Meadowlarks

Ellyn Peirson

I am immensely grateful to Andrew Ruhl, Evelyn Dunsmore and Sheila McLaren and to my cousin, Carol Smith, for their support and for their ability in the tough times to re-kindle my flickering writing flame.

This story, highly fabricated though it is, is written around my childhood understanding of a significant, singular incident in the life of my paternal grandfather. Because of my grandfather's life in London, England, on the Canadian prairies and in Toronto, I am here and writing this story about an unsung hero, a most ordinary man. I dedicate this book to him, Harry Westley, a mudlark of sorts who loved meadowlarks… and to the memory of his son, my father, Frank…

> *Twas on a Holy Thursday their innocent faces clean*
> *The children walking two & two in red & blue & green*
> *Grey headed beadles walk'd before with wands as white as snow*
> *Till into the high dome of Pauls they like Thames waters flow*
> *O what a multitude they seem'd these flowers of London town*
> *Seated in companies they sit with radiance all their own*
> *The hum of multitudes was there but multitudes of lambs*
> *Thousands of little boys & girls raising their innocent hands*
> *Now like a mighty wind they raise to heaven the voice of song*
> *Or like harmonious thunderings the seats of heaven among*
> *Beneath them sit the aged men wise guardians of the poor*
> *Then cherish pity, lest you drive an angel from your door*
>
> *[William Blake: married Catherine Boucher in 1782, saving both of them from having to return to St. James Workhouse in Soho, London]…*

MUDLARKS:

Our death certificates called it phthisis, Hippocrates' word. We called it "the white plague" – it was our Blitzkrieg, killing who knows how many and turning the survivors into mudlarks, a new community of sub-humans, sifting the filth of the Thames for a living. [Harry Westley, October, 1947]

MEADOWLARKS:

Did you hear that, Nell? That's the prairie meadowlark. When we first moved to Swift Current, a friend explained to me that they sang when the buffaloes roamed the prairies. [Harry Westley to Nell, June, 1947]

Table of Contents

London

I wander thro' each charter'd street,
Near where the charter'd Thames does flow.
And mark in every face I meet
Marks of weakness, marks of woe.

In every cry of every Man,
In every Infants cry of fear,
In every voice: in every ban,
The mind-forg'd manacles I hear

How the Chimney-sweepers cry
Every blackning Church appalls,
And the hapless Soldiers sigh
Runs in blood down Palace walls

But most thro' midnight streets I hear
How the youthful Harlots curse
Blasts the new-born Infants tear
And blights with plagues the Marriage hearse

       William Blake

William Blake, visionary, artist, poet, was born in Soho, London, England in 1757. Blake was profoundly affected by his mother's role as his teacher and with the consequences of the Industrial Revolution. Unrecognized and unappreciated during his life, Blake now stands as one of the most outstanding artists and poets of his era.

Harry Westley, youngest of eight children, writer, musician, father, was born in Mile End New Town, London, England in 1882. Harry's London, the Cockney slums of squalor, disease and workhouses, was the London Blake foreknew. Harry's gift to his progeny was to establish life in Canada and to take the family Bible with him across the Atlantic.

Every line of Blake's "London" is also Harry's London. It is time for his story to be told.

Nell Westley, Toronto, 1994

1. *There are times when ancestors make themselves known*

Ah! The sense of completion was profound. After sitting on the steps and becoming encapsulated in un-time, I moved into the sanctuary. I took the Schoolboy in. And I whispered to Harry! I went up to the dome, and I whispered into the whispering gallery so that I could be heard 45 metres away, across the dome. "Are you happy to be here, Grandpa? Are you?" And Harry heard me. I knew it. And probably Sarah heard me. Only I didn't know her then. Bless Sir Christopher Wren and his harnessing of angels.

And so I now "see" that the angels of St. Paul's heard me. And I know it was meant to be. For Harry's soul and Sarah's soul. And for mine. I can do this "seeing"... because I've heard the whispering energy of angels in other places.

(Nell Westley, April, 1980)

Nell sat down at her desk to write an email. The keyboard clicked away as she established a rhythm. It was after 11:00, her best time to write. Happy "night hawk" that she was, she was intent on something important. With unruly blond hair and in blue pyjamas, she looked as though she were trying to meet a deadline for a university course.

May 3, 1999

My dear friend,

The time has come, your body says. And you wonder if you've been with an angel and if you've had the omen you've been looking for in this long migration of your soul, and I tell you, yes, you have been in communion with an angel, a particular angel. And I have reasons for knowing.

Ellyn Peirson

So, the other day, when you were waiting for more tests, and that man peeked his head around the screen? Well, you were right on both counts. He was an angel. And the event was an omen. Here was this ordinary, soft-spoken man, appearing out of the blue to tell you to go West, of all directions, for your transplant. In less than five minutes, you had the crucial choice of your whole life to date presented to you through this man who appeared on the other side of the hospital curtain and disappeared, leaving nothing but everything. And doors are opening. Dare I say once more, "Out of the blue"?

And the most I tell you initially is that I know exactly what angel it is. Your angel, I say, is the hospital angel who visited me in a Toronto hospital a few years ago, wanting an end to an old pain. I knew your experience was with this angel from the moment you began to tell me what happened at the hospital. Once you opened the door with your wonder about an angel and an omen, I knew I would eventually have to tell you. The truth.

Now it's time for the truth. Let me tell you about my hospital angel before you decide.

And all of this will be woven into a story, for you, the consummate story-buff.

Let me introduce you to the hospital angel. You need an understanding of this before I let the story unfold. I've never attempted any unfolding with this story, so I have no idea where we'll be going.

As I say, almost five years ago, I was visiting someone in hospital in Toronto. The circumstances are irrelevant. What matters is that it was old and repetitive and therefore painful. Transformation was necessary. At the moment I was feeling saddest and this dearest person was in pain, I was compelled to look up toward the door into the busy hospital corridor. A man walked by the door. He had thick, wavy black hair with a few streaks of white in it. Although rather short, he carried himself well, appearing taller. He was well-dressed with a sienna-orange, long-sleeved shirt on, his left side toward me just enough for me to see the small breast pocket with a couple of pens peering out. In his mid-sixties, he was handsome, with a neat moustache, and he exuded a rather serious and very solitary intent. He was oh, so definitely alone.

5

The sense of non-time was strong. And I almost got it. But no! That could not be! I stared at the doorway in disbelief after the man had disappeared. He must have been someone coming to visit some patient, a hospital visitor detracting me from the truth and steering me into fantasy… that "wishful thinking" that my mother had often accused me of exercising.

And then he walked by again, oppositely profiled, seeming to be now the only person in the whole hospital.

Dad?

But you've been gone for a decade and more, though not gone. I have your ring – here, on my middle finger – to prove it, to prove that you're gone, though not gone.

And he was gone. I hurried to the doorway.

Gone. Like the train station angel he told me about when I was little. Gone. Though not gone. Gone, leaving the promise of life.

Gone. Though not gone. Gone again, now leaving you, dear friend, with options and choices and life.

And have I not often told you how much you remind me of him? My Frank.

And when you told your father, Frank, about this, did he not say, in complete opposition to what you've ever known about him, "Was this the omen you've been hoping for?"

Indeed, dear friend, indeed. You are in the best of company as you begin this difficult, final leg of your healing journey. My angel, Frank, recognised by your Frank, is less than a breath away.

This is a strange story about a small family becoming smaller. As I think about – because I can't stop now – I realize I need to set off on the story of an English explorer, coming to Canada, with a framework and some directions. Producer and director, my parts in this story-come-movie.

There will be invisible markers along the way because I'm beginning to see your point about markers. I was surprised when you asked me about my thoughts on markers some time ago. You provoked me to think about them when you said that perhaps my feeling about not needing one when I'm gone wasn't "correct", that others might want one about me. From me? Over me? To me? Prepositions fail. You cited your need to visit the marker for your grandmother on occasion and how you feel close to her there.

I wonder if you've considered the possibility that it's the invisible markers that count. Have you? Some stories are invisible markers. I'd venture to say that all poetry is replete with markers.

And our time frame? We'll be travelling back and forth, hither and yon, across the Atlantic, from the prairies to Toronto and London, and especially into the cloistered nooks and crannies of the mind and soul. There will be no constraints nor any need for meticulous, linear chronology.

Ah, and characters! I promise you characters full of character... and repression, love, repulsion, joy and sadness... all those common human chattels. And we'll simply let them talk and move and have their being and unobtrusively watch and listen to them on the invisible platforms of their lives.

You're probably wondering about genre now that I have you thoroughly confused. "Get on with it," did you say? Since you have such a love for stories and an eye for imperceptible nuances, I'm going to tell you that kind of story - a fable about invisibility, a novel about finally being heard, a saga about extraordinary markers where markers had appeared to disappear.

That's what we'll be following here - invisible markers. We can approach all of this in your territory of images and scenes. After all, who doesn't know about Shakespeare's truism that all life is a stage?

As with any stage, markers, visible and invisible, are important. After all, without props, there would be no play. Ah, but with books, we slip silently and seamlessly into the realm of invisibility.

As with any story, the clay is the guts of humanity. Blake called it Innocence and Experience. Or, if you will, Lyca, his Little Girl Lost, his signature Blakeian anagram, Lyca.

2. Some ancestors have completions to carry out

Awake, awake my little Boy!
Thou wast thy Mother's only joy:
Why dost thou weep in thy gentle sleep?
Awake! thy Father does thee keep.

O, what land is the Land of Dreams?
What are its mountains, and what are its streams?
O Father, I saw my Mother there,
Among the lillies by waters fair…

… "Father, O Father, what do we here,
In this land of unbelief and fear?
The Land of Dreams is better far
Above the light of the Morning Star."

[The Land Of Dreams, William Blake]

"Find me."

I heard a voice. I was sure of it… plaintive… far away. I'd been organising some old papers into 'pitch' and 'keep' files, and one had surprised me – a poem my grandfather had written the day I was born. Welcoming me! I'd never seen it… ever! I sat back in my chair to clear my head. And the plaintive voice had whispered. English, but not my grandfather. This was female.

"Find me." There it was again.

I wasn't sure what I was hearing (or was it feeling?), and I knew I was making this up, in a sense, in my head. But I let my curious, jumbled thoughts nudge me toward the basement. Why? More papers? Pictures? What? I ended up at the bottom of the stairs wondering why that poem had brought me here. Grandpa. The poem affirmed the connection we'd shared. And it now raised an old question. Who really were the Westleys in London? Why had Grandpa seemed so often sad, so often on the outside of things? Perhaps it had been our shared quieter natures that had created such a strong bond between us. Oh yes, he could bond, this excuse-me-for-being-here, brilliant, quiet Englishman.

No longer puzzled at finding myself in the basement, I looked around and up. Had I missed more Westley papers. All twelve and a half pounds (I weighed it before heading upstairs) of the book upstairs to my office, laid it down on the floor and wiped it off with the rag I'd been using to dust my computer. Merging the two time lines, so to speak.

So, there I was with the Westley family Bible. Just the two of us, with a century and more between us. I'd never looked at it since my sister had given it to me years ago. I'd merely known it shouldn't go astray. And now this little voice kept repeating her plaint, "Find me."

Who? Who are you?

The Bible opened up to the first in a few pages of hand-written family documentation. And there, in careful handwriting similar to my Grandfather's beautiful script, was the documentation of his family in England. His name amongst his seven siblings, his mother and his father.

MARRIAGES

Arthur Westley, aged 23 & Sarah Pegg, aged 22, February 10th, 1867

Arthur Westley (2nd marriage) & Lucretia Sharp, (2nd marriage), August 3rd, 1891

Arthur Westley, Jr., 24, & Alice Mosden, 22, August 27th, 1893

Charles Westley, 24, & Alice Tickner, 22, March 31st, 1900

Harry Westley, 28, & May Graham, 26th, September 7th, 1910

CHILDREN'S BIRTHS, *22 Buxton Street, London Mile End New Town*

Arthur, August 14th, 1868

Edith,   December 31st, 1871

Ernest, April 25th, 1874

Charles, June 1st, 1876

Herbert, August 3rd, 1878

Walter   , December 22nd, 1879

Ellen, April 22nd, 1881

Harry, August 26th, 1882

DEATHS

Edith, February 8th, 1873, 1½ years

Ellen, 1881

Walter, November 28th, 1881, 2 years

Mother: Sarah, February 13th, 1888, 43 years

Herbert, November 24th, 1891, 13¼ years

Ernest, April 30th, 1892, 18 years

Arthur (Jr.), November 19th, 1894, 26¼ years

Father: Arthur, December 13th, 1896, 53 years

I stared at the sad statistics of Grandpa's family's life, the impetus for his emigration to Canada for good things in a New World. I felt overwhelmed at what had led to my family life in Canada. There, within the pages of an old Bible, was the name of the voice that had been waiting patiently and persistently for over a hundred years to be acknowledged and believed. And heard… above all, heard—listened to—because we can't fully leave this realm until our story is acknowledged and finished. Someone must hear us and weave our story into some kind of fabric, receptive and complete. Sarah Pegg, wife of Arthur Westley, mother of eight children, two of whom survived into enduring adulthood. Sarah Pegg, dead and gone from her family's history at age forty-three. I had never heard of her—from anyone—and had never taken the time to delve into the Bible (how did it get here, to Canada?) and find this modest genealogy. But I knew it was Sarah's voice I'd heard—Sarah who had spoken to me. I had a compelling sense that she was speaking and needing something.

Oh, Sarah, how patient of you! You must be so very weary.

I couldn't escape her voice. Nor did I want to. I became wilfully possessed by this woman who had made it possible for me to be here, this Sarah Pegg, of whom I knew nothing. Nothing.

This Sarah Pegg, of whom I must know everything. Everything.

Help me find you, Sarah. No one but Sarah could hear me. No one but Sarah, sad mother of eight children. Sad mother of six dead children and two who had left for Canada because the rest of her descendants must be born there, across the great Atlantic Divide.

And so began my journey of listening, to the inaudible, to the stories of one of London's tattered children.

3. Ancestors visit in dreams

Spadina Road Dream

I was with a group of people on a boat, going to Toronto Island, when someone began talking about a "museum tour" of a house on Spadina Road. We all became enthused and decided to forego going to Toronto Island. As happens in dreams, we were then at Spadina Road, and it all seemed so familiar to me. It was a huge old home with wonderful woodwork. I recognized it as 176 Spadina Road. As the group and I began to walk around inside the house, I noticed pictures outside the doors in the house. I went closer to inspect. There was Auntie Ada's picture with a write-up on her under the photo. She looked lovely and vibrant. There were a number of people reading the article and looking into the room. I was so happy for her - that she was finally recognized. I began to tell my group of people about the house and the history, and we all moved on together while I told the stories. All the other people in the house joined us to listen. As we all moved along, there were doors for Fred Bowman and all the others – Auntie Ada, Grandma, Grandpa and rooms for Susie and Tom, whom I couldn't remember. I was very happy to see Fred's door and loved telling stories about him – his New York accent and mannerisms, his big and happy presence, the way he could cook and tell stories and "fluff up" the rooms where guests gathered. It was such a blissful time with all these people, moving with and telling them the stories of all the fabulous photographs and rooms. There was a wondrous, silvery light permeating the house. I had the sense of Grandpa being there, almost behind me, rather than being invisible. And I had the sense of Grandma being up the stairs we had yet to climb. When I woke, my abiding impression of the dream was celebration and connection.

And then I wondered why none of the pain had been present.

Nell, 24/05/2001, Lake Huron

SCENE ONE—Regina, June 7, 1947

Regina is parched and hot. The omniscient eye of the camera pans down on a mother pushing a toddler in a pram and our four-year-old, dressed in a yellow gingham sun dress and straw hat and riding a kiddie-car. Nell stays ahead of the pram. There is no talk as the little trio crosses a huge barren field, walks past what is euphemistically called "The Cow Palace", a building used for farm exhibits and auctions, and onto Dewdney Avenue with its pride-inducing hand-planted trees, and passes by the front of the Grey Nuns' Hospital, where both children had been born. After this long trek, it is easier travelling to Elphinstone Street, where Grandma Westley lives in a small grey stucco house. No garden here, just a brutal caragana hedge and a few vegetables struggling to survive.

LOIS *(there at last, the thirty-four-year-old mother, with the long, long chestnut hair rolled into a knot and the blue dress patterned with large fuchsias, takes the baby out of the pram and cautions Nell.):* "Stay put!" *(She is tense and hot. She walks up the stairs and enters the porch door to knock at the inner door. Nell doesn't budge.)*

MAY *(a conventional sixty-year-old woman, wearing an apron over a crisp white house dress, opens the door):* "Ah, good, you're here! *(She takes baby Meg and ushers Lois into the house; turning, she speaks to Nell.)* Now you just do what you always do, dear, and don't go any further than the water pump."

NELL *(smiling wanly, is obviously hot and thirsty):* "Yes, Grandma Westley." *(Off she pedals on her little kiddie-car, out from the yard onto the street, with its typical wooden sidewalk, to begin the routine she has come to accept. The camera pans out to take in the other small houses, some of them wartime houses, and the communal water pump at the end of the street. The street is empty. Nell goes as far as the water pump where she stops and alternates between looking and appearing to wait for something. She perks up when she eyes the "foster girls" who work for her grandmother, walking her way.)*

FIRST FOSTER GIRL *(pulling the wagon with her left hand and pointing with her right):* "There's her granddaughter again, not allowed in because she might move the furniture out of place. Poor kid! Sometimes I think we would be better off back with our own families, instead of living with Mrs. W. She's so fussy!"

SECOND FOSTER GIRL *(shading her eyes with her left hand and looking at the little girl at the water pump):* "Yah, you'd think the kid's mother would speak up for her. But I wouldn't want to get Mrs. Westley mad at me. Once was enough! Anyway, you have to feel sorry for her with her husband going back to England. They're almost all packed for the move. Hey – maybe we're her new husbands!" *(Both girls, wearing identical house dresses, one in yellow and one in green, are laughing as they approach the water pump. The teenagers smile at Nell and begin pumping four pails of water that they place on their wagon.)*

NELL *(Waiting, she smiles eagerly in response. When the pumping is complete, the First Foster Girl picks up a cup from the wagon and scoops water out of a pail, offering the cup to Nell. Nell drinks without stopping.):* "Thank you. It's good!"

"Bye, Kid!" *(The girls say good-bye in unison and trundle off, slopping minimal amounts of water into the wagon. Nell watches until they go into Grandma Westley's yard. She resumes her routine. Back again to the opposite corner. Back and forth, back and forth, obediently, knowing that Grandma Westley cannot let her in for fear that she might move one of the chairs in the living room off its designated floorboard. Back and forth…)*

END OF SCENE

4. *All ancestors are migrants, seekers, weavers*

97 degrees today. The children and I went downtown by taxi with Mrs. W. to see her off. Frank and Dad also went to the station. I kept the kiddies and we stayed to see the Arcade to start off the Fair. Home at noon. Tonight Dad was feeling in fine form so he went out to get a dozen beers. Poor Dad. We enjoyed the evening.
[*The Lois Diaries, July 28, 1947*]

The first child of his parents' progressively loveless marriage, Frank Westley was born in Regina, Saskatchewan, on July 15, 1911, ten months after his father had married his mother on rebound.

His father, Harry, had come to Canada from London, England, to prepare the way for his fiancée, Annie, of whom little is known, except for Harry's quietly ardent and lifelong love for her. Frank's mother, May, an officer in the Salvation Army, was as thoroughly Canadian as anyone could be in those early pre-WW1 years. Oddly enough, Harry, who believed in the Mind as Supreme, found and married May, who believed in Hell, Fire and Brimstone as the tenacious offerings of a Supreme God (Mind, if you will) shortly after his Annie wrote to say that she wouldn't be coming to Canada. Her father was ill, and she must stay to look after him. May in Canada lived with the spectre of Annie in London for all of her troubled marriage to Harry and, I suspect, never let him forget it.

By the time Della Iris arrived, five years after Frank Edgar, May's pattern of antipathy had fixed itself firmly and repetitiously to Frank's intelligent and sensitive soul. Della Iris (Harry called her Della, May called her Iris) involuntarily opened the divide between the parents to manifest itself in a split down the centre of the family. May and her daughter, Iris, shared a bedroom from then on, and Harry and his son, Frankie, shared another bedroom, or what constituted as one, in their history of Ontario and Saskatchewan homes. Needless to say, these homes were all humble. For, despite his brilliance, Harry had left school in London when he was eleven to hawk newspapers on the steps of St. Paul's Cathedral and to light fires for

Orthodox Jews on their Sabbath Days. And to plunge into books, books, books—a genetic condition passed along—from whence, I wonder?—in the Westley family.

The split-arrangement wouldn't have been all that dreadful, if it hadn't been for, as I say, May's projection of her antipathy toward Harry onto young, spiritual Frankie.

How this mismatched, quietly seething couple got themselves trekking between Toronto, Ontario, in the centre of Canadian development, and Regina and Swift Current, Saskatchewan, smack-dab in the centre of the God-forsaken Canadian prairies, will become evident as we go along on this true journey of wandering and loosely-connecting lost souls.

There are other earlier souls to hear from, in particular, my Great-Grandparents, Arthur Westley and Sarah Pegg, and the earlier, pastoral Westleys in Essex. Arthur moved this story from the quiet town of Little Bardfield in Essex into the dark heart of Victorian London and books, books, books. Was it he who brought about the fall of the Westleys into Cockney poverty and the sound of the Bow Bells? (One is not a Cockney unless one is born within the sound of the Bow Bells, my father explained.) Perhaps. Or was it Arthur, rebelling against his father's control over his destiny? Perhaps. Or was it Sarah Pegg, creating another love story and throwing out a pattern that I, as her great-granddaughter, had to discover, listen to and rectify? I'd opt for this one. It has the strongest likelihood of being true. And it has to do with love and therefore pain and poetry.

But back to Frank Edgar. His belief in angels is key to this whole story.

"Read it right!" Meg's vocal frustration could be counted on, without fail, to be the penultimate factor in this repetition-compulsion of the books, books, books of our childhood. And without fail, the ultimate factor kicked in—our father's infectious, ageless giggle. How he loved his own jokes! Especially the one where the story started with, "Once upon a time, there were two little girls who lived at 1836 York Street in Regina..."

"Read it right!" Indignation!

And back we would go, Dad's arms securely around us, his hands drawing us into the oneness of trinity, pages turned by us at the tap of his finger. The heavy-handed frost might have thickened the windows; the prairie wind might be howling and stretching its fingers in through the gaps in the doors and windows, seeking us. But we would be safe and comforted, within our father's hand span, so to speak. And inspired. Books became the heavenly portal to life, fear, survival, grief and triumph in the oddly arrogant fledgling province of Saskatchewan. I say arrogant because any entity or being would have to be somewhat audacious to give survival even passing consideration in a place that had once been named "Pile Of Bones", after the rotting carcasses of plundered buffaloes. More arrogance.

And I say Oneness because, with my father, all things entertained the Heavenly.

Part of this possibility of opening the heavenly was because of his delight in life, his laughter, his openness. Another part of this was because I needed it in the face of a mother who was brilliant, tempestuous and sometimes wildly frightening and in the face of an acute sense of dislocation... an unbelonging.

But the essential part of the heavenly was because of Dad's hands. Well-groomed, fine hands. Not delicate. Not big. Above all, not ordinary. Immaculately clean, tender hands. Rounded nails. The hands with the one ring, on the ring-finger of his left hand. The only jewellery he ever wore. With the "W" on it, the "W" that will be forever associated with his hands for me. I took that ring, the only physical part of him I could keep, the day he died. If you ever happen to see me wearing it on the middle finger of my left hand, you'll know I'm in a state of needing steadiness.

Safe hands. Nurturing hands. Hands that made a belief in God simple. Hands that collected rain water and washed my hair tenderly. Hands that prepared a lemon rinse to keep my hair blond. Hands that showed me how to plant seeds and let them sleep until they were ready to wake up. Hands that helped make a bridge from the window of the streetcar so that I could sit on his arm and watch out the window. Hands that gently hushed me when I saw my first nun in full habit and called out, "What's that?!" Hands that never hurt. Hands that were incapable of hurting. Hands that, despite his big eyes, were the window to his soul.

Hands that spoke.

The hands that opened heaven for me, made it accessible.

And so it was that my first lesson about my father's experience with angels came about when he had his arms around my sister and me, with his hands drawing us into the oneness of trinity. I might have been in school by then; but I was still young enough to believe and never doubt. And while I may have moved away from the truth of this story at times, I never doubted that truth.

"Once upon a time, when I was a young boy— Della was very young—my Father left Toronto and went out West on The Harvesters' Excursion." This was going to be a Big Story; I could tell by Daddy's face and tone of voice.

I looked up earnestly, "Why were you in Toronto? What's an excursion? Who are harvesters?" I remembered Toronto so well. We had been there— near Casa Loma—last year, at his Auntie Ada's house. Auntie Ada, who had inherited the house on Spadina from her employer. Auntie Ada, who with happy Fred Bowman, the chauffeur, and Tom, the quiet butler, continued to live there in the three-story Victorian house with—of all things!—two staircases. Auntie Ada had been bequeathed the house by the woman whose "companion" she was. Toronto had, for me, the reality of fairy tales. Wilting heat, even for a four year old, intoxicating fragrances, trees that met overhead, traffic, stores, streetcars and the awesome touch of a different accent, even though I understood the language. "You told us you were born in Regina!"

Dad continued patiently, "Yes, but we moved to Toronto to try to make more money. Saskatchewan wasn't an easy place for a skilled penman like my Father to live. However, neither was Toronto. So, my father decided to believe in what was being offered in The Harvesters' Excursion. Go out West, be given some land and make money. So, Dad was gone, and Mother and Della and I waited in Toronto to hear when to join him."

I felt sad for them. I knew what it was like when my Daddy had to go away "on business", although I had come to trust these disappearances. But, I wouldn't let go of my hatred of them. "Were you sad for your father?" I needed to know.

"Yes, but I understood. It seemed as though everyone was struggling for money, especially after The Great Flu Epidemic and all that it..."

Oh—WHAT?? The Great WHAT? "What was that?" I had to know. It sounded mysterious and scary and important.

Dad laughed, "One story at a time. Back to The Harvesters' Excursion." I filed The Great Food Demic in my memory and settled into the story. Meg may have gone off by now to find our mother. "At long last, my father, your Grandfather, wrote us to say that we should come out on the next available excursion. I remember my excitement when I thought of seeing him again. And to be going back to Saskatchewan by train!" (Time for the fabulous train whistle Daddy could make by cupping his hands together and blowing into the crack between his thumbs while slightly opening and closing his hands!)

"Just once more! Pleeeease, Daddy!" Wonderful! I could feel the locomotion and taste the soot.

"Well, finally the day came, and Mother and Della and I went to Union Station in Toronto. What a tremendously big and beautiful place! But the crowds! Thousands of people, all wanting the same thing—to go out West and become rich! Free land! Free travel! Go West, Young Family! And how quickly it turned dangerous!" Scared, I curled into Daddy's safe arm.

"Before we knew it, we were herded—it was like we were cattle—into a long, wide stairway, carried along with the force of the crowd's madness. We came to some kind of platform. I could hardly hold onto Della's hand. Della let go and went down. Mother screamed and reached for my sister. And mother went down. I felt like a lamb fighting off dragons, dragons who were just going to knock us down and trample over us and kill us. 'Mother! Della!' I tried to reach them. Della looked up at me, her eyes wild. She screamed something I couldn't hear. A big man stepped on Mother. 'Stop it! Look after my mother! Help us! God, help us!' Where was God? Mother had blood coming from the corner of her mouth. I fell down."

Oh, my poor Daddy! How could this ever be fixed?

Daddy turned to look directly into my eyes. His eyes were so big and kind. "And do you know what happened?" I shook my blond curls, my eyes, I'm

19

sure, as big as his. "Well, it was like time stopped. Suddenly, I felt something very strong pick me up. Della and Mother were standing up, too. Our hands were joined, as though we had never fallen, except that Mother's mouth was still bleeding. And, we were carried along—that's all I can say to explain it—we were carried along and up into the train. As Mother and I looked around, we saw the back of a man—perhaps around my mother's age... longish hair... good clothes... moving quickly back through the crowd... against the crowd. And he was gone. Just like that, he was gone! And we were safe! Safe to go out West to be with my Father."

I couldn't talk. I just stared into Dad's eyes. Because I knew.

"That, my little lady, was my first encounter with an angel."

5. Ancestral herds are called clans or tribes

mr. Andrews, head Brewery clerk, will
retire next month—refusing to be
budged
from his desk. you know the man—
the one in the dingy nicotine-stained corner. there
by the filmy window repelling
the seekingsun. the one—yes! the one moistening his
pencil, the familiar habit born of a familiar
longing for some bosom he
never had or perhaps lost. his mother lover pencil
breast.
he leadsips the numbers into his
head
selfcomputing digits that move exponentially into his
brain and onto
paper.

poor old retiring-next-month-andrews what
is his story? this retiring chap with no
life
that we know of here—
no friend here there anywhere—it seems

caught-in-the-middle Andrews, purveyor of
pittance to the draymen, two-legged horses he
calls them in his Whitechapel
superiority… no friend here there anywhere—
it seems

you know the man
he creeps day after mediocre day into work with
the filtered flecked dust in the new

bornmorn
sits down at his desk—the meagre orderly table set for him by
him at the end of the before workday

what will he do in Whitechapel, filthchapel when he has no
where to go? poor retiring paperlark…

[Nell, thinking back, 1993]

When I was twelve, I had this burning desire to become an archaeologist. Burning. To the point of obsession, I dreamt of going to Egypt, Italy and England. There was nothing I desired more than to unearth evidence of pre-Christian civilizations. It had nothing to do with fame or fortune. The positioning of that desire within a prairie girl made me an oddity in my social group, not that it bothered me. And now here we are, you and I, crossing the sea with Harry in search of "markers". Because Annie is a powerful marker in his life. How odd that your probing into markers would activate my early desire to do archaeology.

Because, as I say, here we are, discovering that markers, visible and invisible, are in fact artefacts. Is that what we each become somehow? Artefacts, unknowingly brewing and strewing artefactual pieces of ourselves along the pathways of our lives, leaving work for future archaeologists?

How neat really. How very neat.

So, here I sit with Westley artefacts strewn about me, as I produce more. It gives chaos theory ample space to reveal itself, doesn't it?

From way out there in and beyond the stratosphere, I'm pulling that swirling, dissolving lostness of the Westleys together, plucking fragments out of the air and nailing them down, virtually, and then moving them at will until they fit. I've always loved jigsaw puzzles. They're all very ordinary pieces, but, that's always the way, isn't it? The chemical formula of any intriguing story is one part Ordinary and one part Alchemy.

Here's what I have so far, except for the stuff that doesn't yet fit or make sense. I'll save that info for later. I have the family Bible, pictures of Harry and Mavis and Frank and Isabelle, Harry's meticulous tonic-sol-fa "edition" of Frank's school songs, various samples of Harry's penmanship, a 1919 water colour by Frank entitled "Sled Party", memories that made it my way for depositing, and my own memories. Oh! And Ernest's academic medal.

I may not have mentioned that one yet. The medal. "All Saints' National Schools, Buxton Street East, Ernest Westley, 1886, Reward of Superior Merit", it declares in its perfectly preserved, ornate Victorian inscription. It's a stunning silver tooled medal, about an inch and a half in diameter, in perfect condition in its original leather box. Somehow, this artefact made its way to me. Does it have a will of its own? I have no recollection how I got it. I think I must have been given it before Dad died; but I'm not sure. Nevertheless, for making it across the Atlantic if for nothing else, it deserves substantiation for having persisted. Obviously, it was not going to rest until Ernest was acknowledged, one way or another, in this so-called real world. I have more to discover about this youth who died six years after receiving the award. All I've learned so far is that the school itself was demolished in the 1950's, not long after Harry's return to his homeland. (I hope you approve, Ernest, of what I'm doing in marking you and your family and in getting to know you. Why and how did you die so early?)

Do the markers I've mentioned so far - medals, photographs, handwritten notes, Bibles - qualify as markers for you? Are they not more significant than gravestones? More important than some spot under a tree or facing out upon Lake Huron? If we go digging, we'll find the markers we need. If someone needs to be found, she'll eventually be found and anchored. I could imagine you photographing this family, this family of no gravestones, marking them for posterity, your eye keeping them alive. I suspect you'd anchor Harry first.

And now we have Harry alone on the ocean or alone as a five year old in London. Take your pick. Although, I doubt that it matters which you choose. I'm learning that the child is father of the man, mother of the woman, and that Harry as a sixty-five year old is the same, essentially, as Harry as a five year old.

Do you see him as I do? Look at this photo of him with Frankie in December, 1911. What do you see? That's his handwriting on the photo… "Daddy, Frankie and Teddy-Bear." When you look at his way of holding his firstborn, do you see both his pride and his awkwardness? Look how he toes in slightly, with just a modicum of self-consciousness. One arm around Frankie and the other around the Teddy. Immaculate hands. He's quite dapper in his presentation, isn't he, with the long jacket and the high-necked shirt? Polished shoes. Shoes! Sarah Pegg's prayers have been answered. No shades of Cockney poverty here. No hint of having to find his way in a brutal world. Genteel, you could say. Yes, a perfect and perfectly groomed gentleman.

I wish I had known him better. Longer.

I wish you'd been around to photograph him properly. To catch his soul.

6. Sir Alec

It is nice to know Frank will have such a nice trip only I will be lonesome without him and don't like it. Imagine Frank being at both coasts in less than six months. He is getting grand experience. We took Dad to see "Waltz Time," an English picture.
[The Lois Diaries, August 5, 1947]

Perhaps, then, the best way to put Harry in the context of that remarkable family Bible is to build an ark and float with him back across the Atlantic to London, back to his roots, back to Annie.

It's a massive steamship we're on for these few moments, one that separates and connects. One that travels through the panes of glass and smoky mirrors constructed and shattered in the minds and dreams of a family rapidly becoming extinct. I would say that we're about mid-Atlantic on our Journey Home for Harry. I can see him. Can you? He's the one on the canvas chair, off by himself, with the striped blue and white blanket placed carefully over his midriff and legs. Right there – dapper hat with a visor (he always wore a visor in the sun), dark glasses, and reading, of course. If you get a little closer, you'll see that he looks uncannily similar to Alec Guinness, especially Sir Alec as he was in "Lost Weekend." Look! He's pulling something out of the breast pocket of his tweed jacket. It's a letter. He carefully reads all three pages, holds the letter against his chest and looks up into the wide, blue, eternal sky. It must be a letter from Annie. How long have they been communicating, I wonder. His thoughts appear to evolve into the puffs of clouds weightlessly dotting the blue heavens.

I know this story, you see, because of one of my earliest, clearest memories. Always accessible instantaneously at my command, the scene appears now and moves me away from the Atlantic idyll to its prairie prelude. This memory is now playing like a movie trailer.

Back to "Take one!"

I've drawn on this setting, with its touch of the exotic (at least for me, blond dreamer back at Pile of Bones) numerous times.

Just look with me, if you will, over here… almost straight ahead; but just a touch to the left. Yes – right there.

SCENE TWO—Regina, Saskatchewan, August 5, 1947

The prairie sun is brilliant in the early afternoon. The shadows are sharp. Two people—a four-year-old blond girl, with red bows in her hair and wearing a red plaid skirt and matching hand-knit sweater, and a sixty-four-year-old reserved, somewhat elegant Englishman, wearing sunglasses and a visor—sit together on a dark green blanket on the well-manicured, tender lawn. A white tablecloth, embroidered with yellow flowers, sits squarely in the middle of the blanket. Despite the location on the wrong side of the tracks, this garden is exquisitely incongruous in the dry, forbidding locale. Deep purple irises are still blooming, breaking trail for the embryonic brown-eyed Susan. Behind the little girl is a burgeoning blue spruce tree, planted by her father the day she was born. Behind the man is an older maple tree that, replete with promises of climbing and hiding to come in the little girl's newly evolving life, has split into three about four feet up the trunk. The air is redolent with a summer perfume of dying bonfires and the pungency of a locomotive as it chuffs its way into the east. The northerly wind carries the soot away from our al fresco characters, letting the freight train consume itself in its own diminishing song.

HARRY *(reaching down to a bowl of ice cream in the centre of the tablecloth and spooning out servings for his granddaughter and himself)*: "Well, your mother has made us some lovely ice cream. Chocolate. What little girl, and indeed what grandfather, could resist that?"

NELL *(smiling sweetly and placing her bowl down in front of her)*: "Thank you, Grandpa."

(A grassland meadowlark sings its intricate, multi-dimensional melody from somewhere nearby.)

HARRY *(holding his bowl of chocolate ice cream out toward his granddaughter and looking up)*: "Did you hear that, Nell? That's the prairie meadowlark. When we first moved to Swift Current, a friend explained to me that they sang when the buffaloes roamed the prairies. Now, little lady, back to our ice cream lesson – allow me to show you how properly to eat ice cream. One takes one's spoon like this (*placing it toward the outside of the two scoops of ice cream and very gently stirring the ice cream, making small circles while the ice cream softens.*) Go ahead now; you do the same."

NELL (*in awe of her grandfather, picking up her bowl and following his instructions and his lead*): "Am I doing it right?"

HARRY (*stopping his stirring and lifting a spoonful toward his mouth*): "Precisely right. One wants one's ice cream to be like this—not too soft, mind! Now, eat, dear!" *(Harry politely sips and savours his proper ice cream.)*

NELL and HARRY (*sipping together, share a dignified giggle and relish the ice cream, Nell making a few polite sounds of amazement at the wonderful flavour the ice cream has developed.*)

NELL *(becoming serious)*: "Grandfather Westley, why are you going away?"

HARRY *(taken aback, his spoon in mid-air)*: "I… I didn't know you knew. Did you overhear your mother and father talking?"

NELL (*nods her head, her eyes big and questioning; appearing to have much information within her.*) "Yes. They were trying to be secret."

HARRY *(finishing his ice cream)*: "Delicious! Your mother is an excellent cook. Yes, I am going away, across the ocean, to a place called England… where I was born. I leave tomorrow. I shall take the train from here to the East and then a ship across the ocean. It will take quite a while." (*He places his bowl and spoon carefully inside the serving bowl and reaches for the wet cloth on the tray.*)

NELL (*compellingly)*: "Is Grandma Westley going with you?"

HARRY *(flustered, meticulously wipes his hands with the cloth)*: "No, my dear, she is not. That's why she went to Toronto to be with her sister."

NELL [*innocently and sweetly*]: "Then who is Annie, Grandfather?"

HARRY *(even more flustered, stands and brushes off his trousers)*: Come now, my dear, I hear your mother calling you to come inside. It's rather chilly after the ice cream."

NELL *(big teardrops spilling onto her cheeks)*: Grandpa, I don't want you to go away.

HARRY *(disarmed, assists Nell to stand; he wraps his arms around her and gives her a kiss on her forehead):* Oh, dear Nell, we won't be parted forever. You see, I left England a long time ago. I have some pieces of myself to return to. And Annie is a friend I used to know. That's all, dear heart. It's something I have to do. I do hope you understand.

NELL *(smiling bravely):* Forever would be a long, long time, Grandpa. And Grandpa, you have all of your pieces… arms and legs… and everything on your head you're supposed to have…

HARRY *(with a little laugh and a hug)*: Oh Nelly, I do love you! Of course, I have all those pieces, sweetheart. But you'll see as you grow older that relationships, how you become attached to certain people, give you strong feelings and sometimes strong messages to finish things up. You must pay attention to your feelings as you grow up. It's an important thing to do.

The curious couple look into each other's eyes directly and briefly. Harry wipes Nell's hands and mouth with the cloth. He pulls out his handkerchief and wipes the tears from her eyes. And then he dabs at his own eyes. Grandfather and granddaughter fold the tablecloth and the blanket together. Harry drapes the tablecloth over Nell's right arm and the blanket over his left arm. He gathers the tray of dishes, holding them in his left hand and reaches for Nell's free hand. They walk hand in hand the short distance toward the front porch of the modest insulbrick house.

END OF SCENE

I had indeed heard much for a three year old. All of it has lingered within me all these years, unanswered. I recall very clearly that my grandfather was going to visit Annie, his love who could not come to Canada so very long ago. My parents whispered about the scant details they knew, oblivious to my keen hearing and perception. Could the trip have been the reason Harry lived with us for a while before the trip? Could he and Grandma have separated? It was all so secret.

In all the years that my parents continued to live after this scene, we followed protocol impeccably on this matter as with all big matters of the heart. Thus, we never discussed the reasons for or events of my grandfather's departure for his home. It was as though this remarkable story had never happened.

7. Dip into the ancestry pool

Cool and a bit rainy looking. Got up and got the fires going. Washed today and things went well. Took the pillars down between the dining and living rooms. It looks grand – the rooms bigger. Mrs. Dodges over to get the wheelbarrow. Dad was delighted with his presentation – a wallet and $25. It was fine for him. His last work day.

[*The Lois Diaries, August 25, 1947*]

Harry Westley, grandfather, father, husband, son and orphan, breaks his reverie. How long has he been looking into the eye of God, questioning himself and his sinfulness? He drinks in a great gulp of the briny air, shivers a little in the cool, late afternoon mid-Atlantic sun and clutches his chest. Ah… Annie, her letter. Folding it perfectly, he stops the procedure just short of returning the letter to his breast pocket. He unfolds it again and places it back against his chest, securing it against the capricious breeze with the flat of his hand. The ship's engines drone dully in the background of his mind. He must read the letter again – to touch her, to understand her, to understand himself. What madness has he undertaken? On the other hand, what restraint he has exercised in not returning to her years ago! And what a miracle that their twice yearly letters through all these years have kept them connected. Annie who married late, and Harry who married in anger. Annie whose marriage died with the first Great War, and Harry, whose marriage lived in misperception. The old, well-known, acute pain rises in his chest again. Despite its severity, it, like a go-between, has kept him close to Annie, in this current eternity, with a stunning immediacy.

Harry pulls another blue and white striped blanket from the unoccupied chair to his left and wraps it around his shoulders. He'll go for the second sitting of supper. Food holds no charm at the moment. In fact, it hasn't for a long time. Everything in his life has become so very utilitarian. Except, of course, for that interlude with little Nell on the lawn the day before he left Regina. Funny little wise granddaughter, she seemed knowing, and he had felt an acceptance from her. It was all right that she had questioned him.

Closing his eyes, Harry breathes deeply and focuses, moving onto his well-worn pathway to silence, his doorway to reading and thinking. This discipline (family called it "escapism") has been his salvation, part of his painstaking working out, as the Apostle Paul, whom Harry has lately come to understand, admonished, of his "own salvation in fear and trembling."

He opens his eyes, smells the letter and sinks into reading, or more precisely, listening to, it:

May 16, 1947

Dear Harry,

I have waited so long.

You are coming home! I find this so hard to believe, after all these years. I'm excited and afraid. You left England and me forty years ago, Harry. That's an enormous amount of time. But when I think just of you, it's as though no time has elapsed.

How will we look to each other? I'm frightened when I think of you looking at me. Why is that? We have both changed physically, of course; but how else have we changed? Will we know each other in the ways we used to? This scares me, Harry. We've led such separate, divergent lives. Or, have we? I'm not sure. I haven't been able to tell definitely through our letters. Perhaps the very fact that there have been letters for the interval – the long interval – tells the story. I really don't think I've changed much in these forty years. I'm sure you have. Or have you? Do you see my fear? I feel it right now. I dislike it.

Well, I've never shied away from fear. I'd almost like to right now… tell you not to come… tell you I won't be here waiting.

How foolish that would be! I – and you – need to see this through.

I hope that you will not miss your family too much. They'll always love you. I have never told you this before, Harry; but I keep your children close to my heart. I allow myself to think of them as mine. The photos have helped. After all, Frank was the name we dreamt of naming our son. When you wrote, so long ago, to tell me of his birth, my heart broke. I didn't know whether to be angry or sad about his name. So I chose to be honoured. And now I have at last told you this. And I simply don't care how you feel about it.

Harry, this is a London now completely ravaged by two world wars. Add that to the poverty you knew, and you've got a tough picture. Finally, though, we seem to be winning the war against the white plague. We lost so much to that brute, didn't we, Harry? I guess in many ways it's what ruined our life together.

But I haven't changed much. Honestly. Since losing you, I have not needed much... only what I could not have. We're so close now to finding out what has changed and what hasn't. Remember that I won't be home until 6:00 on the fifteenth. This apartment is working out well. I think you'll like it. I was able to find a single woman to move into my house in Leigh-on-Sea at a no rental cost because she'll be responsible for its upkeep. I wish you had let me meet you at the station. I could have taken an extra day off work. But I understand your need to get here on your own. Buxton Street is still Buxton Street. It's my waiting-place.

Is this really happening?

I wish you a safe, peaceful journey. For once, the vast ocean that separates us is our friend. May it help you remember us as we were and accept us as we are. These are the things I ask for.

As I always have, I love you, no matter what,

Annie

This time Harry folds the letter perfectly and places it in his breast pocket. But, rather than going for supper, he sinks more deeply into the past. "It must be the boundlessness of the ocean," he thinks as he drifts further and further back. Annie, laughing and as beautiful as Elgar's music, floats up to his face and disappears into the placid ocean. His father, Arthur, his face set bravely against all the losses, moves in and away only to be replaced by the image of his mother, *Sarah Sarah, Shrouded Sarah, Sweet Sarah of*

Whitechapel, Swaddled Sarah; Sanguine Sarah; Woman, where is thy son? Mummy grieving, grieving… She cups her hands and extends them to him, pleading for something that no person can give and God refuses to provide. *My babies; give me my babies; oh dear little Harry, I want them back,* and her eyes burn black holes through the crimson shroud… *Help me Harry, Harry, Harry, Harry!*

The loves and the losses of his youth become beings that taunt him, mocking his belief in personal triumph. "You see, don't you, Harry," cry out his dead siblings, "you are as dead as we are; you are dead like us? You joined us before you left England. Your soul will have no peace until you come home. Come home, Harry! Come home!"

"Harry! Come home! Harry!" He could hear his mother's rich voice calling down the street, as he walked home from the Goldbergs' place on Pelham Street. It was an especially chilly, dark Friday evening in February of 1888, and the five-year-old boy had just finished his Jewish Sabbath job of lighting fires in the homes of three Jewish-Orthodox families.

On his fifth birthday last August, his father had suggested he could help the family by earning a little money. "I've spoken to the Goldbergs, son, and they are willing to have you take over the job that Bertie has been doing. Bertie will do it with you until you feel secure—he started when he was just a little older than you are now—and then he'll go on to the fish market every day before school and on Saturdays." His father extended his right hand, "Congratulations, young man!"

Harry had felt proud and grown-up as he shook his father's hand… until he looked over at his mother. She, who had been so excited at giving the sweet family supper to acknowledge his birthday, had tears in her eyes. But a birthday was a happy event!

"It's all right, Sarah," his father had walked over to his mother's chair and put his hands on her shoulders. "Our Harry is five now, already so much older than the other three. It's all right, my dear." And then Arthur had bent down to place a lingering kiss on the golden curls of his wife's head. He pulled a loose curl into place behind her ear, "It's all right, my love."

"Harry! Come home!"

The five-year-old returned from August musings to the February chill and began running. "Coming, Mummy! I'm all done! I did three all on my own tonight! Three fires on my own tonight—doh doh me me sol sol fa; doh doh me me sol sol fa; three fires on my own tonight." As he skipped around the corner onto their unlit street, the fog clamped its hands over his face. He stopped to peer through the shrouded darkness. There she was – his mother – a few doorways down the street, crouched, her arms open. Harry quickened his pace and threw himself into her embrace. She was always so happy to see him, so happy that her "baby Harry" was safe and happy. No matter how awful her cough was, she would be there to meet him on his way home. Always.

Hugging him tightly, Sarah laughed and planted a kiss on his forehead. "Oh, Harry, I missed you! And here you are—so grown up. Well done!" She stood and clutched his hand as they headed home. "I wish these streets were safer and well-lit. Harry, I have tea and a biscuit waiting for you."

"With cream this time, Mummy?" Harry loved the safety of his mother's handclasp.

"No, my love. I'm sorry. Cream is a little too expensive yet. But soon, Harry, soon."

Oh, please don't be sad, Mummy; you mustn't be sad; you mustn't. Because then I feel sad, too, and I don't know why. I love it most when you're happy, Mummy. "I love them without cream! I do! And even without butter! Are you and Daddy going to have biscuits, too? How many did you make?"

Sarah laughed and held her son's hand more tightly, "Oh, Harry, you do make me happy! I made a dozen, and so—let's see... If Arthur and Ernest had three each with gravy for supper, and Charles and Herbert had two each, how many are left, Harry, how many?"

Harry giggled, "I have to decide things like that when I do the candles, Mummy. So, if I had candles, I'd have two left, wouldn't I? So that must mean that there are two biscuits left. Is that right, Mummy? How can two left be fair to you and Daddy and me?"

Reaching the front door of their lower tenement home, Sarah swung her son into the hall and knelt before him to help him take off his jacket and shoes. *Oh, my little one, look at your cold feet. Oh, would God, would God, would you, God, fill these soles, fill these holes with your mercy, and fill our souls until we need no more, and again I plead, Amen and Amen until I can utter it no more.* "You are so very clever, Harry—the cleverest Westley yet! Now, lean on my shoulders, Harry, so I can put your slippers on, please." Feeling the imprint of Harry's still plump hands on her shoulders, she slipped on the blue woollen slippers she had knit from her unravelled sweater for his Christmas gift. "I'll tell you how two biscuits can be fair for three people. The littlest person gets one and the two big people get one-half each because they're finished growing!"

Listening at the kitchen table, Arthur Senior felt the anger rise in his chest. *When would Sarah have enough; when would her health improve, her face fill out again with happiness, her breathing be less laboured? When would the life she had forfeited be given back? When would life be easier for all of them in this hell-hole, this shame-hole of London?* In this brief indulgence in passion, Arthur, a gentle soul, was amazed at the anger that rose like a fierce inferno from his gut and tore upwards, blasting through the top of his head. He wanted to smash the walls and bring all of Whitechapel down with his voice, like a mighty thunderbolt. Squash the stench and the fog and kill the filth that had made them all so sick. But he knew that if he started to shout, he would never stop.

More than that, Arthur knew his fury would die a sudden death, taking more of him with it than he could afford.

"Where's Daddy?" Harry giggled, likely from Sarah's gentle play.

And as always, as he listened into the words of these two, his anger dropped away, and he began to hear and feel the joy that this little son continually brought into their lives. It was a joy that had been mitigated when little Edith died in '73 and that had disappeared completely when little Ellen and Walter had died last year with the disease that made them cough and convulse until they could breathe no longer. The return of joy was a joyous thing, indeed!

On Friday evening, February 10, 1888, Arthur Westley, born January 12, 1844, into a brood of five sons and one daughter in Little Bardfield, Essex, father of eight and now five, counted himself, truly, as blessed. Harry Westley, his last born and only five years old, had brought joy back to this struggling family.

8. Poor Dad – he seemed fit

*Woke at seven to get Dad off to the east. Poor Dad. He seemed
really fit. I bought a new hat and handles for the dressers and a few
other things. Kay is coming soon to stay with us.*
[*The Lois Diaries, August 27, 1947*]

On Saturday morning, February 11, 1888, young Harry woke at 5:00 to the
sound of voices. Yes, it was Mummy and Bertie getting ready to go to work,
Bertie to the fish-monger's and Mummy to All Saints' School at the other
end of Buxton Street. Charlie would be next up, preparing to go to St. Paul's
to hawk newspapers. And then it would be Daddy, Arthur Junior and Harry.
Daddy and Arthur would leave for Fleet Street at 9:00 to clean floors at the
newspaper offices. Daddy would then "leave Arthur to it" at 10:00 to go to
the Old Truman Brewery on Brick Lane for the rest of the day. And Harry?
Well, Harry would stay at home, tidy here and there, draw, make up a few
songs and play with Percy, if his Mummy would let Harry come in. Ernest,
now almost fourteen and no longer ever called Ernie, would spend the day
studying literature with Mr. Deacon and music with Mr. Sitwell. Because of
his prodigious talent in both areas, All Saints' School had requested that he
not work other than at his studies. "Yes, yes, we realize that your other sons
are bright, Mr. Westley; but Ernest has exceptional talent… perhaps—and I
do not say this easily or lightly—genius. And we must conserve his health.
We've arranged for the Major Booth's programme to provide him with a
little more food here twice a week. I do wish we could do it for everyone;
but we can't. No, no, Mrs. Westley, we can't." Mr. Deacon, principal of the
school, understanding that the Westleys were in need of the money that
Ernest's newspaper job brought into the family coffers, offered the mother a
modest task at the school to be paid in the same amount that Ernest would
have made hawking newspapers. And so it had transpired that Sarah Pegg
Westley spent Saturdays at All Saints' School mending and baking in order
that Ernest could excel. She harboured a deep desire that one day she would
be asked to do the same again for Harry, the brightest of her children.

Harry drifted in and out of sleep for the next few hours. It was delicious to have the mattress and blanket all to himself, without Arthur, Charlie and Bertie taking up space and pulling his share away. Mummy and Daddy had the mattress on the other side of the curtain. Young Harry had been known to crawl in with them if his brothers got too greedy with the covers! In the morning, no one was eager to have him up and in the way when so much had to be done. He dreamt about fires and horses and how tomorrow would unfold at St. John's Church and what they would have for supper. Always, always, Mummy would turn Sunday into the best day of the week… tripe, gravy and biscuits… more than one biscuit each!

Once everyone was gone but for his father and Arthur Junior, Harry arose, used the slop pail in the little shed just outside the back door, got washed in the cold soapy water left over by the others, dressed and scampered into the kitchen to make certain that the oatmeal porridge was warm. The two men, for Arthur was nineteen now and involved in his apprenticeship at the newspaper office, ate their oatmeal quietly.

"Well, Arthur, we had best be off," Arthur Senior placed his watch back in his pocket and ruffled Harry's wavy black hair. "Mrs. Givens expects you will check in with her on the hour every hour and that you will have lunch with her at noon. Understood?"

"Yes, Father," Harry always found it best to be formal with his Daddy at times like this. "And I won't go off our street."

"Oh yes, and speaking of the street, Harry. Don't forget to empty the slop pail into the street, son. It's very full," Arthur ruffled his son's head. "And mind you don't slop and slop!" Harry tried to match Arthur's laughter; but he couldn't do it… not when he thought about the stench. Harry almost gagged then and there!

And Harry was precisely obedient... which wasn't hard because he enjoyed his own company and delighted in having a day where he could read and think about music and play with his toy soldiers. Mrs. Givens, who had "taken quite a shine to young Harry," according to others in the neighbourhood, had bestowed upon him a wonderful little toy collection. "You put me in mind of my little Edward, Harry, you do," and her eyes had filled with tears as she opened the treasure box. "He'd be a young man, he would, by now, Harry. Make sure that you grow up to be a young man,

Harry. Your Mum needs that. Make sure." And so it was that little Harry had come to have a significant relationship with "the richest lady" in the whole of Buxton Street.

While lunch with Mrs. Givens was very special and time with Percy was fun, time with Harry by Harry was the best time of any Saturday. On this particular Saturday, Harry did play with Percy for an hour and chat with Mrs. Givens over watercress and cold pork pie; but, most importantly, he wrote out three new songs from school in tonic sol-fa. How he loved figuring this out and then singing what he had written. He hadn't told anyone—not even Bertie—but he had something very special tucked in the bottom of his dresser drawer! He was writing a song himself! He had the tonic sol-fa written out for most of it and the words for half of it. People would love it, and soon he would sing it for everyone. It was called, "Never Be Afraid; Just Sing".

When the Bow Bells called out 5:00, Harry was quite happy with himself. He had been all over the world in his imagination and had even done some dusting and set the table for Mummy. And now he was ready for people to come home. Would Mummy be first today or would Ernest?

Within minutes, the front door burst open and Ernest charged in. "Harry! I'm home! How are you?" Harry ran to the door, eager to see Ernest, who clapped him soundly on the back. "Mum's not home yet?" Harry shook his head. "Well then, I'll put my books away, read the newspaper for a few minutes and then be back to play with you, Harry," and off Ernest went, newspaper in hand, to the other side of the curtain.

Five minutes later, Harry peeked past the curtain. Aha! Just as he had thought! Ernest was asleep. Harry thought of jumping on his big brother; but decided first to see if Mummy might be coming. She should be here very soon, or how would they ever have supper on time?

Reaching the front door, Harry opened it just enough to peer up the street in Mummy's direction. He knew Mummy wouldn't like this because of the danger on dark streets; but he was being ever so careful. *"There are bad people in The City, Harry, and you must be careful! Never wander out without knowing that I'm watching for you. If you aren't bothered by bad people, you'll be bothered by the fog. It brings sickness, Harry. It's what has made my lungs so bad. Nothing must ever, ever harm you, dear Harry."*

Harry looked carefully up the street.

What was the commotion up there? It sounded like Mr. Givens' voice yelling, "Arthur! Arthur Westley!" It was Mr. Givens! The shadows were becoming people—three people. Mr. Givens, still shouting for Daddy, and two other men Harry didn't recognize. What was Mr. Givens carrying? A huge sack?

Harry screamed for Ernest, "Ernest—help! Mr. Givens is yelling for Daddy and he's carrying Mummy! Ernest!" Harry ran out onto the street.

"Harry—go back inside. Get your father! Now!"

And then now disappeared into never and forever. For Harry saw his mother, and the world went mad.

Mummy's white scarf was splashed with red, and there was red all over her coat and dress—wet, bright red. And some women came near and tried to pull Harry away. And Harry screamed and screamed and screamed. And Ernest was there. And then Daddy and Arthur were there. And Daddy screamed, "Sarah", until the name would never end. And they were in the house, and a doctor clucked over Mummy on the mattress and packed white cloth around and around her neck, and Harry wondered if this was like swaddling clothes. And Mrs. Givens brought a bottle of whiskey to the house and made everyone, including Harry, take a sip.

And then Harry looked. And Mummy—his beautiful Mummy with red on her fair hair—took a sip, too, and it seemed that room itself took a deep breath.

And Mummy looked over at Harry, her face as white as the cloths around her neck, and she said, "Oh, my little Harry, I'm so sorry" and she fell asleep.

On February 13, 1888, Arthur awoke very early, at 4:26 to be precise, to find his wife, Sarah Pegg Westley, cold beside him, her pale face partially framed in the red that had oozed into the pillow and settled into her hair. She had succumbed to the injuries inflicted on her by what the police called "a person or persons unknown" as she had walked happily home to her family from All Saints' School two days before. The doctor said that the wound simply would not stop bleeding and that infection had set in. He kindly chose to enter the disease that was killing her as the reason for the death. "This family has had enough to manage," he said to himself. "They don't need a permanent record that foul play was the cause." And he wrote "Phthisis", as he had done for those she had joined.

Harry, who would not be six for another six months, was not allowed to attend the funeral. All the adults agreed that this would be best for the tender little tyke. Only his brother, Charlie, disagreed.

Harry Westley, who would live much longer than the others in his family, decided that day, when "affection set in", and he knew that he would always have affection for his Mummy, that he would give no further affection to God. It wasn't that he didn't believe in God. Oh no! It was that he didn't like him. In fact, he hated him. "Dear God… God…" How could he pray to that kind of a God?

"Sir, sir," Harry felt his shoulder being gently jostled. He sat up quickly and regained his bearings, wiping his eyes... because they were wet.

"Yes? Yes?" It was difficult to feel composed, and composure was eminently important.

"Sir, it's after 9:00. I thought that you might be rather chilly, still out on the deck." The steward smiled kindly. "Could I bring you a cup of tea, sir?"

"No, no. Thank you. Thank you very much. I'll be off to my cabin." And Harry Westley, motherless Harry Westley, folded the two blue and white striped blankets carefully, laid them on his chair and exited from the deck.

9. *Made in England*

This should be a "red letter day" for me as after dinner, Frank and I went to Simpson's and got me thoroughly outfitted. New shoes – lovely walking ones, a new hat – one of those little ones with flowers on the crown and a new dress – a real good one, and a nice new beige coat – of pure wool, made in England. Am I proud. Dad Westley was in.
[The Lois Diaries, March 30, 1946]

Did he dare go back to the bank of deck chairs that had transported him yesterday to the truth?

Harry walked yet another circuit of the deck. If he were going to take the plunge again into being at the mercy of his memories, he should do it now. The evening was cool—perhaps a little too cool to sit out with his backside having nothing more than canvas between it and the dampness. Why couldn't he do this part, enter this pain, during the daylight hours? He'd known this would happen, so why was he allowing it only when the light slipped below the surface into the innards of the sea? Well, what did it matter anyway? At least he, and not the night, was now in charge. The night could not compare with the darkness of his soul's acquaintance, that archaic, perpetually nodding acquaintance.

Once again, Harry was simultaneously amazed at and shocked by his audacity in undertaking this journey. The sharp, fresh smell of orange wafted up toward him and brought him back to his senses. Here he was looking out over the black, fathomless sea.

Ah, he had stepped on an orange peel. He picked it up and tossed it into the void. Too many people on this vessel were unthinking… ungrateful.

The band played faintly and dreamily from the inside sparkle of the ballroom, reminding Harry of his relentless loneliness. The reflected shimmer from the ship's lights winked and danced up at him, mocking him from the forbidding anonymity and mystery of the ocean. Two world wars and forty years had passed since the earlier steamship had carried him and his tears and anticipation toward the promises of Canada. The tears remained. The anticipation had been replaced with monotony.

And here he was doing something that he felt compelled to do. But what were his motives? Selfishness? Yes. Grief? Yes. He had not been a good husband to May. The marriage had been a sham. Living apart these past few months had finally brought about a visible, public recognition of what many had known for years. And now he was leaving her completely, abandoning her for Annie. Of course, that element had been there from the beginning. If only she could have been less severe. If only he could have been less sad. What did it matter that he had encouraged her to move to Toronto to live with her sister? Whom was he fooling? Only himself... and that not well done either. In fact, what had he ever done well? His thoughts drifted painfully to his little granddaughters.

No! He would have none of this. He must see Annie again. And he must live in London again. He must go home. He had known this truth since Annie had not joined him in Canada so long ago. Frank and Della had relieved the pain during their childhood years; but they were gone now into their own lives, and there was nothing that remained between May and him. Nothing but bitterness toward each of them. A salty spray reminded him that he should have let her know that he was going home. He owed her that. It was just that he didn't want to hurt her in the way that she would perceive so terribly personally. *Poor, dear May, you have been the casualty of my heartache.*

Harry went to the same chair that he had occupied, or that had occupied him, yesterday. The chair of recollection. Fastidiously, he smoothed the woollen blanket into the length of canvas. He sat down and took a blanket from the next chair, put it over his knees, pulled over a footstool and put his feet up. Ah... he took a deep breath and closed his eyes, his hands a prayer tent over his chest.

With clear intent, Harry Westley took command of his memories, sinking into the deep indigo of his own personal dark waters.

Mummy... it all and always came back to her, didn't it? She was the key to his life, and there was no way to reach her and plead with her to open the doors to understanding. And no one, after she stopped breathing, would answer his unasked questions before they all died and joined her. No, they were all so enslaved by the brutality of Whitechapel that, had anyone opened those doors, the truth could not have been endured. All breathing would have stopped simultaneously.

Harry's solitude became the light below the sea's surface – "full fathom five thy mother lies, Harry, full fathom five".

10. *Don't die in vain*

*Very warm again. The rooms really are beginning to look fine. Dad
out doing a bit of shopping for me. We enjoyed being lazy today.
Frank got me a money order and I sent it off to the Viavi people for
Dad and his ulcers.*
[*The Lois Diaries, August 2, 1947*]

On the last day of rest of his remaining life, on the Sabbath that rent the veil
forever for him… Harry… Little Harry … sat with his back against the
door, his knees held firmly in the clutch of his clasped hands. His arms
shook with the physical effort of holding himself together. He returned to
rocking back and forth to alleviate the pain in his belly. He knew no other
way to contain the crushing fear.

Only his father remained in the bedroom now. The older boys had visited
Mummy and left. His turn would come soon, Daddy said. Daddy promised.
But why was it taking so long? He could hear their voices once in a while,
so why? Why? Charles and Ernest had tried to drag him away from the door
to go out and play; but he had kicked and screamed until Daddy had said to
"leave well enough alone."

Earlier Harry had heard Mummy say something about "not dying in vain".
Why would she talk about dying when the doctor had come by again to fix
her neck? She had mentioned Jesus, too, and said that she was "well aware"
that she had "sacrificed" her soul. And Daddy had said not to talk like that,
Sarah, and started to cry. What did they mean? Harry shook until he thought
he would fly apart.

And then the crying had stopped and there was nothing. That was the hard
part: when there was no talking, his belly hurt something fearful and his
heart ran around inside him and he thought he couldn't stand it.

Uh! Shhh…. They were talking again. They were alive! Harry put his ear to
the door. Daddy was comforting Mummy, telling her everything would be

"all right." Harry felt some relief, the same way he always did when Mummy told him everything would be "all right."

And then Mummy said, in a scratchy, whispery kind of voice, "Arthur, it's all right, Arthur. Please don't cry. You must listen to me. Hush… it was for the children."

"But," Daddy's voice still had tears in it. "I should not have allowed it. I should have found another way. Your work at the school was enough for you."

"Arthur!" Mummy sounded louder than before, and she said very clearly, "You know full well I am not the only Whitechapel mother who has done this for her family, Arthur. I made the choice! Not you!"

Oh, Mummy and Daddy, don't be quiet again! Please talk. Please. Stop coughing, Mummy. I'm scared. I'm…

"The attacker was a stranger. Do you understand, Arthur? I had never seen him before. Just please never let the children know. They must never know… oh, please, dear God! That would…" Mummy's cough started again.

And then his father made soothing sounds and began humming. Harry listened and listened to the humming until his arms loosened and he leaned up against the wall and closed his eyes. It would be all right. It would be all right. Daddy had said so.

Harry sat up. "What?"

"Harry, would you like to see Mummy now?" His father was leaning down, offering his hand. Harry took his hand and stood up, dazed from being wakened, and walked into the room with him.

"Sit down next me, Harry, over here." Harry's eyes began to accommodate to the darkened room. It wasn't easy to breathe in here. Why? What was it that didn't feel right?

He looked around. It all seemed the same… the box for clothing, the mattress, the picture of Jesus, the table, the big Bible gleaming away on the table so that it could be read and written in. Yes, it was all the same. Except for a new smell that made the fear start tumbling around his heart again.

"Harry?"

"Yes, Mummy, I'm here." *And where are you, Mummy? It's hard to see you.* Mummy held the sheet up around her neck with one hand and offered her other hand to her youngest child. What did a little boy say to a Mummy who seemed so far away? Harry felt the overwhelming terror again.

"Oh, my little Harry, I do love you, I do."

Was she really there? She seemed so far away, as hard to see as any light in the fog. "Mummy, are you getting better, Mummy?"

"Harry," Sarah's voice was barely discernible. "Harry, my sweet… Harry, don't die young, Harry. And never forget me. I wanted to be your mother longer, Harry…"

Sarah closed her eyes, moving again toward some distant place. Harry let his head rest next to his mother's.

"Harry…"

"Yes, Mummy…"

"Harry, wipe your tears away. You just won't be able to see me. That's all, Harry. I'll always be at your side, Harry. Always, Love… I promise… You'll see…"

Still holding her hand, Harry drifted off to sleep again.

And Harry, aging Harry on the great ship Aquitania, came out of his trance, folded his blanket yet again and trundled off to his second class cabin. How long had his mind been dwelling in the ocean of Whitechapel?

If you'd been nearby, listening very carefully, you would have heard him softly singing, "Children of Cheape, hold you all still, For you shall have the Bow bell rung as you will." His was the light, flawlessly pitched tenor tone of a young man.

11. Duplicity

Letter from Mrs. W. for Dad! Oh dear! Caroline called. I telephoned for some paint and rollers, etc. Oh dear, the money goes through my fingers. Painting today. Finished roll of films and hope to send them to Frank soon. He's in Edmonton today. Mrs. Winn had me in for a cup of tea. Trudy and I are planning to go the show "Welcome Stranger."
[The Lois Diaries, September 4, 1947]

The night was particularly placid. In fact, the tenor of the entire trip had been one of gentle blessing for Harry, as though the very elements were easing him back to where he belonged, to where he had left his heart. And his soul. Because it was his last night on the ship, Harry decided not to hold back any longer. Having repaired to his cabin early, he now hung his blue dressing gown on the back of the door, sat on his berth and picked up his snifter of brandy from the night table, downing the honey in one gulp. *What would May think.* Removing his slippers and placing them carefully at the bedside, he reached to turn out the little light and slid under the covers. Restless at first, Harry at last calmed when he lay on his back with his hands clasped behind his head. After all, he had decided that this night would be the one to let his thoughts of Annie come and go under their own volition. His eternal nightly self-discipline of controlling his thoughts in order to manage his dreams could fly out the porthole and sink to the bottom of the sea for all he cared.

That being said, Harry's mind went blank.

An amorphous recollection from the day tried to surface. What was it? "Well, if I can't do it, I shan't force myself." Harry spoke aloud to whatever sea urchins might be present.

His thoughts floated back to the dining saloon and the final dinner of the voyage. Yet again, Mrs. Archer had called out to him as he attempted to make a discreet entrance, "Oh, Mr. Westley! Over here! Over here, Mr.

Westley!" She beckoned him to her table, pointing out the chair next to her unremarkable, middle-aged daughter. The atmosphere at their table was laden with repression and fragrances of roast beef and heavy, sickly-sweet perfume. Mrs. Archer wore the lavender silk dress and stole that her daughter wore in green. They should have switched colours, Harry thought. The high ornamentation of the saloon and its tones of cream, pink and rose, punctuated by the Havana velvet of the mahogany chairs, conspired to create a sense of the lingering incongruity of a disturbing, half-forgotten dream. Harry was eager to get to his table, privately tucked in near the wrought-iron balustrade.

Why did this woman insist on hurting her daughter this way day after day? The only reason he had ever sat with them a few times was because he pitied the daughter. Feeling it again now for this young woman, who was in all likelihood destined to be permanently unattached, Harry made his way to the table, acknowledging first the daughter and then the mother with a perfunctory bow. Harry held out the book he carried in his left hand, "Thank you, madam; but I've made myself a promise that I shall finish this book before we land. Enjoy your dinner."

Just as he was turning toward his table, the daughter spoke for the first time without solicitation, "It's worth the read, Mr. Westley," she nodded toward the book. "Du Maurier does not give Lady Dona – nor us - easy excuses for duplicity. Does she?"

Harry felt suddenly known. He was unprepared for a comment, any comment, from this woman, let alone the bold statement she had uttered. He looked directly at her, nodded his head slightly and smiled, "Quite right, Miss Archer. I agree."

Harry was struck by the woman's eyes. She looked into him with a clarity he had not experienced for years. He turned and left.

Had it been her eyes? Her voice? Her intuition? It didn't matter. The recollection now took Harry to the old feelings he had been trying to invoke. Yes, re-living the moment – the clear statement and the surprising beauty of her free, deep voice – opened the floodgates long held up against intimate memories of Annie. Harry looked up at the ceiling in his tiny cabin and let his sense of Annie flood over him. He was going home. He closed his eyes and looked into Annie's eyes.

Yes, Miss Archer's eyes were like Annie's eyes, actually – hazel with a black rim around the pupil that gave the gaze an intensity. And, yes, Annie would have made a statement like that, going straight to the truth, without deviation. And, yes... yes, Annie's voice. Miss Archer's voice had a musical quality to it, like the deep tone of the bells of his childhood. The bells of his Annie's voice. And laughter.

It had been the resonant, clear voice he had heard that day so long ago... that day when the world had opened up for him for the first time since his mother had died.

12. Leigh-on-Sea

Rainy but I decided to wash anyway. Letters from Frank and an air-mail from England from Leigh-on-Sea from Dad. Put a furnace fire on as it was real cold.
[The Lois Diaries, September 16, 1947]

At almost eighteen, Harry had been relentlessly reduced, in terms of family companionship, to the exclusive company of himself. Home now consisted of a room in his stepmother's home at 8 Commodore Street in Mile End. For Harry, that made Buxton Street now a short physical distance and an eternal cognitive distance away. It must groan with the collective sighs of Mummy and her children, he thought… whatever was left of it… Buxton Street, the pearly gates of Hell… and then Dad alone trying to breathe some life into the coughing, heaving, dying walls of Buxton Street. How did one revive a corpse? Even the move from 22 to 81 had made no difference to the appetite of the White Plague. Nothing in the life of the Westleys was impermeable to the fog as it seeped in through the windows and the chinks in the walls, bringing with it the most feared and prolonged death imaginable. If Mummy had sacrificed anything, he thought, she had sacrificed her breath so that others could breathe. And if – if – there was a God of compassion, that God would never punish Mummy for whatever it was that had made her feel she had moved beyond the pale. And she had kept them all breathing for a while; but the task was too onerous, even for a departed mother. Herbert had died three years after Mummy had died. Ernest had died less than a year after Herbert. The younger Arthur had died two years after that. And their Dad had died two years after that, over three years ago now. Only Harry and Charles remained, and Charles, who had left Harry to his own devices a year ago, would marry his Alice in March of this year, 1900, to be precise. In Kingston-on-Thames, a lifetime away from Buxton Street. To date, he and Charlie had escaped any footprints of the infamous, insidious killer. Neither, though, was yet as old as young Arthur had been when he had died at twenty-six. However, both of them were, and always had been, stronger than Arthur.

That was life – and death – in Whitechapel. Harry had become inured to it. Early death was a Cockney habit.

Arthur's had been a particularly brutal death, culminating in what Dr. Hastings diagnosed as "gangrene of the lung." Harry and his father and the incumbent widow, Lucretia, had been there with the younger Arthur at the end. Words were often inadequate, Harry had found, to describe pain and its effects. How in God's name (because Harry still recognized the existence of some force) could anyone say there was a loving God and at the same time watch a kind, intelligent, hard-working young man die in dreadful stages of unmitigated, incremental pain and suffocation? As commonplace as pain was within the sound of the Bow Bells, Arthur's pain surpassed any Harry had witnessed. Arthur's and Mummy's deaths might, he realized, be impossible to eradicate from his memory. *Perish the thought! I shall keep forgetting them.* Following Arthur's death, Harry had seen his father intentionally wither, despite the caring attention of Lucretia who had married him in 1891 to help with his vanishing family and to ease her own White Plague lonely widowhood.

And now here was Charlie, planning – no! – pledging to marry at the same age young Arthur had been when he had married his Alice. Harry, who routinely scoffed at superstition, nevertheless found himself wondering if Charlie had considered he was marrying a woman with the same name as Arthur's widow at the same age Arthur had been when he married. "I wouldn't do it!" He'd uttered the words aloud. As a stylish passer-by looked startled, Harry tipped his hat and enjoyed the moment.

No, indeed, Harry wouldn't marry at all. He'd seen enough pain and loss. He had better, more rational things to do. No woman would find her way into his heart and mind and live there. His brief relationship with Dorothy last year had helped him make his decisions and develop a set of skills. Dorothy had wanted nothing more than marriage. Harry had wanted everything more than any marriage he had ever seen to date. Working one's way, decently, out of Whitechapel must come first, he had told Dorothy, who had passively disagreed and aggressively pursued her prey. It had been the passivity that had irritated Harry more than any other quality. It was more Dorothy's passivity than her aggression that had done her in – struck her from any list in Harry's plans. He wished her well and had no regrets.

There would be no early marriage for him and certainly none with any young woman who had no vision beyond what Whitechapel offered.

These were the thoughts that occupied Harry Westley's mind as he made his way along Farringdon Street on the fourth Tuesday evening of February in this new century. He was on his way to sample the politics of the Fabian Society at a meeting of trade union and socialist groups. After his years of blind bondage to poverty, Harry was discovering alternatives, alternatives he hoped might open the world for him and take him further west and out of Mile End.

Education had become his first avenue of escape. He knew that all success would depend on this. Both Ernest and Arthur had illustrated and promoted the power of education and intellect. If they'd only been well, they would each have managed to rise above the high tides of poverty. Ernest had become a commercial clerk. Arthur had become a printer compositor. Never had Harry been so impressed as when Arthur's Association, the London Society of Compositors, provided all expenses for the funeral. Finally, the brewer's drayman had a child not buried as a pauper. *And you, my Dad, you should have been buried in Westminster Abbey, you should. Why did you have to go, too? Why? To be with Mummy, you told me. Are you there with her now? Where are you? Have you made your peace with God? Has He made His with You? Has He?*

Harry picked up his pace. Yes, despite having had to leave school when he was so young, he'd never abandoned his intelligence. Both Arthur and Ernest had warned him not to. With the help of his step-mother, he'd achieved acceptance into The City of London School in Cheapside. *Poor Lucretia now in her befuddlement; she'd been a kind stepmother, caring for Dad, never trying to replace Mummy… always having to live in Mummy's sad shadow… Mummy's shadow…* As "the son of a poor man," he'd been awarded a John Carpenter Scholarship and completed studies in shorthand typing and penmanship. In Harry's assessment, these seemed the best skills to perfect to give him speedy, fruitful egress from Mile End. And, indeed, just before Christmas, he had secured a modest position as a shorthand typist in the Records Office of Old Bailey. To augment his studies, Harry had continued his inexorable consumption of books and questioned people he sought out as informative and bright.

And here he was walking along Farringdon Street. This was a world thriving with life, not sinking into decay and death. Here was life – particles and slices and great slabs of life – vivid and loud. Loud with the constant, aggressive din of London's true pulsebeat. A far cry from the seething, skulking, muffled noises and utter stench of the Cockney domain. Dare he hope to move one day entirely out of Mile End? Surely the painstaking efforts he was exerting in new penmanship classes and in modifying his dialect would help bring this about. Surely! "If our health doesn't give us away, our speech will," his Dad had told him. "Watch your speech, Harry, watch your speech, and find someone away from this bloody cemetery to mimic. Your Mum gave you all a grounding in manners and polite speech. Your Mum was a woman who knew how to read and write, Harry. How do you think you and your brothers became so clever? There must be one of you to carry along her desire for betterment. There must be, Harry. Do that for your Mum… and for me."

Harry sighed and put his hand on his breast pocket. Yes, there was Ernest's medal, his strongest motivator. *I'll do it the way you would have, Ernest; you, of all of us, could have done it.* In his quest for meaning, Harry had yet to find personal fervour, something that would carry him beyond the Christianity of his childhood. To be fair and true to his Mummy and Dad, he had attended meetings to hear Major Booth speak and had come away with respect for the man and for the changes the Salvation Army was effecting in Whitechapel. But, truth be told, Christianity did nothing but enhance his excruciating loneliness, his sense of having no "fit" anywhere. So, the Salvation Army brought him personal pain, and the major denominations held no meaning for him. It was easier to keep Christianity as his personal ogre, far easier than exploring the pain. And, there was still that great anger toward God that gripped his heart and prevented any softening. Yes, it was much easier to think, and hope, that God Himself could be punished. He'd become skilled in exercising this anger despite the closeness he felt toward Mummy at times and her example of blind faith. Or had it been blind? The frequent haunting of long lost words threatened to surface. With the perfection borne of exacting practice, Harry evicted them.

Dad would be happy about one thing. Harry had found someone admirable and real. In Thomas Robertson, a robust, honest, genuinely happy fifty year old, Harry had found the person his Dad had told him to watch for, the man to mimic. Just last week, he had been speaking with a few mates after work about his interest in Secularism and Theosophy, and Thomas had suggested tonight's meeting. "Harry, my man, come and hear what the Fabian Society has to say. You're bright. You'll understand, and, more importantly, you'll find it less based on nothing than Secularism. And, do please stop calling me Mr. Robertson. We're colleagues."

"Well... Thomas... I've read some writing on the Fabians. What makes common sense to me, in any theory, is the pre-eminence of the Mind. It's our minds that will save us, not some God who allows the kind of poverty we see in this city. If anything were going to save Londoners and eradicate London's scandalous poverty, it must be based on reason and its application," Harry hadn't felt this zealous in conversation with anyone since Charles had left for Alice's home. "That's the key, though, I suppose. Reason must guide reasonable action."

Thomas enjoyed this thoughtful, guarded, perhaps too idealistic youth. He had it in him to develop politically. "As long as you don't tell me that God is Mind and Mind is God, Harry! You'll enjoy Edward Pease; he'll be compatible with your thinking. The meeting is on the 27th at Memorial Hall on Farringdon Street. There will be a debate and then a vote. You won't be eligible to vote; but the experience will be good for you."

"What will they be voting on, Mr.... Thomas?" Harry felt awkward in trying to relate to this experienced court clerk as a colleague.

"The delegates will vote on a motion to establish a separate, distinct Labour group in Parliament. Don't be put off by the details. Just come along as an observer and keep your analytical skills sharp. See if there's anything in it for you. Memorial Hall is that Congregationalist building I pointed out to you on our walk a week ago. The one that used to be Fleet Street Prison, just beyond the bank at St. Bride Street. Shall I see you there, then? Eight o'clock!" And off Thomas had walked – westward – to his home in Westminster.

And here now was Harry – at the meeting place of the bank and the Hall. Glorious buildings! He'd been home first to feed Lucretia and settle her for the evening. He walked up the stairs and into Memorial Hall. And he was only a half hour late. It wasn't difficult to find the meeting. He simply followed the noise and found himself in a great hall. There couldn't have been many more than a hundred people; but their jeering and clapping filled the vast hall. A man, seated close to the door, got up and approached Harry. "Are you a delegate, sir? One has to be twenty-one years of age or older."

"No. No, I'm here to observe." Harry felt ill-at-ease but keen to watch the proceedings.

"Then would you go up to the gallery, sir, with the other spectators?"

Harry looked up and was immediately relieved. There was only a handful of spectators in the gallery. He made his way up and took a seat toward the back.

What ensued was the most overwhelming and energetic experience Harry had ever had in his life. This was not the quiet, mannerly presentation of new ideas he had experienced in Theosophical and Secularist presentations. No, this was a rip-roaring, loud, confusing exchange of ideas that was creating something in the order of a palpable, new entity. Out of what Harry could vaguely make out as Socialists, Trade Unionists, Independents, and Fabians came some radical proposal to form a Labour Representation Committee. There was talk of women's rights, poverty, equity and "a party for ordinary blokes." Even with the keen sense that he knew so very little, Harry felt something within him loosen and spin itself into a desire to get involved. This was an entirely new feeling for Harry, and it made him… well… giddy, he supposed. At least that is what he suspected he felt, given that he'd only read about giddiness. And, for Heaven's sake, he felt alive. Connected! Passionate? Yes, passionate.

The evening – whatever this evening was – seemed to be over when Harry heard his name being called out from the main floor. "Harry! Harry Westley! Down here, my man!" Ah, it was Thomas, waving vigorously at him to come down. And off Harry bounded, making almost rude headway to meet his friend below. He elbowed his way through the crowd to Thomas.

Thomas put his arm around Harry's shoulder. "Well? What did you think? I saw you come in. Were you impressed?"

"Impressed? Indeed. But more than impressed, Thomas. Inspired." Harry was animated. "I've never seen nor heard anything like this. I had no idea politics could be this exciting – that there could be anything for – well – for the ordinary bloke!"

"Then come over here, my friend, and meet Pease." Thomas steered him through a few chattering groups to a line-up of people waiting to talk to the man whom Harry recognized as Edward Pease. "He always has people after him for more, after he's spoken," Thomas guided Harry into the line-up. "No doubt you can understand that after hearing him tonight."

Harry nodded in agreement, trying to formulate in his mind something intelligent to ask Pease. The group of four people in front of them gave up the wait and left. Harry and Thomas promptly stepped ahead into the vacated space.

And that was when it happened. It was at that precise moment that Harry heard her clear voice and her intellectual repartee with Pease. Something was being said about how the "inevitability of gradualism certainly didn't happen tonight, did it?" and then, "How are you going to honour the perfect character in you while this business is going on, Edward? Power can be intoxicating. No one functions well while intoxicated."

This was a woman speaking. A beautiful woman, plainly and neatly dressed, with wild golden hair spilling out from the green ribbon attempting to pull the curls back. A woman, if older than he, certainly no more than a year or two older. A woman speaking on equal ground with a man. A woman as confident as any man her age, and certainly more confident than he. A woman with lustrous traces of pure Whitechapel in her voice.

Harry was mesmerized. He followed Thomas's direction in nervous, and yet mildly happy, obedience.

"Edward. Anne. I want you to meet Harry Westley…"

And that was how it had all started. That was how it had all started – the beauty and the pain – forty-some years ago.

Harry left it at that for his last night on the Aquitania. *Best to leave it here, best to stay with us together… yes, that was how it all started… and how will it end?… because it never ended, Annie… If only, Annie, if only we could start again, Annie, I am so sorry, so sorry…* With Annie's face, framed in gentle golden curls and surrounded by green, her hazel eyes shining into his like that first night so very long ago, Harry drifted off to sleep. The gentle undulations of the ocean played the ethereal treble clef of an old melody. And as the supporting, strong bass clef, the Aquitania's engines droned reassuringly along.

13. Theosophy and Secularism

> *Rain, and boy it is wet and cold, too. It is a bit monotonous. Kay has taken a job at McGavin's Bread from 4:30–7:30. Got a letter from Mrs. W., also an airmail from Dad. By myself and it is still raining.*
>
> *[The Lois Diaries, September 17, 1947]*

The aftermath of his dream clung to him, pulling him down. Harry felt as though he lacked the strength to return from this heavy, opaque place that wanted to pull him down until he could breathe no longer. It seemed so much more powerful than he.

He sat up and looked around. Yes, here he was, on the ship. He took a deep breath. There would be no more dreams on this ship – only the dream that was called life. But Harry couldn't shake a sense of doom. Its malevolent odour filled the small cabin, as sour as the disease of Whitechapel. It was old and all too familiar; but it was the first visitation of it on the Aquitania. A flash of anger was quickly routed by an explosion of overwhelming panic. Gasping, he slipped his legs over the edge of the bed and found his slippers.

Harry, forlorn, sat for a few moments to settle his breathing and rid himself of the panic and pain in his chest. He felt little.

What had the dream been? At first, all he could remember was the sense of death. And then he remembered Ernest. Ernest had been calling him from across an abyss... *"Harry!"* He had called desperately. And then all the children had gathered around Ernest, and then Dad had parted the group, like a wild Moses of Whitechapel. And Dad had called to him, *"Stay away from us, Harry. Do what you must do at home, lad."* And – ah, yes, mother. Always, Mummy. Just as she had arisen in the dream with her supplications, he had woken. Harry lay back on the pillow, his hands clasped behind his head, slippers still on his feet. He closed his eyes.

"Harry. Harry."

"Yes, Mummy."

"Harry, I'm here. As I promised. I am never far from your side."

"I'm troubled and yet so close to home, Mummy. I'm committing an unforgivable sin, I am." The air was dense and electric, as though it had substance.

Sarah smiled into his trance, all liquid gold, and rich, like manna. *"No, my son. You are doing what your soul needs to do. You will find peace for your soul only in one place, Harry."*

"Yes. At home? At home. Yes."

"Harry."

"Yes, Mother."

"Harry. Open your eyes."

Harry opened his eyes.

"Mummy!"

"Yes, Harry. You see, I am not simply in your imagination. I am here. Always."

"I do see."

"Harry, I am the angel round your head. As I promised."

And as Sarah smiled and Harry's heart settled, the white and gold lights spread out, surrounding and vaporizing his mother. And Sarah disappeared into the light, leaving a trail of sweet perfume.

A light-hearted Harry sat up. "Good morning!" He felt like shouting. "Good morning, Life. I'm coming home, Annie! Home!" He put on his bathrobe, laid out his clothes – his Hello England clothes – and prepared to shave.

For the rest of that day, while the Aquitania moved stolidly and unwaveringly toward Southampton, Harry felt released from an old, indefinable weight. He wasn't sure just what it was; but it had been heavy to the point of death, and it was gone!

Unfettered and as buoyant as the Aquitania itself, Harry even deigned to have lunch with Mrs. Archer and her daughter! Not only that, he dared to pick up on Miss Archer's prior comments on his reading. As poached pears were being served in the Grand Old Lady's sun-drenched Verandah I, he dared to entertain the difficult remark about his reading, "Why did you say that Du Maurier doesn't give us easy answers for duplicity, Miss Archer?

Angela, undaunted, leaned forward into the question. Had she perhaps been hoping for it? Her eyes danced, truly alive – and, yes, beautiful. She was actually pretty! "Perhaps that was forward of me, Mr. Westley; but I've seen you on this trip as someone doing something new and frightening. You had told us you were returning to London, and, almost in the same breath, told us there is nothing and no one left there for you. I have the sense, you see, that there is someone there for you." Her eyes still steady, she relaxed into her chair.

When Miss Archer took it upon herself to talk, Harry mused, she didn't mince words! And yet, in the vitality of her smile and words, she was possessed of a compelling intensity that matched Annie's. "Well, you're very perceptive," he spoke quietly. "I am indeed going to see someone I haven't seen for over forty years. And I am going to a city I abandoned when I didn't know what I was doing." Harry was utterly surprised at himself as he spoke freely for the first time in years.

"Well, Mr. Westley, Angela and I thought you were most likely a very interesting man. And, indeed, you are," Mrs. Archer, ever the woman of manners, attempted to steer the conversation onto a less private path. "But, Angela, my dear, don't you think that you might have asked if you could ask personal questions like this?"

Angela withdrew. Harry could see it happen because he knew it – the cycle of covert castigating and shrinking – so well, so intimately. Her mother had some hold over her daughter's confidence, and Harry abhorred the resulting self-diminishment in Angela. It took her beauty with it. This was the meekness, the drabness, Harry had sensed before… because he knew it himself. It happened when Mrs. Archer took over. Angela's poise had turned to embarrassment. She was about to offer an apology when Harry responded directly to her, "Actually, I'm quite prepared to have a challenging conversation like this. I have perhaps been quiet for too long on this trip.

And, I suppose that this as the last day provides me with a sense of freedom. Go ahead, Miss Archer, and I shall have some questions for you." Harry's sense of surprise at himself was developing into wonder. His reward was Angela's resumption of interest and energy in getting to the heart of a matter. Following her own senses was good for her, Harry realized. Her rather square face softened, allowing the burnished gold in her hair to light up her hazel eyes. Yes, indeed, her auburn hair and her quite dazzling smile transformed the tight caution he had always detected in earlier, cursory exchanges.

"Fair enough, Mr. Westley. I, too, have remained distant for the better part of this passage," Angela succeeded in quieting her mother and impressing Harry. In her speedy return to composure, he saw his misjudgment of her depth. Like Annie, this woman perceived deeply and, in a context that allowed it, stood her ground. "Mother is correct. You are a much more interesting man. As I suspected. I hope the venture exceeds your expectations. Perhaps, in terms of duplicity, you've put an end to being dishonest with yourself."

"Perhaps," Harry acknowledged. "And you, Miss Archer? What are your plans when you return to Cambridge?"

Angela's look was as steady as Annie's had always been. "I'll return to my studies… and perhaps to the man I crossed the sea to forget." Ever so briefly, Angela's eyes revealed her sadness and vulnerability. She quickly recovered. "And now we are even, Mr. Westley. We know each other's secret motivations. Of course, we are also now more human." Mrs. Archer's evident disdain and shock couldn't penetrate the dialogue.

"Indeed, Miss Archer, we are… very human… a condition I've found to be a painful one on the whole," Harry's shy smile broadened and developed rapidly into laughter. "I do take myself too seriously at times!" Angela and, yes, Mrs. Archer, joined in the laughter.

"And you see now, don't you, Mr. Westley, what I mean about Du Maurier's use of duplicity?" In Angela's interruption of the levity, Harry realized how laughter had, for him, become a lost treasure. He'd had that treasure in spades with Annie. And never since. Except with Frankie.

Harry savoured the last bite of the poached pears. "What, Miss Archer? That it shows and can be read?" It was amazing how much better food tasted when one was in the company of stimulating people. Harry had not enjoyed food so much for years.

"Except when one is very clever or too deeply preoccupied, Mr. Westley. You missed mine," Angela dabbed at the corner of her mouth with her napkin. Harry recognized her need for self-control. "We all have ways of artifice that only serve to confuse us. I saw it in your composure because I know it myself. My intent was not to hurt you. I wanted to see who you really are. Thank you for joining us today."

"Well, enough of the confessional! If Angela hasn't pushed you too far, she has me, Mr. Westley," Mrs. Archer kept her fork poised over her dessert. "Do tell us what you expect to see on this trip, Mr. Westley. Our steward told us that you were Canadian; but we recognized your fine English accent. Where is home for you?"

Harry's smile disappeared. *Mind your words, Harry. If our health doesn't give us away, our speech will.* The time had come. "In a place called Whitechapel, Mrs. Archer. Have you heard of it?" There! He had said it. He had said it!

Mrs. Archer was silent, for a moment. Speechless, really.

The remainder of the luncheon continued in energetic dialogue. Except for Mrs. Archer's disappointment that her daughter had not met someone who could divert her from James' unreliability, it was a perfect ending to life on the Aquitania.

In point of fact, both Harry and Angela found in the interchange mirrored qualities of their lost loves. Thus it was that the easy friendship that developed and that would drift away with the Southampton tides served to strengthen Harry's and Angela's separate, but similar resolves.

For Harry, it was as though his Mother had woven gauze tendrils connecting him to her dreamworld and to England. He felt reminders of the connection throughout the day of approach to docking on England's shores. And his invisible tears of reunion were softened and gently wiped away by these imperceptible fingers.

As he assisted Angela and her mother, later in the afternoon, from the deck of the Aquitania and down into the excited throng of people waiting for passengers, Harry was grateful he had broken his habit of restraint. He had missed so many opportunities in life. "Thank you, Mrs. Archer for your persistence in asking me to share a luncheon with you."

He turned to Angela and smiled into those eyes that made Annie real. "Miss Archer, your company, late though I allowed it, has been the highlight of the voyage for me."

"And, Harry, your company has been my highlight. Thank you," she extended her hand to Harry. "I am so pleased we did not miss each other's souls."

And, as Harry continued to surprise himself, he took Angela's hand and kissed her. "You are a beautiful woman, Miss Archer, in all ways. Be certain that the man you love is worthy of you."

"I shall, Harry," Angela whispered. "Thank you." She squeezed Harry's hand, let go and turned to her mother.

Mrs. Archer put her arm through her daughter's, and the women left to find out if indeed James was waiting.

And Harry! Well, he could go boldly on toward London. Harry Westley was no longer alone. He turned for one last look at the four proud funnels of the Aquitania, saluted and turned to find a taxi to take him to the train terminus.

He was home! Land of Hope and Glory, indeed!

14. Questions about destiny

> *A Robin Red breast in a Cage*
> *Puts all Heaven in a Rage.*
> *A dove house fill'd with doves & Pigeons*
> *Shudders Hell thro' all its regions.*
> *{Auguries of Innocence; William Blake]*

The exhilaration of yesterday's landing in England had been replaced today with a brooding homesickness. *Strange, given that I am home. Ah, yes; but they've all left. Gone and left me. Is there another home, then? Have they gone there? Perhaps. I feel less inclined to see that as delusional now. Everything's an illusion, anyway, in one way or another.*

London poured in around Harry. In spite of the passage of time and the War, it was the same. Noisy. Lonely. Crowded. Acrid. Sooty. *Would Elgar write a different Cockaigne, a new London Town? Perhaps not. But then, so much has been destroyed. Levelled.*

He'd made his way from Victoria Station that morning, taking a cab from Whitehall to the Courts of Justice. He wanted to walk from there, to follow Fleet Street east to St. Paul's. And here he was, sitting on the same steps where he'd stood so many years ago, hawking papers. *My platform – stage, if you will.* The forbidding columns of so long ago continued to keep him in his place and prohibit entry. With his two bags sitting in front of him, he'd read Annie's letter once more. "As I always have, I love you, no matter what." He read these words again, as though the very reading would make them permanent, as though Annie were with him, speaking the words to him, not writing them across the Atlantic after a lifetime of separation. And they would, they could, they should, be back again, talking, holding each other in the darkest night. Safe.

How can we know how we'll feel now? How dare we think we know?

For the first time on the journey to Annie and to himself, he took another letter from his jacket pocket and opened it. It was his short-hand copy of the letter he'd sent to her to say that he was coming – truly coming – home. Had he ever left?

Regina, Saskatchewan

August 15, 1947

Dearest Annie,

May moved to Toronto July 28th. Lois and the children went downtown by taxi with her to see her off. Frank and I went separately to the station and stayed back from the send-off. It was all right – in fact, Lois told me after I seemed "in fine form." My last day at work will be August 25th.

I'll leave for the Aquitania on the 27th, the day after my birthday. Frank will take me to the train terminus here, and I'll take the train to Halifax, a long journey. Frank has travelled it on business a few times since the War, so I'm following his directions. The Aquitania will leave from Halifax on August 28th and will arrive in Southampton September 6th. I shall take the overnight train to London from there and arrive at Victoria Station early in the morning of the 7th.

Thank you for understanding my need to find my way to you along the pathway of my youth. I'll go to my lodgings on the 7th and walk to your place on the evening of the 8th. During that day, I'll visit Buxton Street. Well, I've written it now. And so, I'm committed to doing it.

I share the same thoughts that you have had, Annie. How will we see each other? How will we know that we love each other as much in person as we do in writing? This will not be easy for either of us.

And there is so much for me to move past. Although I found it easy to say that you had let me down, I truly was the one to cause the desertion of our love and our life together, Annie. You were so right that I could have waited for you or returned to you. Somehow both options seemed impossible to me. And look at the length of the interval I created! How could I have been so short-sighted? I understand your anger. I ask you, please, to let it go. If you can't, nor won't, I understand. I am asking, I see, for forgiveness, Annie.

Is it not incredible that in these questions time has fallen away? We're back to my passivity, or stubbornness, of forty years ago. It makes me wonder about some of the idealist teachings that were important to us so long ago... questions about destiny and perfect character. How could I have purported to believe such theories and not have put anything I believed in into practice?

Annie, I'm concerned that I sound insincere to you when I write about how very much I loved you. Please know that I said it back then from the depths of my heart and that I say it from there now. And, Annie, in all that time between then and now, I have loved you.

Love always,

Harry

Harry put the envelope carefully in his jacket pocket. He was so close to Annie now.

"London Times! Worker killed in Blackwall Tunnel excavation! Read story in the London Times!" The caller made the words sound like Cockney music. Good for him; he was doing the chant correctly. A lifetime away and the cry was the same.

Where was the voice coming from? There! That young boy over there. *Brandishing a newspaper just as I would have done so long ago*. Harry was compelled to get up and walk down a few steps to listen more carefully to the boy. He'd like to ask him a question or two. But everything had turned to sepia. Blast the fog! He'd go to the boy anyway. It seemed impossible to get there, even though the newsboy was a mere dozen steps away. He'd do it, though, before the boy disappeared. *I must ask him what it's like selling newspapers these days.* Harry struggled toward the boy. Odd get-up... the boy wore a tattered tweed jacket and a matching cap. His pants stopped below his knees, and his worn knee-stockings fit into shoes that were well-polished and full of holes. A little too thin, he was. The crowd became a single sepia organism as Harry stopped directly behind the boy. "Excuse me, young man, I used to sell newspapers like this right here. On this spot! I wanted to let you know that you're doing a fine..." The boy turned around and looked boldly at Harry.

"Do I know you, Guv?" He was about ten years old, clean, proud, sharp, gaunt.

"No, son; but I know you," and his eyes brimmed and burned with salt.

And then the boy did the strangest thing. He began to cry in unison with Harry and pleaded, "Where's our Mum? Our Mum? Where's our Mum? Bertie needs her."

As Harry reached out to him, to help dry his tears, the sepia bled into reds and blues and dark greens, and a modern youth stood in front of him. "You all right, Guv?"

Harry stepped back, shocked and embarrassed, "Yes. Completely. Yes. I'm sorry to have bothered you. I thought you were someone else... another newsboy."

The boy blended into all the rest of a present that Harry wasn't part of, that he was blind to.

And Harry, disregarding any thought of entering St. Paul's Cathedral, picked up his bags and made his way up to Cheapside and St. Mary-le-Bow while the Bow bells, all that the Blitzkrieg had left of old St. Mary, tolled out noon.

He was home. He'd never left.

15. White + Chapel

Blue Thursday for me, but otherwise it wasn't bad. Mugsie a general nuisance. She broke four dishes today. Nell was supposed to have taken a box of candy in for Bob's birthday and when Trudy wasn't home, she kept it and ate it. I made more and she took it in safely. Frank home tonight.
[The Lois Diaries, October 2, 1947]

He'd hurried home the day of that headline.

Dad's comment on the building of Blackwall Tunnel was that if they could build tunnels under the Thames, they could figure out how to save Whitechapel from the White Plague. But no one cared about Whitechapel, despite Poverty Surveys and help from the Salvation Army. As long as the rest of London was safe, Whitechapel didn't exist… except to be thought of as the carsey of the city.

Dad couldn't do it all alone any longer at home, especially with young Arthur gone most of the time, so he'd married Mrs. Sharp that summer. She had lost her husband and both children to the White Plague. And she was strong and loving and needed to help, she said. She said it would give her a way to get over her grieving. Harry wondered how more grief could help anyone get rid of grief.

Both Bertie and Ernest were struggling hard to beat the disease that the fog brought through the very walls. It seeped in through brick and stone and glass. It couldn't be stopped because Whitechapel breathed it in and breathed it out, in and out, in and out. Bertie wasn't as strong as Ernest, not nearly as strong. He looked so wretched now that Harry actually thought last night it might be good for Bertie to be with Mummy. She'd look after him better than this little family could do down here on earth.

Harry burst in the front door. The stench of sickness made him cough. "Dad! I sold all the newspapers today! Dad! Here's the money, Dad, and a nice gentleman gave me a half crown! Dad!" Harry had never been given so much money. It must have been because he was nine now. Once he'd turned nine in August, he'd actually felt so much older. "Dad!" Harry bent down to take off his shoes.

"All right, my man, Harry!" Arthur came through the curtain they'd put over the kitchen door to hold the heat in for Bertie. "Good for you! But pipe down. They can hear you back at St. Paul's now!" He put an arm around Harry. *Good, you still feel solid, my prince! Not like Bertie; not like Bertie.* Arthur knelt in front of Harry and looked into his eyes. *Ah, Sarah, you still live in those eyes; you do, Sarah.* He put his hands on Harry's shoulders. Was it to steady Harry or himself? "Bertie's struggling, Harry. You should know that. In case he doesn't make it."

Harry was immediately afraid that his thought of Bertie going to Mummy had made his brother sicker. He shouldn't have thought it; he shouldn't have thought it! "Is he dying, Dad? Is he?"

"I'm afraid so, son. Dr. Slimon told us on Monday night that Bertie wouldn't survive this bout; but I didn't want to tell you then. I was sure that Lucretia and I together could nurse him through. But we're losing, Harry, and you need to know." Bone-weary, Arthur coughed and stood up.

Harry's immediate flood of relief over not having caused Bertie's decline was quickly replaced by that old, familiar, terrible feeling in his gut. What would he do without Bertie? *Bertie, Bertie, kind Bertie. Who will draw my pictures? Who will sing to me when I can't sleep? Oh, Bertie, who will make the hurt go away? Stay here, Bertie – it's not fair if you go to Mummy yet! Not yet, Bertie; not yet... please..."*

"Would you like to see him, Harry?" Arthur's voice settled Harry.

"Yes, Daddy. Please."

Arthur put out his hand. "Come on, then." He led Harry into the kitchen and to the cot near the fire in the grate Mr. Givens had given them. "Remember not to get close to his breath, now. Dr. Slimon believes this evil is carried through the air somehow. And he says there's reason to believe we should wash our hands frequently. Well, I say, first you have to have water. And what good is the filth we have to use as water?" Bertie's heaving breaths played an eerie continuo in the background.

Arthur knelt down beside Bertie. He whispered in Bertie's ear, "Harry's back from St. Paul's, son. He's here to see you." Arthur kissed Bertie's forehead and looked over at Lucretia who shook her head. Bertie seemed unable to move, unable to unlock himself from his stare. *Oh, sweet Bertie, what are you looking at? Your face is burning, Bertie.* Arthur wiped his face with the cloth Lucretia had put in a bowl beside Herbert's make-shift bed.

Harry sat on the floor beside his brother. *You're so sick, aren't you, Bertie? Look at your cheeks, Bertie. They're redder than the coals on the grate. And your eyes are going further and further into your head, Bertie. And your breath... oh, Bertie, Bertie.* "Bertie," Harry took his brother's hot hand – how strange, the fingertips were cold. "It's me, Bertie. Harry. A man gave me a half crown today, Bertie. He gave it to me for you, Bertie, because first off, he gave me a shilling, and then I said, 'Thank you, sir, for I have a very sick brother.' And then he said, 'Then give it back to me, lad. And take this. And may your brother be blessed.' Wasn't that fine of him, Bertie? It's a good sign, it is!"

A flame shot up from the grate at the precise moment that a flicker of a smile passed across Herbert Westley's lovely, sensitive face.

"See, Dad! He heard me! Bertie heard me!"

"He did indeed, Harry. Never forget how much Bertie loves you, my boy. Now you run along and find Ernest. Charlie has gone to get Arthur."

And as he left the kitchen, Harry heard Mother Lucretia (for he could never call her simply Mother) say something about "Bertie's diarrhoea being nothing but blood now, Arthur dear; I'm so sorry." The next thing he heard was Daddy crying. *Poor Daddy; crying like he did when Mummy was dying.* Harry refused to let the tears push their way into his own eyes. He ran to find Ernest – to see if he was still getting stronger. And he must be lonely. And scared. Yes, he would help make Ernest better now.

At seven o'clock the next morning, November 24, 1891, Arthur woke Harry as usual. He looked dreadfully tired and troubled.

"What's the matter, Dad? Is it Bertie, Dad?"

"Yes, Harry. It's Bertie," Arthur took Harry's hand and stroked it lovingly. "Bertie died early this morning. I was with him, son, and he slipped away very easily. The pain is over for him, Harry." *And it goes on for us, Harry, in bloody Whitechapel, and I haven't the energy any longer to be angry.*

Later that day, Harry looked at the certificate Dr. Slimon had written about Bertie. Bertie's and Ernest's reading lessons had given Harry a reading ability far beyond his years, even if, at times, he wasn't sure what the meaning was. He understood the meaning of these words, though. "Tubercular peritonitis, 3 months; Diarrhoea, 8 days, 81 Buxton Street, Mile End New Town," it said. These words meant that an awful murderer had killed his beautiful, kind brother. And the same God who had let Mummy die had done nothing to save Bertie from this foe.

So ended the record of Herbert's once-promising life. He was thirteen years old.

And Harry, Aging Harry, Returned Harry, following the same path Home that he had run along the day of the half-crown, felt the length of the years and the weight of the grief he had hidden for so long. How could anyone in Canada know the Cockney burden?

It was a burden that had greater mass than either World War or the Great Influenza Epidemic.

It was more ponderous and heinous because it received no recognition, and it had no end. All he had to do now was to give in to his surroundings as London's geography pulled him inward and eastward, along Cheapside to Old Jewry and into the very guts of The City. London's buried shame would unfold the rest of the undertaking for him.

As would Annie.

Harry had intentionally positioned himself in lodgings adjacent to Bishopsgate and Wormwood. In planning, he had felt that being midway between Annie's flat and Buxton Street was a wise place to be. And being within the old heart of London was somehow fitting. After all, his life was undergoing its most rigorous trial. All elements had now been brought together in a crucible, of sorts.

And here he was, once more sitting forlornly, on the edge of another bed. It had been a difficult night. He'd been monumentally unsettled all through the night and could not now shake a lingering sense of dread. Perhaps his desire to be near the old Synagogue and Spitalfields Market had been foolish. How could he have foreseen the changes? How could he have prepared himself for the devastation both of war and time in this ancient territory? He'd heard tales of people's surprise at how tiny their places of childhood felt when they revisited them years later. This was not the case here. Whitechapel had been eviscerated and spread-eagled around yawning holes, scattered debris and the brokenness brought about by war and poverty, where the only colour was venous red, visible and invisible, splattered and contained.

Heaving a great sigh, Harry stood up and forced himself to move into a morning routine. And what would that look like, he wondered, forty years later in the now of blankness? This was his day to meet Annie again, his day to come home! In some ways, he had never felt so alone.

Ah! Imagine running water in Whitechapel! Harry dragged himself into the present and made ready to go out for breakfast and his walk north and ever so slightly eastward... up to Spitalfields, onto Princelet, over to Brick Lane and straight up to Buxton. He had committed to visiting Buxton Street, hadn't he? He could never in a multitude of lifetimes forget the route home, the route young Harry took to fly into Mummy's arms.

But all that Harry did that day was wander. Whitechapel took control, and Harry succumbed. He quite simply could not go to Buxton Street. It was too onerous a task. A profound sadness descended upon Harry and bore down, down into the depths of his being. Old worldless, formless entities took hold of that vulnerable spot in his chest until he found himself, almost running, hell-bent southward, away from his stalemate with the old Synagogue.

What in the name of all that ever might be holy had he thought he was doing?

He sped along London Wall and down Moorgate until his body forced him to stop and breathe. Gasping, he leaned against a wall.

At last breathing more easily, Harry looked up. Now, where was he?

He looked around. Why, he was looking directly into the face of St. Olave's Jewry! The survivor with the pentacle and spire intact! He'd taken himself into the area of old halls and walls of justice, to safety and to sanctuary. He laughed. He'd always known westward was safer, stronger. Although he'd gone too far west in this day's quest for strength.

And - yes! He'd taken himself to the area that he and Annie had loved. Would the tea shop they'd frequented still be there? He headed toward St. Olave Park. And – yes! There was the shop. Or, at least an updated facsimile of it. Harry walked down the street, crossed the corner to the shop and entered.

The inner workings were indeed similar to his and Annie's times of meeting and talking and dreaming. The gentle ambiance and the soft light were the same, welcoming and quiet, musty and familiar. Would she be there?

Yes, there she was! Over in the far corner, holding hands across the small table with a young man and speaking passionately into his equally intent gaze. Ah, how well he knew that look, that green jacket, those curls.

"Yes, Harry, yes! We'll go to Canada. Charlie has a good head on his shoulders. And Alice has, too. They wouldn't mislead us. And Charlie is the only family you have," she pulled Harry's hands to her mouth and kissed them, "except for me, Harry."

Harry leaned into her gaze, "Annie, it's the way for us to break from the poverty of Whitechapel. There truly is no other way. London is unforgiving when it comes to one's place of birth. Good heavens – England is unforgiving! Canada offers us freedom… a fresh, new beginning." He touched her cheek and stroked a stray curl away from her forehead. "I love you, Annie."

"And I love you, Harry, with all my heart. I think there's a lot of the Blakeian soul in you, Harry… tender, artistic, perceptive. The same boy in different centuries and in different Londons. Somehow, the same boy with the same mother. Blake's mother educated him at home. Sarah did the same, in another way, for you. For another thing, Blake prophesied your life a hundred years before it happened."

Harry looked shocked. "What in the world do you mean, Annie?"

"Well, Blake was grieved over the Industrial Revolution. Your family was killed by its effects," Sarah took Harry's hand again and smiled. "Look at you, my Harry – you're the Blake Schoolboy. 'Ah, Harry,' whispers William, 'ah, Harry... How can the bird that is born for joy, Sit in a cage and sing? How can a child when fears annoy, But droop his tender wing, And forget his youthful spring?'"

Harry felt intensely connected to Annie, Annie with the blond curls and the smile that would take any man's breath away. "Shall we finish our tea and go to your place?"

How beautiful she is. How in love we are.

"Tea, sir?" The proprietor intruded.

"Yes. Please. And two scones," Harry felt irritated. "And I'll sit over there in the corner by the window." *With the young woman. And never, never bother us again!*

Harry put his cap and jacket on the clothes tree by the table and sat down in the very spot where he and Annie had coalesced the dreams of their life into one.

I am back, Annie. I'm coming home to you. The heaviness in his heart fell away. And he looked eastward toward Mile End. He could feel her waiting, waiting... for him. She had waited so long.

Only our bodies are older, Annie... only our bodies.

16. Bow Bells

A parcel came from Mrs. W. and Aunt Ada in Toronto – a plastic plate (bunny) for Margaret and 2 pair of panties for Nelly and a doll made from shells. Went downtown and cashed cheques and paid some bills. Saw Dorothy Moore and she told me Mrs. Rowley has polio. Ironing this P.M.
[The Lois Diaries, October 7, 1947]

The longest walk of his life behind him, Harry stood at the door to the flat, staring at the little brass door-knocker... *Stratford-on-Avon*, it said, around an image of Shakespeare's birth home, with Shakespeare himself as the knocker. Only Annie would care to make the exterior of her door artistic in the midst of East London's mediocrity. He removed his hat and held it in his left hand, slowly twirling it with his right. *What if...* Harry could get lost in the eternal echoes of this fundamental question. He breathed deeply and knocked. This, then, was the defining moment... a tentative knock at an ordinary door.

The Bow Bells chimed out a seven o'clock response.

Harry had never felt this kind of anxiety – the fusion of anticipation and dread that threatened to obliterate him. He heard her coming to the door. His heart hammered against his chest.

The door opened wide.

Harry, his hat clasped by both hands, looked steadily into the eyes of the soul he had abandoned... the soul that had forever since possessed his. Annie stood still and looked at him. Yes, Annie. Annie, her countenance framed still by wild curls and the reddish hair that would never turn completely grey, stood before him, after all these years, her eyes at once misty and challenging.

"Harry," she whispered in the voice of their past life.

And, somehow... somehow... Harry, still looking into the compelling green of her eyes, still looking for the traces of his fingerprints on her lovely face, let his soul speak to hers, "Annie, Annie..."

And they were in each other's arms, behind a closed door, crying and holding on as though there would be no other expression of togetherness left in their lonely, yearning lives. And then Harry realized that Annie was buried in his jacket, sobbing and immovable. He kissed the top of her head, overcome with love and old, old grief.

Her voice was muffled against his chest. "I have not truly lived without you."

Harry held her as though she would become one with him and buried his face in her curls, "Nor I without you, Annie; nor I without you."

Back where they belonged, they soothed away the years, each holding to the other more than humanly possible so that neither would let go and sink away. The bridge over forty years was without height and length. And so they clung to depth, tentatively, to give that depth time to re-awaken.

Harry led Annie to the sofa, seating her at his side. With no words, the old lovers fit with each other and dispensed with the years that intervened. Annie curled up at this side, and Harry removed his jacket while still holding her close to him – one arm, then the other, and the jacket flung over the far arm of the sofa. He slipped his left arm around his curled-up soulmate, to bring her into the place where she could listen to his heartbeat. It had always, always been her place, her refuge. Annie, keeping her face turned to his chest, slipped both arms around Harry. This had been her shelter in an often brutal world. She re-claimed and inhabited her space now to keep him there. Forever.

And for the next hour, all that Harry and Annie did was to cling in oneness and offer up the syllables of their love and their grief... sibilant utterances and tender gestures speaking for the words they did not know.

Harry did not leave that night. Rather, he stayed where he belonged, with Annie, the woman he had deserted a lifetime ago. The wonder of it all was that in their reunion, he and Annie, the somewhat crumpled Prince and fading Princess found a timeless, unshakable base that still existed for them in the vast, wordless world beyond what had seemed like silence. Each time they tried to bring the conversation into the linear and chronological, they would look at each other and let go of the words that were no more than irrelevant intrusions into their language of intimacy.

And so it was that their healing easily and sweetly found its way along its archaic, complex, sheltered path.

Neither Harry nor Annie had been sexually intimate for years. Once all attempts at finding a comfortable love had been discarded from his marriage, Harry had accepted a shrivelling of the soul. After all, he deserved it. As difficult as May could be, she was honest. She did not carry another love with her in her back pocket. And he did. Annie was his touchstone, his measuring rod for evaluating all forms of love, a constant presence and source of comparison. Yes, mea culpa.

Annie, on the other hand, had been honest and direct. She'd had a very brief marriage, just under two years, and had been almost brutally honest in her letters in saying she'd had "a fling with marriage, finding it highly unsatisfactory." She had been very clear with any man who wanted to court her that there would be "no marriage on any horizon."

Because both had privately assented to their undying love for each other, both had feared the mysterious and frightening part of their reconciliation. But all fears had evaporated in their first touch, so that when their tears ceased and Harry wiped away the dampness on Annie's face and her hair curled around his fingers, they simply yielded to what was theirs. In re-joining the kiss that had truly never ended, Harry claimed the breast, button by undone button, he had forsaken.

As Annie had many times so long ago, she took Harry's hand and kissed each finger, her eyes peering into and seeing his soul. And then she stood and led him by the hand to her bedroom. Ah, coming home – the elusive perfection Harry had sought for so long! It was as simple as that. It was as simple as the beauty in Annie's aging body. It was as simple as the re-awakening of the old, powerful desire he had left with Annie so long ago. It was as simple as returning to a shared soul. In their complete nakedness, simple honesty allowed re-union of skin and soul, ecstasy and stillness.

Perfect sufficiency. The path into reckless abandon and fusion was old, well-known and seamless.

In that sufficiency, the old lovers drifted off to sleep together, breast to breast, Annie's face buried in Harry's chest.

Just as he felt Annie's letting go to sleep, Harry noticed, in the flickering, shadowy night of Mile End, a sketch framed on the night table. There he was, waving to his soulmate from the deck of the Empress, sending elation and promise to Annie... knowing that it wouldn't be long for Annie to follow him to Canada.

Harry drifted off to sleep, his lips lingering in her hair, the familiar scent of Annie consuming him.

17. Chin Up

> Each outcry of the hunted Hare
> A fibre from the Brain does tear.
> A Skylark wounded in the wing,
> A Cherubim does cease to sing.
> *[William Blake]*

SCENE THREE—Regina, late November 4, 1947

STAGE: the Regina living room, late afternoon light, with the dining room beyond. The rooms are separated by the trendy painted mock pillars of the day. The dining room table is cluttered with books. At stage left, in the dining room, the mother, Lois, in concert-accompanist style, is playing "Sunrise and You and the Soft Morning Dew, Like the Tears on Your Cheek When We Parted" at the piano. The father, Frank, and daughter, Nell, are sitting, centre-stage, in the living room on the maroon sofa. Frank has his right arm around Nell, who is crying softly.

Lois, her hair pulled back in a bun as usual, is wearing a black dress with wide bands of red taffeta at the neck, sleeves and hem of the slightly flared skirt. She sports a tortoise shell comb atop the bun and a large rhinestone brooch on her dress. Frank wears navy pin-striped pants and suspenders over a white shirt with upturned sleeves. There are two pens in his breast pocket. Nell wears a blue gingham dress, a white hand-knit sweater, white socks and brown oxfords. She has a blue ribbon in her neatly brushed hair.

FRANK *(sitting forward in the sofa and pulling a handkerchief out of his pocket and dabbing at Nell's eyes)*: All right—chin up! We didn't mean anything hurtful, little lady. We just meant you'd have to wait until I finish practising for us to do the Christopher Robin songs. That shouldn't make you this sad. What is it?

LOIS *(still playing "Sunrise and You")*: There's no need to cry over something silly. You can wait for your songs. You think about two that you'd like to hear, and we'll do two for you.

FRANK *(turning more toward Nell with his back now to Lois)*: Yes—good idea. But you're not really crying about that, are you? What is it? What's making you cry?

NELL *(finished sobbing, looks up with big, wet eyes at her Daddy)*: Grandpa.

FRANK *(smiling broadly)*: Is that all? Why are you crying about him? You know he's in London now. Why does that make you sad? *(Frank tilts Nell's chin up and dabs away the remaining few tears.)*

NELL *(suddenly very serious, looking directly and defiantly at her Daddy)*: Because I heard you say that he isn't coming back. I heard you say that to Mummy. And... and... nobody told me that! *(More tears)* And then I heard Mummy say to you, "We got a letter from Mrs. W. for Dad. Oh, dear!" I heard it when you got home from work. And Mummy seemed upset. And then I was upset because Grandpa... *(more tears)*

LOIS *(having moved now to "My Little Gray Home In The West," another of Frank's solos... loudly...)*: Do we have to spell everything? Does she have to know everything? *(She stops playing and turns toward Nell...)* Listen, dear, just because you're our Little Woman, it doesn't mean that you should listen to everything. You really should try hard not to overhear. However... no! ... your Grandfather Westley is not coming back. He has gone home. And, yes – we did get a letter. Everyone gets letters!

FRANK *(quietly fierce)*: Lois! Stop! We do not know anything for certain. *(Turning to Nell and putting his arm around her; Nell wipes her eyes)* Nelly, my father... your grandfather... had to go back to England to collect old pieces of his life. If we love him and pray for him, he will come back. *(his voice trailing off...)* He will come back to his real home...

NELL *(strongly now, for she sees that her own Daddy is sad)*: What does it mean "collect old pieces," Daddy? Will he bring them back here?

FRANK *(laughing again, plants a kiss on Nell's forehead)*: Yes, my dear, I think he will bring them back! Your grandfather left some happiness and sadness in England a long, long time ago. And so, he needs to go back. He deserves to do this. Now! *(rubbing his hands together and standing)* Now! What two songs would you like? We'll do two for you and then we must get back to practising for the concert.

NELL *(jumps up, excited and smiling)*: I want "They're Changing Guard At Buckingham Palace" and "There's a Cabern In The Mountain... hammer, hammer, hammer"! Hammer... hammer... hammer! Will Grandpa Westley see Buckingham Palace? Will he?"

FRANK: Indeed, he will. *(Laughing, he turns toward Lois, who has been watching the magical disappearance of tears, and speaks to her...)* Come on, Lotus Bud, on to A. A. Milne we go, all three in a row.

Frank, Lois and Nell unite their laughter into one big musical chord. Lois turns to the piano, opens the book of FOURTEEN SONGS from When We Were Very Young by A. A. Milne to page 14, runs her hand down the centre to ensure flatness, creates an elaborate, funny introduction and Frank joins in with the words, while Nell is filled with pure delight...

FRANK *(in his clear tenor voice, vivace con spirito)*: They're changing guard at Buckingham Palace / Christopher Robin went down with Alice / Alice is marrying one of the Guard / A soldier's life is terribly hard / says Alice...

DISSOLVE

END OF SCENE

18. *Mustard Plasters and Pears*

A lovely holiday. Frank is home. He took some muffins, 1 quart of pears and grape jam to Mrs. Moore. She has a terrible burn from a mustard plaster and she has a real old cold. He took some Tan jelly over later to help the burn. We all went to the Evans' for the evening and took a taxi home.
[*The Lois Diaries, October 12, 1947*]

On the fourth day of his return home, Harry sat on the curb, across from what was left of 22 Buxton Street as he had known it in the previous century. He had waited until Annie was back at work to visit. This was something he had to do alone… this step into the fine points of his life… into consciousness.

Having approached Buxton from the East, Harry had found himself unprepared for the devastation. Great gaping holes allowed sights of London that had never been seen here before, like a view into the viscera of war. Although what was left of Hughes Mansions after the bombing of two years ago had been rebuilt, nothing could cover over what had been amputated from Whitechapel's body. *The killer plague continues*, he'd thought, and he walked, dazed, from the Hughes' skeleton, past 81 Buxton and on to 22.

Annie had wanted to be with him…

… He'd had a dream last night and had woken to Annie's voice, "Harry – it's all right. I'm here. You're here… with me."

She kissed him, and he settled. "You called out for Ernest and for me… do you still dream of Ernest?"

Harry enclosed her in his arms. "Ah, Annie. I was dreaming I'd lost you. It was in my childhood on Buxton Street, and so I wanted to find Ernest to help me. And then all of Buxton Street began… became… as though it were some amorphous organism which began crying until the road was flooded, and I let myself go in its waves to see if it would take me to you and Ernest. But I couldn't find either of you. And I couldn't get out of the water. And then I knew I was drowning." He held her more tightly and kissed her neck. "I thought I'd be rid of the dream here."

Annie could feel his breath, warm and still familiar against her neck. His heartbeat steadied her now as it had so many years ago. And just as he had done forty years ago, Harry traced her ear with his fingers, again and again. She pulled his hand toward her mouth. "Oh, how I loved your hands, Harry." She kissed his fingers. "You still dream your old dream, do you? Is it what it used to be?"

"Yes… with Ernest needing me, calling me. It always starts that way. We're supposed to do something, and I've let him down. And then I see him disappearing into the fog, and I run after him, and the fog becomes a thick wall. But, this time," Harry let her hair fall around his fingers, "this time, the fog became water and you were gone, Annie. You were gone with Ernest, I think. And I think I wanted to drown, to drown in all the grief I've caused."

"So you still believe you caused his death," Annie defined his boundaries. "You didn't. Harry, I'll go with you to Buxton Street. It was too much for you to try to go alone yesterday. I don't want you to go alone."

… But it had to be done alone. He must sense it alone, the position of childhood.

And here he was on the old curb, with his back turned against the school, his eyes fixed on the green doorway which gave relief to the brown tenement brick, caked with layers of London's grime and soot. The street was quiet. Most of Buxton Street would be at work.

The door had been black back then, hadn't it? And, regardless of the current vestiges of the Blitz just down the street at Hughes Mansions, the stench had been more acrid and the noise more insufferable back then. Hadn't they?

What had been the incremental weight of the heartache of going in and out of that door all the multitudinous times of his childhood. It had been a childhood, hadn't it?

Yes, indeed, he had had a childhood, more so than many other Whitechapel children. There had never been a doubt that Mummy and Daddy had loved their children and that the children had loved each other. Never! But the sickness and death hovering and swooping, the relentlessness of it all, had robbed them of any ample sense of life. Always taking, taking, these thieves, until there was no breath left in anyone, except Harry and Charlie.

Edith, one year old, had died nine years before he was born. Ellen, three months old, had died a year before he was born. And Walter, two years old, had died nine months before Harry's birth. Shrouded in the grey gauze of grief, these little souls were mentioned only in hushed, secret tones… "There's no need for our little Harry to hear about those who've gone before. It will only make him fearful." And so it was that Harry, then, could not mention them either, for he wasn't to know about them, was he? How then could he ask his questions? And to whom?

They'd all been born, all the other Westleys of Buxton Street, before Little Harry. Arthur, the Big Brother and second father was fourteen when Harry entered the family. Charles had been six and Herbert had been four years old. With Walter, his closest sibling in age gone, Bertie thus became Harry's playmate. Sweet, delicate Bertie. But – no! – tears were fruitless for the eight year old Harry losing his playmate and for the man who still missed artistic, delicate Bertie.

Unclear whether he was saving the best till the last, or leaving the most difficult, Harry finally allowed his thoughts to stretch out to Ernest. Ernest, eight years and one day older than Harry, the exceptional sibling. Always, it had been Ernest providing meaning to life, Ernest being a shining example, Ernest telling Harry the family story about Little Bardfield and Mummy and Daddy's great love for each other, Ernest explaining that "you, Little Harry, are Mummy's special child, her gift, her solace, her joy in the midst of her love and melancholy." Ernest the poet and scholar. Never had Ernest failed…

Ah! Harry left his reverie. *Why, there they were now!* Harry had known that if he waited patiently and quietly, the boys would come out again. He had caught sight of them as he had approached the school earlier; but they had noticed him and had dashed back into 22. Look at them! Clever boys. Arms over each other's shoulders, heads bent toward each other, chattering away.

Harry leaned back against the tree trunk, hoping to blend in with it. If only he could tune his ears more finely…

"Bertie, you need to tell Mr. Crow that you get tired. I'll do it for you; but, really, you must begin to speak up for yourself! He'll let you stay in and do your artwork. He will! Now, don't be so morose – cheer up!"

"Thank you, thank you, Ernest! I do hate speaking up."

"Look! What's Harry doing by the tree?" Charlie seemed excited. "Harry! What are you doing over there?"

The boys ran up to him. He hadn't wanted to be seen; he'd just wanted to run away for a little while. Mummy seemed so sick lately, and tired, so tired that she didn't want to play with him when she got home from work. The winter had seemed very long and dark. And truly, everyone was very, very tired. He had come to understand happiness as a very difficult mood. Ernest had explained that "this is the way life is, Harry; some people are born poor and have to work dreadfully hard, and some people are born rich. It's not our lot to be rich. But we have love, Harry!"

Bertie and Charlie sat down on either side of him, and Ernest kneeled in front and extended his hand, "Come, Harry. I'll take you back inside the house. Mrs. Givens will be over soon. You won't be alone for long. Take my hand." Ernest smiled.

Harry crossed his arms over his chest, looked down at his feet and shook his head.

"Bertie! Charlie! You run along to your class. I'll stay a little longer with Master Storm Cloud here."

Bertie ran into the school, calling back, "Go home, Harry. Go home, and let Ernest come to school!"

Ernest sat beside Harry. "What's bothering you, Harry?"

"I've runned away, that's what."

"Oh, I see. Then perhaps you'll be fine if I leave you here until you're ready to go home. We all have to run away once in a while, Harry," he ran his hand through Harry's wavy, auburn hair. "But four year olds do have to decide to return when they get hungry. Don't forget that."

Harry peered through the shock of hair that tumbled down to his nose, "All right, Ernest. I'll go back when I'm hungry."

"Good boy, Harry!" Ernest knew better than to use any form of levity. This was a serious matter. "And, Harry, Mummy's all right. I can tell that she's improving. And tonight, Harry – if you've returned home – I'm going to give you something to keep for me, something I'm getting at school tonight. I'm going to give it to you, Harry, to keep for me." Ernest put his arm around Little Harry, "Well, I must be off. One can't be late for school, Harry. Don't forget that when you start next year."

Harry, pouting a little to maintain his point of view, relaxed and looked at Ernest, "All right, I won't. And… Ernest…"

"Yes, Harry."

"I shall be home tonight to get my present from you."

"All right, lad," Ernest bounded off in Bertie's direction.

Harry felt the rough bark of the old tree against his back. Where was he?

Yes, yes. He remembered. He remembered Ernest's promise of the gift. Mummy and Daddy had let Ernest wake him up that night after he'd been given the "reward of superior merit", the highest prize at the school. Ernest had opened the box and allowed him to hold the medal, all shiny and beautiful with Ernest's name inscribed on it.

"It's for you for now, Harry. You're the brightest of all of us, you know, lad. So, I want you to keep it safe for me."

Harry had closed his fist around the cool silver, his eyes shining into Ernest's, "I'll keep it ever so safe for you, Ernest, and I'll never, ever lose it."

And he had kept his word. With Annie's assistance. She had kept the medal for him all these years. The plan had been for her to take it along with her to Canada when it was time to join Harry. Along with the big family Bible. "With this medal and Bible, I thee wed, Annie." He'd told her that before they left for the Empress. And he'd smiled into her camera as he sailed away from her life and love.

"I do thee wed, Annie." Harry collected himself and strode west on Buxton, away from Number 22. He didn't need to stop at Number 81. No, he'd seen Bertie and Ernest. And he'd felt the presences of all the Westleys. What more could he ask for?

Only the spirits of the departed saw the tears that streaked down his cheeks. *Ah, the children of Whitechapel...*

As soon as he felt the tears, Harry pulled out his sunglasses and hat from his jacket pockets. These old companions would take care of things. Wouldn't they?

19. Because of the children

The Bat that flits at close of Eve
Has left the Brain that won't believe.
The Owl that calls upon the Night
Speaks the Unbeliever's fright.
            [William Blake]

"Harry. Harry."

Harry realized he'd missed some conversation. "Annie?"

"You're doing it again," Annie laughed, "you're staring at me and not listening."

"Ah; but you know why. Sometimes I can't believe you're there… that I'm here," he reached across the table to hold her hand. The soft yellow of Annie's small kitchen complemented Harry's mood. "I do honestly think at times that this is a dream."

"Do you remember how we always said that everything was a dream, that we create our own lives? You re-visited Buxton that way last Tuesday, didn't you? Is that why you feel you're done with it? Is it that or is it that it's too painful?"

Harry was silent for a moment. "It's both. I did come to terms with Buxton in a certain way. I needed to see the physical remains. I'm done with that. The other part of it is not as simple, as concrete. There is pain left, Annie; but it's a pain that clings and that can't be satisfied by the physical viewing. Do I make any sense?"

"You do… at least, I think I understand," Annie concentrated. "I think there are two things here for you to resolve – your grief and your regrets. Grief can be explored… shared. But regrets? That's a whole different matter. And

I sense that you have regrets about your life."

"Isn't life a rather regretful matter?" Harry grinned.

Annie smiled and sat back, pointing at him. "Aha! It's still there, isn't it? Harry Westley, you're still rooted in your old Cynicism. I've seen it a few times, sir," she looked directly into his eyes, and Harry flinched. "And no old sardonic smile is going to convince me otherwise!"

Harry mellowed, "I know. You're right, Annie. But, I may find it happen more naturally, rather than trying to make it happen, once I start working and get back into being a Londoner. Not that I ever stopped being one." He reached over for Annie's hand again and held it firmly. "I won't let things slip away again."

"Your work may parallel some of what you want to resolve."

"Well, in the re-building, but not the reforms, I suppose. I like Attlee's reforms; but it's the rebuilding and retrieving of records that I can help with. Who'd want a repatriated sixty-five year old to work on new reform?" Harry smiled, "But I've got a job, Annie, and it'll be fine. I don't need much. Which is good, because it doesn't pay much! I've been sending money through Frank and Lois to May since she moved to Toronto, and I'll keep sending some."

"She doesn't know that you left Canada?" Annie looked shocked. "Harry, I thought you would have told her!"

"Annie, I never wanted you to know much about that part of my life; but May and I long ago fell into a pattern of living separately in the same house. Separately... very separately. While the children were growing up, we exchanged pleasantries for their sakes... at meals... at church... and so on," he stared at his hands and seemed lost. "And, once the children were older, that became unnecessary. Although, I'm sure we never fooled them anyway." He looked up at Annie, "She seemed to hate me, Annie. That's the only explanation I can give. And I suppose I never blamed her for that. It was a wretched relationship we had."

Harry's forlornness was almost more than Annie could bear, "Why didn't you blame her, Harry? Why didn't you tell me?" For a moment, Annie was as lost as Harry. She felt her anchor was gone, that truth had never been true. "The lost time, Harry! And I thought… I thought I knew… I could always see you within a family I had built in my imagination. Why didn't you tell me?"

"Because it was all my fault, Annie. All of it… losing you, marrying someone I shouldn't have, not telling her the truth…." Harry felt a strange necessity for forgiveness. He needed to see – he must see – understanding in her gaze. "Oh, dear God, Annie, don't let this all come between us!"

Annie clasped her hands around Harry's fist, gently kneading the tension away. "Harry, look at me. I'm shocked, that's all. I have to rearrange the picture I've carried all along. Yes, I feel deceived; but it's more from the enormous amount of time that we've lost, time we could have spent together. Why? Why did you wait this long?"

"Because of the children, Annie. And because I was never fair to May. I never loved her. She came into my life when I felt lonely and angry with you…" Harry put his hand out to silence Annie, "Hear me out, Annie. I'm trying to tell you what I felt, what I wrestled with. I know I was very unfair about you. But I couldn't see a way to return to England, and I couldn't imagine, from what you said, that you'd ever find your way to Canada. You seemed so final in what you were saying."

"But Harry, I may have at first seemed that way. I mean… I was shocked at how quickly my father became ill. And that's all I could think of at first. But I told you that I'd come," Annie's anger was immediate and raw. "I told you."

"No, Annie, you didn't! I have your letter here," Harry reached over for his jacket on the chair beside him and pulled the letter out of his breast pocket. As he unfolded it, the rustling of the old paper felt like thunder to both of them. Thunder ushering in an old epoch as it crashed its way through the years of aging and distance. He gave the letter to Annie.

Annie glanced over the letter. "Yes, this is my first. It hurts to see it again, Harry. I wish you hadn't kept it." She threw it into the middle of the table. Her tears angered her further.

"Well?" The anger had found life in Harry as well.

"Well! You say, 'Well'?" Annie stood and began pacing from the table to the door and back again. "I can't believe that you hold that letter up as some kind of evidence against me, Harry Westley! Yes, it was devoid of hope! I was in shock. You had gone, and my father was dying. I needed you, and I wasn't thinking well. That letter," Annie snatched it from the centre of the table, crumpled it and threw it back on the table, "that letter is irrelevant! And you know it! You know it, Harry, and you never responded to the following letter. No! Instead, you waited for a few months – abandoning me! – and then had the audacity – the audacity – to write me that you'd met another woman!" As Annie paced again to the doorway, Harry stood up and moved toward her. "And don't you come near me, Harry… don't you dare come near me! Did I ever – ever! – hold that against you? Did I? No, instead…" Harry's strong arms around her made it impossible for Annie to move. Struggling, she began to hear Harry's words and settled.

"Annie. Annie, hush. Hush," he pulled her head into his chest and let her sobs subside, kissing her hair. "Annie, what letter? What following letter?" He kissed her face over and over again. Old music played in the background of his mind… "What following letter? Oh, Annie, there was no following letter. Oh, Annie, Annie…"

"Oh, dear God… Harry…"

Annie looked up at Harry and believed him. "Oh, dear God, Harry… you didn't get the letter, did you?"

"*Melt, melt my pains….*" Why did this old song start singing itself over and over in his mind as he brushed Annie's hair away from her face. *Dear God, would that lost words and letters had never revealed themselves.* "No, Annie, I didn't get the letter."

20. As I love thee

Baking a bit today. Still have to be careful as there's no shortening around to be had because of the strike. We did the last ducks so as to have them for Sunday dinner. Frank quite busy doing odds and ends around outside.
[The Lois Diaries, November 8, 1947]

Annie and Harry were numb, shocked, mystified. They had to let these facts settle and find agreement again. Annie's tears and Harry's intense anger brought clarity. Assumptions fell away. Their shock over what had been prevented began to bring them even closer. Harry simply took Annie's hand and led her to the bed. It was as though with every movement of their love-making, healing happened and the life and family they might have had could be briefly and beautifully brought to life. Their energy was the energy they had possessed before Harry had left for Canada. Harry threw himself over onto his back, keeping his hand on Annie's breast. "Dear God, Annie, at this rate, we're going to kill ourselves. We're in a bloody time machine!"

"And die happily, Harry, or simply disappear," Annie claimed this rightful, restful place of hers, where she could whisper in his ear. "I'm so sorry I was angry."

"As am I that I was angry with you, Annie. It was a powerful anger, wasn't it? As powerful as our love-making, I suppose," he kissed her. "Perhaps it was part of our love-making. All I've ever known of anger is its divisiveness."

Annie raised herself to look directly into Harry's eyes, "That's not true. We argued with that energy in our past life! Remember how angry you were over my views on why you chose the doctrine of cynicism?"

"Scepticism… it was scepticism…"

"See… I rest my case!" Annie laughed and sank back into Harry's embrace.

"Look at us! Here we are on a late Sunday morning. And a sunny morning at that, now that I actually look at it. What shall we do with this day, my Annie? Let's do something before we're both working blokes tomorrow!" To Annie's delight, Harry had lapsed briefly into the Cockney dialect he had so meticulously abandoned long ago. "Let's do something fun… free… it's been so long."

Reluctant to let go of her place, Annie kissed her lover with a force that surprised both of them. "You're right; our talk has been all too serious." As she sat up, Harry kissed her back.

"Annie," he put his hands on her shoulders, "and let's promise, now, that we won't succumb to that kind of anger again."

"But the regrets, Harry," Annie looked out the window, "the regrets in knowing that you never got that letter…"

"No, Annie, we have no choice but to let go of those regrets or we risk losing our way again. Look at me," he turned her to face him, " and promise not to regret… there isn't enough time for regret… ever." *Dear God, what difficult medicine.* "I am promising, too."

"I promise… with a kiss. All right, I'll get ready." Her smile was free and tender as she picked up her dressing gown.

Drifting luxuriously in and out of the present, Harry lost any sense of time and place.

"What are some things you'd like to do simply for pleasure? Like the outings we used to have, Harry," Annie returned from the bathroom wearing her white chenille dressing gown; her hair wrapped in a yellow towel. She jumped on the bed to sit beside him while she rubbed her hair dry with the towel, "Are you always this lazy?"

Harry laughed and took over the job of drying her hair, "I'm not lazy.

Cynical, perhaps; but not lazy." He kissed the nape of her neck. "No, Annie. I'm not lazy; I'm at peace. For the first time since I left you at Southampton. I'll get ready now."

Annie loved the sound of the water running as Harry prepared to shave. "You haven't answered my question," she called. "What would you like to do simply for the sake of doing it?"

"Ah, yes," Harry, razor in hand, came to the bedroom door, one razor-track drawn through the lather on his face. "I have the rest of my life to come to terms with London – and only now to play. There are places here I should have seen as a boy. I want to see them. Like St. Paul's. But that's a sombre prospect. On a happier note – your door-knocker made me think of this – I've always wanted to go to Stratford-Upon-Avon. And by the same token, I'd love to see The Globe and a few other places in London that the bard knew well. All the time we were in and around Blackfriar's, Annie, and I never took the time to explore the remainder of the Playhouse."

"I wondered if you still loved Shakespeare," Annie walked up to Harry, scooped up some suds with her index finger and placed them on his nose.

"As I love thee, fair maid, I love him more."

"All right, then, Harry, let's go today!" Annie went quickly over to sit at her little desk and began to search intently through the slots.

Taken with the scene, Harry realized that this was Annie, his lonely Annie of the forty years of letters. Dear God, he loved her and her intensity. "*'When forty winters shall besiege thy brow, And dig deep trenches in thy beauty's field,' Annie... how I do love thee now*," Harry spoke so softly that Annie, lost in her quest, didn't hear him. "What are you looking for? How could we go today?"

Triumphant, Annie held up a pamphlet, "I knew I had this! The rail schedule!" She scanned through it while Harry savoured the moment. "If we get to Paddington by noon, we'll catch the 12:20 train and be in Stratford by

2:40. And – look! – there's a train back at 8:30. I know what's best to see. Who cares whether or not we should have more time. Let's do it, Harry! Shall we?"

"All right, Annie – yes, we'll go!" Harry returned to his shaving. Had he lost all sense of propriety? Good God – yes, he had! "I'll be ready in five minutes. And let's have a quick tea and toast, Annie, before we head out, shall we?"

Ah, this was life... "How much more praise deserved thy beauty's use" indeed!

21. A letter lost

I've seen Blitzed London and learned many things about this city I need come to terms with – to forgive, I suppose. There were 71 attacks on London during the Blitz and over 20,000 people killed. Over a million houses were destroyed or damaged. Londoners moved into the Tube stations and formed communities. This all hearkens back to my childhood. Our death certificates called it phthisis, Hippocrates' word. We called it "the white plague" – it was our Blitzkrieg, killing who knows how many and turning the survivors into mudlarks, a new community of sub-humans, sifting the filth of the Thames for a living.
[Harry Westley, October, 1947]

Annie and Harry sat across from each other in the tea shop in the Jewry in the same place that had been theirs so long ago. It would always be theirs. As planned, they had left work early to meet each other. London's late afternoon sun was partially swaddled in thick haze. What light was able to spin off from it drifted gently through the window and fell on Annie's right shoulder and arm. The air around them was alive with the gentle murmuring of four o'clock words, punctuated occasionally with laughter or a jarring voice.

Could he do it? Could he bear this talk they needed to have? This talk they had agreed was necessary? This talk that would fill in the gaps.

Annie reached for his hand. "We need to talk things through, Harry, and yet I... right now... I don't want to. Do you?"

Harry loved this honesty of Annie. "No, I don't want to, either; but we must," her resistance became a sheer curtain between them. "We must. If we don't, Annie, the unanswered questions will be our downfall. You know that."

"Then where do we start, Harry? Where do we start without hurting each other? Where?"

"Where we must, Annie, at the beginning. At the lost letter," the sun was extinguished by the haze, and Annie seemed to retreat into the shadows. "I've woken in the night a few times with that letter on my mind. We have to retrieve it… and not let hurt feelings or anger get in the way."

As the waiter delivered their tea and scones, Annie appeared to withdraw into the corner of her chair; shrinking from the pain of the moment. She looked down.

Harry thanked the waiter and stirred the tea. "Tell me about it, Annie." The tea leaves released a pungent burst of bergamot that filled the air between them.

"How in the world do we cover the ground to go back forty years, Harry? How do we get there? And then, how do we contain it? Maybe it's better to leave it… acknowledge it, like this, like we're doing right now... and then leave it," she looked up at Harry again. "Not just leave it there; we'd have to agree that it was taken off the path... put in the ditch. We've done well with that, haven't we, since you came back?"

They were travelling now, back to their parting and the assumptions that had been made. "No, Annie, we're only doing well if we revisit the mistakes we made," Harry's eyes conveyed a deep regret.

Annie sighed and once again looked down at her hands. "Well… Father was so ill, and there was no one to help me. I told you all that, Harry. But, I became so... so... bereft. I didn't know what to do without you. We'd been so happy... happy about our plans... and you weren't there... and... it was very frightening for me, Harry. I felt as though I was going to lose everything that I loved." She looked up cautiously. Her eyes pleaded for understanding. "That was the basis on which the first letter was written. Please try to understand that part. It was written on a foundation of fear and anger."

"Why anger?" Harry seemed severe.

Annie met his severity with earnestness, "Perhaps so that I could fool myself?"

"What? So that I would be confused, and you would be fooled? How would that ever work, Annie?"

"Not just that," Annie's thoughts took her attention to the view beyond the window, "I had never felt such despair... never."

Harry took her hand, "Annie, come back. Look at me. I understand. I'm not angry. I want to talk all of this out. I'm not prepared to live my life on some blasted periphery any longer." His words opened a path to re-connection. "Ah, there you are. Keep talking... was the despair over your father or over me?"

"Initially I made myself understand it as being about you. You had been gone for two months. I was due to join you in another three. At that point, that was an interminable length of absence. And then... then... you were the man whom my father always said would never wait for me. You..."

Harry interrupted her, "But we went over and over that, Annie. You knew that I would not abandon you. How could you slip into that kind of belief about me? Good God, Annie! I read your letter – do you remember the part about releasing me to be free? 'Harry,' you said, 'you shall make some lovely Canadian a wonderful husband.' Followed quickly by, 'I shan't be able to move to Canada, Harry; my father must take precedence in my life.' I read your letter – over and over – and I felt like so much jettisoned cargo. I was dispensable. That's how it felt... I was dispensable to you, Annie. I was stunned."

"I know, I know, Harry. I saw – understood – what I had said to you and how hurtful it was. Never once did I believe what I had written, even with Father after me about you..."

"Then why...?" Harry waved his hand, obliterating the question. "Your father kept it up – his dislike of me – did he?" Harry felt an old anger rise in his chest.

Annie felt dizzy, "Relentlessly. Relentlessly. He was happy that I had written you the first letter; but he kept asking if I still loved you. I always told him I did, that I was staying with him to give him a companion in his illness, but that I loved you more than anyone in the world. And then, one day, when he was nearing the end, he asked me to promise that I would never leave England, that I would never go to you. It was at that point that I woke up and realized why my father was so ill. He had a sick spirit. That was his illness. That was how he had lost his sons. That, perhaps, was what had killed my mother. And when I had that realization, when I woke up... that he would want to control me from his grave. I knew that I had to write you. I knew that it wouldn't be too late."

"When was that, Annie?"

"I know exactly," she smiled as the young Annie would have. "It was when I was to have left for Canada, exactly five months after you had left England."

Without calculating, Harry uttered the date quietly, "September first, 1908." And in that very moment of speaking, everything fell in place for Harry. That date had held great import for him as well. He'd accepted a supper invitation from May, whom he'd known for a few weeks. Over dessert, she had offered to mind his apartment for the four weeks he would be spending shortly in Ottawa, working on assignment in the Land Registries Office. Yes, indeed... he had come home to a nicely tied bundle of mail. Yes, indeed... he remembered well where he had been that first day of September, 1908. He'd been so acutely aware that day of Annie. The old feelings poured over him. He could almost taste them. That day in 1908 he had experienced the depth of his perpetual loneliness. May's supper invitation had been a soothing salve.

"Harry," Annie dispelled his daydream. "Harry, what are you thinking?"

"What was in the letter, Annie? Do you remember the gist of it?"

Annie nodded. Leaning in toward Harry, she felt her fear dissipate. Now only grief remained, and it was a grief that they could dispel. "I remember almost verbatim. I didn't blame you for not having responded, although, in my heart of hearts, I had wanted you to. It was a short letter, to the point. I apologized for the meaning you would have taken from the first letter and explained it as being written from foolishness. And then I told you that my father had only a very short time to live. 'But,' I said, and this part has echoed often in my memory… I said, 'But, Harry, no matter when, if you will still have me, I shall come to Canada to be with you for the rest of our lives.' So, you see, Harry, when you wrote later to say that you were marrying May, I took it that you did not want me any longer. That was why I refused to answer your following letters. That was why, when I finally relented and decided to correspond with you, I said that all talk of our past was taboo, that we must stay in the here and now."

"Dear God, Annie," Harry took his handkerchief from his pocket to tend to Annie's tears. "Dear God. I wonder that you ever started to respond to my writing at all." He pulled his billfold from his pocket and put three pounds on the table. The waiter should be rewarded for his part in releasing the truth. He stood up, took Annie's jacket from the coat rack and held it up for her. "Come, Annie, we cannot waste another minute. We're done with the letter. We're done with the past."

Annie's laughed as she almost ran to keep up with Harry. "Where are we going, then, if the past is a thing of the past?"

Reaching out for her hand, Harry felt a great weight fall away, "We're going to my room, Annie. It's time to move all my belongings into your home."

After four weeks of reunion, Harry Westley was home – for the first time in forty years.

Harry sensed Annie's fall into sleep. He turned over, looked up at the ceiling and put his arms behind his head. A distant drunken call and undulating shadows on the wall and ceiling were all that remained of the day. It was almost midnight; but sleep eluded him. There were modifications needed in his emotional geography of Canada.

As Annie had explained the lost letter, he'd known immediately that May had destroyed it. He'd come to know her style very clearly over the years. But he hadn't seen her methods back then. Nor would he ever have thought that her retributive nature would have been active so early. Ardent, brusque, she had incrementally taken over his life. And he'd let it happen. In fact, he'd been flattered that someone in this strange new country had become taken with him. Until then, Annie had been the only woman able to penetrate his fortress of intellectualism.

They'd met when Harry, at a loss after his letter of rejection from Annie, had attended a Salvation Army meeting. Evocative of London's Army work in Whitechapel, a poster had drawn his attention to the needs of Toronto's poor. May had been the informative and efficient, albeit dispassionate, spokesperson for a receiving home on Indian Road. It had been a simple step, in his chronic recall of Mummy's lost babies, from listening to May to talking to her.

From that point on, May had made Harry the most important person in her life. Harry was lonely. Harry was flattered. And Harry was vulnerable. He told May about Annie and about Charles... Annie was not coming to Canada... and Charles had crossed the prairie seas of Canada and might as well have been back in England in terms of proximity.

Above Harry, the ceiling mutated into a movie screen...

September 29, 1908... the train arriving at the waterfront. And there she was, greeting him as he stepped down from the train into the crisp, sunny noontime. "Harry!"

Yes, there she was! How lovely of her to take the time to meet him. Ottawa had been so cold and austere. Except for its odd fascination with planting tulip bulbs, it lacked imagination. And, like all things Canadian, it certainly lacked history. So, there was May, warmer than Ottawa had been. He switched his suitcase to his left hand and moved ahead to shake her hand. Her grip was strong and sincere. As they turned to walk to the carriage, May slipped her arm through Harry's.

And from then on, the relationship had simply gone forward, with May as the leader. She was bright, witty and attractive. She knew what she wanted and didn't mind a more traditional church involvement than what the Salvation Army offered for a couple... as long as church was part of the picture. And soon – there he was! Harry, in a church, when he'd been known as a radical thinker in London, and in a family of pleasant, intelligent siblings. Harry, feeling less lonely and thinking less and less of Annie... in the daytime hours. And the night-time hours? Well, he was used to them, wasn't he? And perhaps, just perhaps, the intense loneliness of the night would fade the longer he knew May and her family. After all, until May, it had never occurred to him that he might once again have siblings. Siblings were rare in London's Mile End.

Harry shifted to his side in bed and looked at Annie. Purring softly, she had turned just enough so that her curls had fallen away from her face. Forty years, and here they were back together. Where they belonged. To the place from which she had been usurped. His anger flared again toward May.

With Frank's birth a year after their wedding, May had changed. Or had she reverted to a condition she'd kept hidden from him? She began to accuse Harry of being distant and wanting to be back in England. And then she had begun to mention Annie. "You're not in love with me, Harry. No! You're still in love with a woman in England who didn't even have the decency to apologize to you for cutting you out of her life!" Now he understood where these words had come from. They had seemed so very out of the blue back then... somehow, judgmentally caring.

And there were incessant complaints about Harry's "passive nature." If she'd only thought, she would have noticed that Harry had simply gone away to an old place in his head. If she'd only cared to understand, she could have seen he was so used to being alone that there were times when he needed simply to be alone. It meant nothing against her. To no avail, he'd tried to explain this to her.

When her anger began to be focused on young Frank as he evolved into a sweet, energetic child, Harry had had to outlaw spanking. "All children are busy, May. Try to forget the mess the toys make. Play with him. I'll tidy up when I get home."

And then, little Della Iris's arrival brought about the odd blessing of splitting the family in half. By the time Della was two, she and her mother slept in one bedroom, and Harry and Frank slept in the other. The perfect metaphor of the split, their daughter was Iris to May and Della to Harry. Always. Unequivocally.

What kind of life had they given their children? At least Della was loved by both parents. Although there were times when May exhibited love toward Frank, there were the multiple occasions when she had been grievously hard on him. Frank himself had taken the broom away from his mother when he was fourteen. "Never again, Mother," had been Frank's only words. And May had never touched him again… physically. But she had known how to reach deeply and odiously into Frank's heart. Not until Frank had left home had Harry heard about May keeping their son from a sled party and spending the money he was saving to buy a clarinet. Frank would not have wanted to burden his father further by telling him things he hadn't noticed.

Harry sighed. He missed Frank. And beautiful Della. Always, always there were oceans in his life separating him from love… the ocean of darkest death or the ocean of deepest water.

Annie stirred.

But no ocean could separate him again from Annie. Ever. He wrapped his arms around her and breathed into her hair.

"Annie…" For the first time in his life, Harry understood the heavenly comfort of white sheets.

22. *Ernest*

Another lovely day. Doing a bit of baking. It is fun to keep house again. No mail as yet. Frank again gardening. Things seem to be coming on OK. Dad Harry was in. Also Mrs. Wilkinson. Frank had to telephone the police about the way a neighbour was beating his wife, etc.

[The Lois Diaries, June 7, 1947]

Caught in the puzzling twilight between waking and sleeping, Harry realized he was drifting, drifting... into another realm. No – he was being pulled by something... a force. He turned onto his back to resist. The rays from the streetlight cast patterns on the ceiling. Harry was unable to pull himself away from the dull, heavy force that now drew his gaze upward. Frightened, he focused on an opaque pool of creamy light forming in the centre of the ceiling.

The light assumed more shape, and a hand reached down. Harry floated up to take the hand, instead becoming part of the light and floating with it into the night sky. He was chilly. The low light pulsated gently and opened up. Now inside the light, he floated beyond the darkness and into another place of soot and dark green light, barely visible. Harry could see chimneys, puffing out meagre trails of odious smoke. Shapes of row-houses became partially visible, organisms trying to be there, to claim space, in this God-forsaken eerie, heavy slime. A dog barked in the distance, its echo sliced in half by a man cursing the dog, echo upon echo, spinning round and round the tops of the houses until silence took over once again.

The light came to rest at the back of a house. And he was alone. Alone, standing outside his Buxton Street home. He looked down at his hands. They were young hands, sensitive hands. He realized he was crying.

And then he heard the noise. Ernest! It was Ernest crying. Crying Ernest.

Dying Ernest.

"Go inside, Harry," the light intoned from above.

The back door began to glow and slowly opened. Harry stepped in. The crying was louder. Where was Ernest? He must find him. He must join him. "Ernest! Ernest! Where are you?" The crying became deeper and modulated into groans.

"Harry! Come!" Harry followed the voice and found himself in a dark hallway with walls covered in dark green vines and tiny pale green buds. There were no doorways. The voice called out more urgently, "Come! Come!"

"Ernest! Ernest!" Harry was shouting, the sound strangled before it could materialize. He desperately ran his hands over the walls. There must be a door somewhere! Desperation became panic.

And then, there it was! A latch and a gate... now a gateway into a garden. The pale green buds burst open around him, turning themselves into huge white flowers the size of pillows, emitting a fabulous fragrance. Translucent green stamens reached out and sang to Harry. And then the broad, silky petals began to flap like wings and the flowers moved upward. "Come! Come!"

Elated, Harry looked up and began to float with the flowers. And, as he did so, he saw Ernest waiting above the flowers, writing words in the air, words that became rainbows of clouds... Ernest happy... Ernest standing and holding out his arms for Harry's return... Ernest ...

Harry moved toward his lost brother with his arms open. "I'm so sorry, Ernest, so sorry..."

Ernest embraced him, laughing, "It's all right Harry, I'm here... Harry... I'm here... it's all right...."

And then he and Ernest fell back together into a cloud, laughing. And the cloud became a bountiful bed spilling over with brilliant white pillows.

And Ernest became Annie. And Harry was awake.

"I've seen Ernest, Annie. It's over. Do you hear me? It's over! He forgives me. He forgives me."

Barely awake, Annie turned toward Harry, kissed his cheek and wrapped her arm and leg around him.

Free at last from the misperceived, misplaced responsibility of childhood, Harry fell asleep, wrapped in Annie's love… Annie's blanket.

23. The white baton

*This morning we got our invitation to Iris and Mark's wedding. Nell
has lost her hockey stick. Poor kid. This P.M. when Mugsie was
asleep, I did the ironing. Frank out to choir practice and I listened
to the Joe Louis – Wolcott fight. Decision to Joe Louis.*
[*The Lois Diaries, December 5, 1947*]

"Do you remember you woke me last night, Harry?" Annie sat down at the
table and poured herself a cup of tea. "It's just coming back to me... you
said, 'It's over,' or something like that. I don't think I was fully awake; but I
remember you talking to me. I think you were awake."

"I had a dream about Ernest. A good dream, a very good dream," Harry
smiled. He loved the way she looked in her blue dressing gown, with her
hair tied back, her glasses barely perched on her nose. "It's coming back to
me in pieces. I can't remember it all; but I remember Ernest in the air,
singing, and telling me everything was all right."

"That's it! That's it, Harry!" Annie's animation was infectious. "You said
you were forgiven. No! You said, 'He forgives me.'"

Harry had not felt so at peace for years. "You're right! Somehow the dream
freed me from the guilt. It's been with me for so long. I can still feel the
relief."

"Why? Why did you feel guilt over Ernest's death? You've never answered
this for me. Try to now... now that it's over. I don't understand it. You were
only ten when he died. How could you have been guilty of anything?"

Harry put his hands around his teacup and looked into the milky drink.
"Perhaps it's time to tell you, Annie. I've always been loathe to talk about
this."

"Why would you not want to talk about him dying – other than the sadness of it, of course? He had the plague that decimated Bethnal. You could never have had any guilt in his death."

"The danger of putting this in words haunted me. Would I get a response of shock or condescension? Would I realize my shame even more and be unable to tolerate it? I knew this wasn't rational, that I was being superstitious; but the sense of blame and regret weighed heavily," Harry began to feel a sense of relief. Could this be why confession was touted as healing? "I don't know what I need... what I've ever needed... around this horrible shame I've had. I wanted so desperately to be rid of it sometimes. But, to be truthful, I knew it also kept me connected to Ernest."

"Harry," Annie put her hands over his and stared into his eyes, his doe-eyes, sensitive to the point of pain at times. "Come. Tell me the story."

They moved to the living room and sat down together on the sofa. Harry put his arm around Annie and she curled into her place, her legs tucked under her and her head against his left shoulder. How else could she hear his heart?

"All right, my Annie. What would you like to know?" He laughed, "This is like Della's or Frankie's bedtime story... 'Tell us a story about London, Daddy,' they would say, 'a wonderful story about London!' And I'd tell them about tripe or kettle broth or cleaning up horse dung from the streets for pay, and they'd think it was all so special and ask for the stories again and again. Imagine feeding stories like that to children and them believing that our London life was exciting!"

Annie cuddled in even more, "Then tell me a London story, Harry. Tell me the story of you and Ernest."

"All right then, Annie," Harry kissed the top of her curls. He rested his cheek against her head and spoke softly. "April of 1892 was relentlessly dank and foggy...

I remember feeling sad, as though the fog were the story of my life… or my captor. Bertie had been dead for five months. And Ernest had been horribly sick for those five months. It was as though our family was in a relay against the white plague, passing the baton from one member to the next, with no hope of anyone reaching the finish line before the disease overcame us. Half of us were gone, and Ernest was tipping the odds in favour of death winning. And both Dad and Arthur had wretched coughs, especially Dad. Actually, I think the fog was deliberately cruel, mimicking the sadness and overloaded lungs of the Westleys… ubiquitous, thick, oozing…laughing in our faces. Ernest had finally succumbed physically and had been bed-ridden since March. I would sit with him in those April evenings…

"Read me more Tennyson, Harry," he could barely get the words out and yet he could smile at me. "Pick it up at 'It is not meet, Sir King, to leave thee thus, Aidless, alone, and smitten through the helm.' I could do with Excalibur myself. Read on, Sir Harry."

And so I opened our book to the bookmark, lay down beside Ernest and read his favourite poem until he fell asleep… "Ah, miserable and unkind, untrue, Unknightly, traitor-hearted! Woe is me! Authority forgets a dying king." Why that passage stuck in my mind, I don't know. I think it helped Ernest to see himself in King Arthur. It's a young man's concept, I suppose, one that was certainly out of place in Canada. I made sure it wasn't neglected in Frank's upbringing.

On that particular evening, a few weeks before Ernest died, I dozed off to sleep beside him.

Suddenly I woke up. I don't know how much later it was. The book fell onto the floor as I sat up quickly and looked at Ernest. Had he called out my name? But he was still asleep… his breathing was laboured; his face clammy.

"His end draws nigh, Harry. Stay with him." I didn't see anything. It seemed to be a part of Morte d'Arthur – Ernest's part. But I knew the

speaker was my mother. And so, that night I vowed to stay with Ernest, the same way he would have stayed with me had the tables been turned.

Ernest wakened a few hours later. His coughing woke me. When I saw him gasping and retching, I knew that he should never be alone, that he should not die alone. I wiped the blood from his mouth and helped him settle. "Ernest," I said, "I'm staying with you every night from now on. And you must wake me in the night if you need me."

"Thank you, Harry. Dying is a lonely business."

I never forgot that phrase. It haunts me still. Here was this young man, eighteen years old, in all senses my big brother, as lonely as a little lost lamb. How many sacrificial lambs did God require of my family? In the name of all that's holy – how many?

From then on, whether it was Tennyson or Dickens, I read to Ernest every night, and then I slept beside him. There were times when he wanted me to sing to him. "Sing me your lullaby, Harry. I need that tonight, I do."

And I'd lapse into the song he had sung to me when our mother died... "Golden slumbers kiss your eyes, Smiles awake you when you rise. Sleep, pretty wanton; do not cry; and I will sing a lullaby." And he'd fall asleep. And then I would. I'd be aware later in the night of Dad's presence in the room. He'd be there to be sure the blanket was covering us both and the candle was out. Always, he'd plant a kiss on Ernest's forehead and then mine.

I remember one day, near the end, when Ernest asked me what I thought about death. I was startled and quickly said I didn't know what to think.

He said that he had begun to think about it more seriously since Bertie's death. "It's very unfair, Harry," he said. "Look at Bertie. The most sensitive of all of us. And a true artist. He could have become a painter. And a poet. How does this God our father who art in heaven allow so much waste of life? Bertie's life was wasted, Harry. Why have someone born with those gifts unless they're going to be used? Why give something and take it away before it's even developed?"

"Just like with you, Ernest!" I surprised myself with my words. "If you're going to die, then that's a terrible waste, too! I don't suppose Mummy's life was wasted because we had her as our mother. But it wasn't right either that she couldn't stay with us. It wasn't right!"

I had started to cry, and Ernest reached over, took my hand and held it. "Harry, don't cry. The sicker I get, the more I realize that there is much we don't see. I feel and hear Mummy's presence. So, I know if there is some kind of welcome when we leave this life, she will be there to greet me. I don't know how to explain it; but I know this." He squeezed my hand. "I suspect that the people who remain here in Whitechapel have the harder time than those who die. I see this. And my prayers comfort me. So, you must be comforted by your tears now, Harry. And by your prayers, Harry."

Rebellion rose in my young heart, and I wanted to scream "No!" to Ernest and rant against this capricious god. But Ernest needed his God. I dared not violate that belief.

I shook my head, "There's no comfort for me. None!"

I could see the weakness seep over Ernest. And I hated it. I felt exactly like I did the day Mummy died when I decided that I would have no affection for God. Ernest was quietly fierce, "That's not true, Harry. Dad and Arthur and Charlie need you. You've a brilliant mind. And you must use it."

"Not without you." At that very moment, I knew unequivocally what desolation was.

"Harry, I must sleep," little droplets of sweat covered his brow. He looked pallid and his breathing had become shallow and difficult. "Harry, I am going to die. You know that."

I shook my head and glared.

114

"Yes, Harry, this is the truth. And I need you to promise me two things. Will you?"

At last, there was something I could do for Ernest. I pulled myself out of my mood. "Yes, Ernest. What do you want me to promise?"

Ernest squeezed my hand again. "Harry would you promise me you will stay with me in bed when I know the end is here? Will you stay awake so that I don't go alone?"

I remember – as clearly as I remember that first knowledge of what desolation is – that Ernest's death became real to me at that moment. "Yes, Ernest, I will stay with you. And I will stay awake with you." I will stay strong.

"Thank you, Harry. You are a good brother." His hand slipped from mine and he began to drift into the slumber of passing.

"Ernest, Ernest."

He opened his eyes. "Yes, Harry?"

"Ernest, you said there were two promises that you needed me to make. I promise I will stay awake with you. What else do you want me to promise?"

"Harry, I want you to promise to live." He eyes closed again.

I leaned close to his ear. "Ernest, I promise you I shall live." And Ernest squeezed my hand in response.

What a strange promise that was to make. I've often had to remind myself of that promise. In the tough times, I've gained some solace from simply remembering that I promised Ernest I would live.

Only a few days after this, Ernest descended in to the final blackness of that euphemistically-named white plague. If it came, as Whitechapel believed, in the whiteness of the fog, it left in the black heart of the Devil. Ernest had dreadful episodes of coughing blood and shaking until it seemed that he would fly apart. I don't know how he survived these incidents. They left him so depleted. He was skin and bones and had no resilience.

But he did find the strength on that Friday – I know it was a Friday because Dad had arranged for Arthur to light the Sabbath fires for me and it was two weeks after Good Friday – he found the strength to tell me that the time had come. He roused from his sleeping state, "It's time to stay with me now, Harry. I'll be going soon."

I remember thinking it was strange for Ernest to ask me to stay with him when that's what I'd been doing. And then I remembered that he needed me to stay awake for him.

I ran downstairs to tell Dad and Mother Lucretia what Ernest had said. And then I ran back up to be with Ernest. I crawled over him and sat beside him, propping myself against the wall. "I'm here, right beside you, and I shan't sleep, Ernest." I put my hand on his arm. "This is where I'll be, sitting here beside you. All right, Ernest?"

"Yes, all right," his voice was barely audible. "I love you, Harry."

Those were his last words to me. His last words. The words and the sound of his breathing and the smell of the room come back to me often in the night.

Dad and Mother Lucretia came into the room. As they had been doing every evening for many weeks now, Lucretia gave him a wash and Dad sat on the chair and held his hand. Dad told him he loved him. "You'll be with your Mum and Bertie soon, Ernest... and the others. There's a brave chap. I wish it could have been different for you, son." Dad was crying the same way he'd cried for our Mother and Bertie... and, no doubt, for the others. This tough man, bigger again than his once strapping son, was losing yet another child. What would eventually remain for him? Would the three of us – Arthur, Charlie and I – get sick, too?

As she washed him, Lucretia was crying, too.

But, I wasn't going to cry. I hadn't cried when Bertie died, and I wasn't going to cry now. I pushed my back against the wall... hard. If I could feel some pain in my back, then I wouldn't feel it in my heart. And I wouldn't fall asleep. Ernest needed me.

Dad and Lucretia got up to leave. "Get some rest, Harry," Dad put his hand on my head.

But, no! Haw dared Dad say that? Didn't he understand that I must accompany Ernest's soul? I remember I had the frightening notion that I might go over some edge with Ernest – leave Buxton Street with him. That's how a ten-year-old's mind can stretch things.

And then I remembered! "I'll be right back, Ernest. This will take only a few seconds." I'd forgotten something, something that would keep me company through the night. I was gone briefly.

I climbed gingerly over my dearest brother and wedged my back into the corner. "Ernest, I have your medal now," I whispered. He stirred, and his breathing became stranger... gurgling... wet... It frightened me. I clasped the medal tightly, hoping that it would reassure me. If I concentrated on the feel of the medal in my hand, made it hurt, rubbed my thumb over it, I'd feel reassured... make it hurt... make it hurt... All I could think of was how alone I felt as Ernest's breath gurgled... make my hand hurt... make it hurt... don't be scared... don't think... don't think... don't... think...

"Harry... Harry." He startled me. "Harry... Harry!" He seemed stronger!

"Yes, Ernest?"

"No, little Harry. It's your Dad." And there was Dad lifting me from the bed. The room was bright, brighter than it had been for weeks.

"Don't take me away from Ernest, Dad! I promised to be with him when he goes – put me back!"

"You were with him, Harry; you were. He's gone now," Dad kissed me and helped me stand. "He went peacefully, son. You see, you didn't even waken.

It was that peaceful."

That peaceful? That peaceful!

I ran from the room, crying, "I'm sorry, Ernest; I'm so sorry!" I was inconsolable for weeks. I barely slept. I had no appetite.

Until I remembered I had another promise to Ernest to keep.

"And that, my Annie, is my great guilt. It is also the reason that I'm still here. I'm here because I promised Ernest I would be."

Annie knelt beside Harry and looked into his eyes. She wiped away his tears, her thumbs stroking outward from his eyes, her lips healing his. "It's over, Harry. You're so right… it's over. You had to come back for Ernest as much as for me," she pulled his head to her breast, "and yourself. It's over, dear one. It was over back then but no one knew to tell you who the light was."

24. The inclination to wait

Nell and Mugsie having a good outing. Made some Cornish Pasties. They were good, too. Nell to a birthday party. Lucille was in and Frank and I out to see "Odd Man Out." Lou had a cup of tea with us. A grand night. Letter from Mother. She sent us apples and pears.

[The Lois Diaries, December 13, 1947]

By November of that year, Harry had settled into a life in London such as he had never enjoyed anywhere. He was alive! Alive! Enjoying himself and not feeling on the wretched periphery of life all the time. Annie, soul of his soul, was with him where she belonged, and his work was more satisfying than he had imagined it could be. More than ever, he had a home, a centre. Headquarters!

And then it happened.

It happened, actually, the same day Frank's third letter arrived. Not that the letter caused it... no... it was rather that Frank's letter released it from where it had merely been camouflaging itself, waiting with the burning, bright eye of the tiger in the stippled shadows. In the heart of his joy, his archenemy had simply lain dormant, waiting for the most opportune moment to spring into action. And Harry, if he were to be completely honest, had known he would be caught by surprise by the fiend somewhere along the line.

As always, he had arrived home before Annie, picking up the mail on the way in. Ah... Frank's handwriting, lovely handwriting reflecting the pride in penmanship he had instilled in his son. How he loved these letters from his children. After hanging his jacket on the hall tree, he'd loosened his tie, put his slippers on and gone into the bathroom to have a quick wash.

He looked at himself in the mirror, a task he had never found easy. Yes, he did look healthier and more relaxed. The darkness around his eyes was gone. Still not much grey hair intruding into the auburn. He took his cuff links out, put them carefully in a dish, rolled up his sleeves, splashed his face and gave his hands a good wash.

Whistling, he went into the kitchen to make himself "a cuppa", so that he could enjoy Frank's letter in style.

He read the letter….

And read the letter again…

Regina, Saskatchewan

October 21, 1947

Dear Dad,

Your latest newsy letter has been enjoyed by all of us, especially by little Nell, who says she would like to go to London to visit you and the King. She remembers Buckingham Palace from her A. A. Milne songbook, which Lois and I continue to teach her, so we're sure that she thinks you're living there with the Royal Family!

We had a lovely Thanksgiving with Auntie Car, Uncle Ted and Phil. Car also invited the Miles Girls, so there was a nice group of us. True to form, Car got us playing games in the evening, after we'd tucked the kidlets into bed, and we went from there into discussions on all kinds of matters, one of them being you and how happy you are in London. All of us, of course, miss you, especially at family times like these.

Nell came out at one point to ask if she could play a game with all of us; but I think she came out because she heard us discussing you. You would have enjoyed tucking her in. She climbed into bed beside Meg and said, "We don't need to say my prayers again, Daddy, do we?"

I said that we didn't need to, and then she said, "Because if I had to, I'd just pray for Grandpa and the King. I hope they're having fun tonight, too."

And then just as I gave her a good night kiss, she looked up at me and said, "I love the smell of Auntie Car. It makes me feel sleepy and happy." I swear she fell asleep as she uttered the last word.

What would we do without Car and her lavender? What would we do without Car and her Welsh songs? Indeed, what would we do without Car? She is more than a friend. In many ways, she's a grandmother to our girls.

This brings me to a rather difficult topic. I hope you will take this not as criticism, but as a nudge on behalf of Della. She is certainly very excited about her upcoming marriage. But I know that she is also sad you won't be there. I hasten to add that she understands your inability and knows that, when you left, she had no idea of marrying by Christmas.

However, there are two difficulties. The one, as I say, is that you won't be there. The other is the delicate one – how will Mother understand you won't be there when she doesn't know you've left Canada? According to Della, Mother expects you will head East with us.

So, Dad, in truth, I have a couple of nudges. Help us with our explanation to Mother. And do send a telegram to Della. The card I've attached to this letter gives you the details of the King Edward where we'll be staying in Toronto, and our room number. If you get the telegram to us the day before the wedding, I can then read it at the reception. Of course, as exciting as this sounds, it begs the question of what we should tell Mother!

My inclination on what and how to tell her is that I write her now with the truth about where you are. I know I could do it well, if you would entrust that task to me.

Lois's inclination is to wait until we arrive in Toronto without you. We could then tell Mother that you became quite ill and had to stay in Regina.

I like my inclination better.

Well, this is complicated, Dad. But you were always the one to tell me that life can be difficult and that it is always "more efficient and caring" to tell the truth.

I'll await your speedy reply to this note.

Love,

Frank

(with love from Lois and the girlies)

Yes, the truth… its time had come. And with it came the need to talk with Annie about the truth. Harry looked again at the last paragraph. Frank's use of his own words against him made him angry, despite their truth, despite the time-worn path of love they opened… despite the longing they elicited in his gut. That was the part he needed to quash. The longing for his own family. He could feel his son's blue eyes looking steadily into his… *"Why, Dad? Why now? Why now when you've resisted this long? Why not simply go back and make your peace with London? I could understand that. Why do you have to stay… with Annie? What about us?"* Frank's bewilderment and hurt sat strongly in front of him as he looked again at the letter. *"She understands your inability…."* My inability? Harry could see the sadness in Della's lovely face. She might as well be there, across from him at the table, sitting with Frank… and Annie. Yes, Annie could be there, too. He took the last sip of cold tea and looked at his watch. Annie would be home momentarily.

Feeling weary for the first time in months, Harry got up to make fresh tea for Annie. It was a ritual that required no thinking. Until now, it had been a ritual of sweet anticipation. Funny how things could change in the time it took to have a cup of tea.

He felt lost.

"Harry!" Annie's call brought him back to the matter at hand. She walked into the kitchen, dropped her jacket over the back of a chair and threw her arms around Harry. "I've had such a good day! How about you?"

Her kiss and the smell of her hair were so good, so right, so his. "I've had a mixed day. Here, sit down for your tea, and we'll talk." He poured the tea. Annie looked quizzical. "Nothing to worry about, Annie. Just something that needs to be talked about and resolved." He joined her at the table.

"Did something happen at work, Harry? You look distracted." Annie sipped her tea, peering cautiously at him. What could she read in his eyes? A sense of alarm took hold of her. There were times, still, when she would slip into an almost pleasant disbelief that they were back together, almost pleasant because the wonder of Harry's presence and touch would be tinged with a visceral memory of old losses. This alarm, though, was oriented to the present, making her fear almost palpable. Annie looked to Harry for relief... rescue....

"No. It was a good day at work. In fact, the whole day was very good. Until I read the mail." Harry handed her the letter from Frank.

Annie looked at the letter and then at Harry. "Has something happened?" She felt alarmed. "Do you want me to read it?"

"Yes," Harry reached for her hand, struggling for words, desperately wanting the letter to disappear. How could one short letter travel across an ocean and carry such power? Did it have the force to destroy? "And, Annie, it's not bad news... it's awkward... uncomfortable information. Please..." he gestured toward the letter, speaking softly, as though his gentleness would neutralize the message. But when had his gentleness ever had power over advancing loss in his life? "We'll talk once you've read it."

What could he see in her face as she read? *Discomfort? Certainly. What else? Fear? Yes, there was a hint of fear.* It resonated with a vague fear inside him. *Why? After all, it wouldn't be hard to respond to Frank's letter. And, whilst it would be onerous, it wouldn't be hard to tell May now.*

Then, what was it?

"Well, Harry?" Annie was stern, her enthusiasm vanquished. Her eyes were probing... angry. *May is doing it again... her power is in others' letters, never in her own. No, she sneaks in through a back door, taking her prey by surprise. Why had Frank suddenly become his mother's champion?* "What are your thoughts?" Annie heard her own fear in the pitch of her voice... an external voice, as though it were separate from her.

"Frank is right." It was that clear.

"He is." And suddenly, in Annie's response, a chasm had opened between them. "Harry, this is the issue we've been avoiding," she spoke slowly, each word measured... feeling control slip away. "I was so shocked when you told me after you arrived that you hadn't told May you were coming home to me. And we've never talked about it since." She stared into the darkness between them. "That was the worst day we've ever had... the argument, the silence...." Annie's voice quavered. *Who am I angry at here? Who?* "Dear God, Harry, this letter is our nemesis! What right does Frank have to intrude into our life? How dare he think he knows what's best for you... for us?"

Annie stood, rigid, glaring at him, her eyes challenging him, angry. Harry felt as though she were joining Frank and Della in their misconception of why he was back in London. In his alienation, he felt an enormous need to withdraw, to go away... it was the ancient call of Buxton Street. If Annie were to slip away... there would be no one left for him in Bethnal... no home... no....

"Talk to me, Harry! For God's sake, talk to me!" A lock of hair had come loose from her headband and fallen across her forehead, serving only to frustrate her. She flicked it back and stepped close to him. "After all these years and years of waiting, I am not going to lose you again. Talk to me!

Harry!"

Annie's command brought him back. She looked like the Annie of forty years ago… *I can't bear it when shut you me out, Harry… talk to me… tell me…."* Which voice was it? Which Annie? Harry felt suddenly angry – angry at being misunderstood, at being the one who had to explain… understand… give up. Grasping her shoulders, he raised his voice. "Stop, Annie, stop! I thought we had resolved that incident! I didn't want this to come between us. I had no idea Della would want to marry. How could I know she would want me at her wedding shortly after I'd returned to London… returned home? Here to you, Annie. Oh, Annie…" Harry saw that she had begun to cry. Her pain melted his anger as he pulled her into his arms. "Don't cry… don't cry. We're both afraid of the same thing… of losing each other again. We're not going to… I promise."

Annie sank into Harry's embrace, "I know. I know." She looked up at Harry with the faint smile and bewildered eyes of a child. "Oh, Harry, I'm sorry. I shouldn't be angry at you. This isn't your fault. It's no one's fault – that's what makes it so frightening. I'm sorry."

Harry caressed her hair and felt her let go of her anger. "Annie, I wanted you to know about the letter. That's all. I'll write Frank tonight and tell him I'll be writing his mother the truth."

Curse the truth, Harry thought, as the possibility of losing Annie again dawned on him… *curse the truth for its destructive ability….*

"We're all right, love, we're all right," Harry soothed Annie. And as she held him more tightly, Harry began to believe his own words.

25. Cornish pasties

The Catterpillar on the Leaf
Repeats to thee thy Mother's grief.
Kill not the Moth nor Butterfly,
For the Last Judgement draweth nigh.
[William Blake]

SCENE FOUR—Regina, December 13, 1947

STAGE: The kitchen in the Regina family home. Stage right – a door to the cellar immediately on the right; in front of the window, the kitchen table with a green enamel top; next, the big, fancy-for-the-day wood stove. The door to the back porch is directly at centre back stage. Stage left – white kitchen cupboards; sink in the centre of the counter; next, the door to the dining room; then, the icebox and a tall pantry cupboard.

Lois, wearing an apron over a dark floral housedress is busy at the kitchen table rolling out pastry. She has the ingredients in dishes in front of her – browned chuck cubes, sliced onions, potato cubes, turnip cubes – and a baking sheet over to her left. The fire is crackling and the girls can be heard playing in the dining room.

NELL *(running into the kitchen)*: What are you making, Mummy? It smells good. *(she peers into the bowls)* Oh no! It's those corn pies!

LOIS *(laughing and cutting her pastry into triangles)*: Cornish Pasties, not corn pies! And yes, that's exactly what I'm making. Your Daddy loves them, and that's what counts.

Nell watches as Lois puts the ingredients in equal amount on half the triangles. Lois puts a triangle of pastry over each waiting bottom triangle and expertly crimps the edges of the pasties together.

126

LOIS: There! Now, just some little slits in the pastry and they're done! *(She finishes her task and puts the tray in the oven.)*

NELL: Could I please, please have my brown sugar pastry… and a little one for Meg, too? Please?

LOIS: Just bring me the brown sugar from the counter, and then in the door below it, the cinnamon… it starts c (not s)…i-n…

Nell quickly follows instructions and puts the sugar and cinnamon on the counter. Lois puts a few spoons of sugar on the leftover pastry, sprinkles on cinnamon and adds two dollops of butter. She rolls the pastry up.

LOIS: I'll just tuck this in with the pasties. *(She opens the oven door, pulls the tray of pasties forward with a potholder, adds the girls' treat, closes the door, and starts to take her apron off.)*

NELL: Why does Daddy like turnip and onions like that?

LOIS *(sitting down at the kitchen table)*: Well, it's a bit of a sad story. With a happy ending, though!

NELL *(sits down across from her mother)*: Tell me, tell me! I love stories!

LOIS: You see, Mrs. W., your Grandma Westley, was not a kind mother to your Daddy. She was very hard on him.

NELL: Why wasn't she kind to Daddy? What is "very hard"?

LOIS: "Very hard" means she was nasty to him. She spanked him a lot. And when he was fourteen, he took the broom away from her and said, "You'll never touch me like that again."

NELL: But then his mother couldn't clean!

LOIS: What I mean is she was hitting him with the broom. And he didn't want that to happen anymore. *(Nell is wide-eyed and quiet.)* Finally when your Daddy was seventeen, he left home. I knew him by then because he had joined my Daddy's church. So my father asked a kind woman, a widow, in our church if she would give your Daddy room and board – that means that he would live in a room there and have meals and pay some money for living there. Mrs. Williams – that was the kind woman's name – was so nice to your Daddy. And she was a grand cook! She was from Cornwall, a place in England. And Cornwall has a special pastry called Cornish Pasties. *(Lois lapses into being alone with herself; Nell listens attentively.)* Mrs. Williams baked them for Frank, and he fell in love with them… talked about them so much that everyone who knew Frank knew about Cornish Pasties… so much that he asked Mrs. Williams to teach me how to make them… after we got engaged. No, he didn't want to give up Mrs. Williams' Cornish Pasties, or maybe he didn't want to give up Mrs. Williams. Funny, I never thought of that. She was like a mother to him, even more than my mother was. He was never bitter about Mrs. W., never. He probably wouldn't say he forgave her. No, he'd say he never felt he needed to. But I haven't forgiven her. No… I won't do that. *(Lois is pensive for a moment and then looks at Nell, who hasn't moved. She snaps her fingers and stands up.)* Come on, Nellie, let's check our baking!

DISSOLVE

END OF SCENE

26. I will sing a lullaby

A SONG OF SARAH'S INNOCENCE

> *Ah, sweet Harry, Joy of my last travail;*
> *Strong in thy meekness, ablaze with Light,*
> *Come to my bosom where Love cannot fail –*
> *Nor vanish in the darkest, dark Night.*
>
> *Oh, sweet Harry, can you see us all here—*
> *O'er White and Green and into this sphere?*
> *Come play, come sing, we'll dance till you come,*
> *See Ernest, see Bertie, with a pipe and a drum!*
>
> *Sweet Harry, thy family lives in your Land of Dreams,*
> *Climbing its mountains and bathing in streams,*
> *Make for thyself a bed on high –*
> *And I will sing a lullaby.*
>
> *All here; all there; all low; all high –*
> *And I will sing a lullaby.*

> *[William Blake & Sarah]*

In the light between the lights, in the space between the spaces, Sarah put her hands on Harry's head. As she sang her lullaby between the separate silences, Harry came to rest, Annie's head against his chest. How much longer would he not listen deeply enough, fail to seek her out, his very mother? *He forgets my pledge: You won't be able to see me. That's all, Harry. I'll always be at your side, Harry. I promise…. You'll see….* Yet again she promised her presence to the Last Born of her Last Birthing.

"The Seeing is so difficult," The First Other chanted. *"Remember, O Sarah, remember how it was for you, for us, for all, in that strange last sojourn."*

129

"These are his soul's lessons," chanted The Second. "This is his chosen migration in the briefness of life in the world of pain and blessing."

The Third Other uttered a benediction, "And you will move on, Sarah, when the last of your children completes the circle. Dear Sarah, it will not be long for you to leave time behind."

"Sarah," sang the host behind the Three Others, "Sarah, dream to Harry; dream to him, dream to him...." Music and words became one in an immaterial array of notes and colours and voices.

And as they sang in this Lost Chord, Sarah knew this was to be, in Harry's Earth Time, the holiest time in Harry's Dream Life. Spinning herself into a pool of light, she became again the incarnation that Earthlings, if they know anything about holiness, call an Angel. She would be there, slipping into Time, when her dearest child went to bed in the day of his and Annie's greatest fear.

"I'm coming, Harry... you'll see!"

Harry shivered. "That was a cool gust, wasn't it? There must be a window open." He tipped Annie's chin up and smiled at her. "I feel better now. Do

you?"

"Immensely! And Harry, we've each needed the other so much... for understanding. But you lost your homeland and had no good-byes you could make." Annie hugged him tightly and walked over to the bag of groceries he had left on the table. "Hmmm... pork pie... cabbage... biscuits. The pie will be all right in the ice-box. Let's go out for fish and chips, shall we? That's what I feel like having! And then come home for tea and one of those biscuits?"

Annie was back. His red-headed Annie, with her uninhibited enthusiasm, had returned from their fear of the past. Because of her, he could do the same. She could move so easily back into the present tense, holding no grudges... ever. "All right, Annie," for who could resist the beauty of her smile and spontaneity? "Let's get ready, then."

As they left the kitchen, Harry remembered. "I'll check the windows. Go ahead and get your coat on." He went through the kitchen and into the living room. The windows were securely closed.

Back in the kitchen, he found the window equally secure. Shrugging, he flicked the light switch off as he went into the hallway. Immediately, he sensed something. Strange… was there another light on somewhere? It almost felt like there was someone else in the room. He turned around. A pool of low, gentle light hovered just above the table. "Odd," he spoke to himself, "it's dark out now... must be a function of the street light." He looked at his watch. It was 6:42 on this November evening.

Glancing again at the table, he saw only the faint outline of the table and chairs. The bowl of artificial fruit gleamed, faintly yellow. "Must be my imagination," said Harry, as he stepped blithely toward Annie.

In the deepest hours of that night, Harry found himself running through a sinister forest. He wasn't frightened. No, he was looking for something, something that lay ahead of him. Where was he going? A force drew him ahead. Three black trees swooped down to push him along the path. A bird screeched wildly, slicing the silence in two.

Suddenly he was at the edge of a lake, a small, misty cerulean lake, paler and diaphanous in the centre where the moon shone down and cast wavering shadows through drooping branches and grasses. He looked round expectantly. Absolute stillness reigned. Except for the flight of a raven across the full moon, he might as well have stepped into a painting.

"Hello..." he called. "Hello! Does anyone live here?" His voice sounded very young to him.

What was that? He looked out over the water to find the source of the noise.

Water gushed up from the centre of the lake and a neutral, melodious voice spoke deeply, "What is it that you want?" At the precise end of the question, a gloved hand, holding a gleaming sword, thrust itself out of the centre of the lake.

Frightened and speechless, Harry stepped back. He wanted to run, but could not move.

And then the hand moved higher until the top of a head appeared. Slowly, slowly, a being emerged, first the silver face, beautiful, inexpressive, framed with glowing, sleek chestnut hair. She, for it seemed more female than male, held the sword high in her right hand, her face immobile. And up she rose as though on a cloud, water dripping like liquid silver from her long white dress. "What is it that you want, my son?" she asked from her hovering position above the lake.

The raven darted across the moon again.

"Who are you?" Harry's voice was weak and tremulous.

"I am The First Other. I am your mother, your father, your sisters and brothers." She spoke forcefully and pointed the sword toward him. A beam of light struck him in the forehead. He fell down, weakened.

"What do you want of me?" Harry was more frightened than he had ever been in any night terror before.

The being spoke more quietly now. "Finish." She smiled, and her face was glorious, lighting up the night sky. "Finish what you must do, dear heart." Her words trailed off and Harry's heart felt warm. The apparition floated into the sky, becoming one with the moon.

"Finish, finish," Harry found himself saying as he woke up. He reached for his glasses and looked at the clock. He'd been asleep for only an hour. "Finish what I must do... what is it that I must do?"

Harry drifted back to sleep, hoping he would find his way back to his lady of the lake again. What must he do? He must find out. He didn't find her, although he did dream about an ancient boat. And he slept soundly and peacefully – "like a baby," he told Annie the next day. By then, he'd forgotten his dream.

27. My dear

7 or 8 days ago, while Frank was sick with earache, I went to the School Auditorium to hear Arthur Hayes and 2 others compete in public speaking. The programme was enlivened by the children interspersing formal harmony with what they call "community singing" of popular songs. One of them, which they sang with gusto was: "I know where the flies go in the winter time." It's a tom-fool song, but as Frank and especially Della, like the "catchy" tune, here's the Chorus.

[Harry writing in his "Songs Learnt @ School" book, where he impeccably recorded his children's song, along with tonic solfa. 6 February, 1922]

May walked slowly upstairs to her Spadina Road apartment. She had a letter in her hand. As she reached the second floor, she looked back at the crimson carpeted stairs and the rich mahogany banister. *My royal walk*, she mused, and turned, taking a key out of her pocket. She was suddenly immensely relieved that she was virtually alone in the house. Ada and Fred were out together on errands and only Adolph remained in the house. Adolph, the strange, silent neighbour who had moved in to Tom's room. Adolph's phantom presence served to increase her sense of aloneness in the big house. The lock relented easily, and she was in her apartment. She locked the door behind her.

Feeling at a loss, May smoothed her hair and tugged her collar snugly into place. She wore a tailored gabardine dress, grey, trimmed with purple velvet. Having chosen her jewellery meticulously, it was perfectly understated, the small marcasite earrings enlivening her thick salt and pepper hair and scant, well-applied lipstick. As she walked past the mirror above the telephone table, she turned briefly to look at herself. *It really doesn't matter how you look now, May; you knew this would happen... you knew.* She pulled the caned chair away from her desk, picked up the letter opener and slit the envelope, turning it over again to examine the writing. She sat down.

Mrs. H. Westley, it dared to say, taunting her. Harry's exquisite handwriting, his modest mark in the world, mocked her. His return address and the stamp stood in stark contrast to her own geography. London? Impossible! No, not really... not impossible... London versus Toronto. As it always had been. For almost forty years, it had been London against Toronto, England against Canada, Annie against May. At long last, the winner had been declared. Farringdon Road... was that Annie's address? May felt ill; her heart pounded.

She took a deep breath and stood up again, pacing. It was hard to be contained, rational. Silly, really. After all, what did it matter? The separation of years had been made irrevocably visible with her move to Toronto.

And now Harry had trumped her.

My dear May...

My dear May? How dare he? How dare he call her – or anything about her – "dear"? She sat down again at her desk, slumping in her chair. Her hands shook. Defeated, May felt lost and overwhelmed. Suddenly the bitter churning in her chest disappeared, and her shoulders began to shake. May, always immune to tears, put her head down on her arms, overcome with her grief.

After a time, she recovered; the tears had had their way and disappeared. She sat back in the chair, pulled her hankie from her bodice, and wiped her eyes and nose. *Well now, what had Harry to say for himself? How could he possibly explain himself to anyone's satisfaction?* At least the tears had relieved her tension. She was ready to read on.

My dear May,

How can I apologize for transmitting what you now have gathered, that I am back in London? Does it help either of us for me to say we always knew, did we not, that I would have to return to my home?

I think not.

Does it help for me to say that this is not something I have done against you, that it is something I had to do to bring peace and resolution to my life?

I think not.

There is nothing I can do to assuage your anger and grief. But I do apologize for my part in these feelings of yours, as I always have.

You knew my retirement would bring my need to return to London to the fore. Our separation last year served only to strengthen my desire... my need. I know you thought it would make me realize my "foolishness." Instead it – shall we say? – made me more "foolish."

And so here I am, May, back home. I should have written you before I left. Instead, I am responding to Frank's request on your behalf. It gives me great pain not to be able to be at Della's wedding. It would have given me even greater pain to ask anyone to lie about that. So, because of Frank, I am telling the truth. Frank has always had that effect on people.

You are loved, May. Your children and grandchildren love you. Ada and the rest of your family love you. I love you, and I know you love me. The unfortunate thing is that our love was based upon deceit and assumptions. You will wonder if I have seen Annie. I have. During our conversations, I have learned of her letter to me so many years ago in which she said she was wrong in deciding against our marriage and would come to Canada to be with me. Love cannot be controlled. Enough said.

For my deceit in my return to London, I apologize. However, May, I do find some rationale for my act in that we had already been apart for over a year and without direct communication for about six months. I chose not to tell you about London because I knew it would be hurtful information for you.

If you wish to write to me, please do, May. It could be healthy for both of us to talk this way. The vast geographical distance between us may serve as a platform for diminishing the longstanding emotional distance between us.

I do hope so, May. Truly.

Always,

Harry

Always, Harry, indeed... *always Harry*. Harry would always be Harry – reticent, elsewhere... in London... with Annie. She had tried so hard. And now, it was over; finally, it was over. She could never have won. After all the years of holding and withholding, loving and hating, it was over.

She looked at their photos on the desk – Harry looking so handsome, she looking expectant and... yes... pretty. Iris about to be married, and she and Harry still married after thirty-seven years... one beginning, one over.

May stood, smoothed her dress and walked to the mirror, pausing longer this time. *Compose yourself, May. Now you know. That's the only difference. What good do tears do? You're no more alone than you've ever been.* Moving in closer to her reflection, she dabbed her eyes with her hankie and picked up a tube of lipstick from a small Moorcroft bowl on the telephone table. Her hands shook slightly as she painted her lips into composure, nice little dip in the middle to make a bow... "There – everything back in order and as it should be!" Sitting down at the table, she picked up the phone and dialled... "Hello, Iris – how are you, dear?" Her voice was firm and steady. "You haven't by any chance heard from your father, have you?...."

28. Morte d'Arthur

Busy getting the clothes dry and put away. Mugsie a great nuisance these days and get everything all over. Tonight Frank and I got some Christmas cards addressed. It takes quite a while. We have a few cards already. Got Mrs. W.'s and Aunt Ada's parcels.
[The Lois Diaries, December 16, 1947]

He'd never felt good enough to sit here. In fact, he'd never felt good enough to darken the doorway. No, the steps had been as good as it got for a newspaper boy. He'd been told that; not in so many words, perhaps, but in gestures and veiled instructions. As carefully as he'd told himself that things were different now and that he could take back what had been taken away from him in London so long ago, he felt the old unworthiness. In fact, he was sitting within it.

As the music wafted over him, Harry realized St. Paul's was the crucible, of sorts, for the resolution he required. The place from which he had felt banned was now the place where his healing could take effect. "Oh, for the wings, for the wings of a dove; Far away, far away, far away would I fly…" the boy sang flawlessly. As, indeed, Frank had sung when he was ten in the land of no history and no music, save the flow of tears through the drought and the whine of the wind through the wheat.

Perfect heaven. Imperfect earth. How did one reconcile the irreconcilable? How did one reconcile his presence – his daring to be present – in St. Paul's in London while his lovely daughter was being married in a church in Toronto? Here he sat at Evensong, Greenwich Mean Time, as Della should be preparing to walk down the aisle with her father in the early winter afternoon in Toronto.

Instead, Frank would walk with her as her father sat far away in London.

Della would look stunning in white against the auburn hair that framed her delicate features… graceful Della….

Yes, he had to admit it, his absence from his daughter gave him great pain right now, on this 17th day of December, 1947. How could it feel so right to be here in London and so wrong at the same time to be away from his daughter?

The organ intruded with its rolling of some lesser know Bach toccata. He must be playing mostly with his feet. Harry's heart lurched with a dissonant chord. Churches should never be allowed male names, he thought – this was the music of the womb… soul music… not a St. Paul or St. Olav or Simple Simon or any other man. Ridiculous! Churches should be called Saint Sarah's and Saint Mrs. Givens and Saint Annie's. Saint Lucretia's, even. The women of his Whitechapel childhood were worthy of that and more, barren though St. Mary's womb had been. He was aware again of the notes falling around him as the healing grace of Mendelssohn took over and sheltered him with its intricate intertwining of voice and instruments. And Harry breathed deeply. He looked up into the domed sanctuary.

So long ago… it had all happened so long ago. All the loss and grief, all the diminishing of family and love. And then finally, Dad had had to go. He was too ill to hang onto life any longer. With young Arthur gone, it was clear that he'd been clinging to life for Harry's sake.

"What are you going to do, son? I can't stay on much longer, you know. You do know that, don't you, Harry?" Arthur looked worse than any of them had looked; his pallor grey like the fog itself; his upper lip wet from the sheer effort of breathing; his breath rattling around inside his chest like a storm looking for the precise timing of major impact. "You'll be all right, Harry. You will."

How strangely the whole experience had unfolded. Young Arthur's death two years previously in 1894 had been too much for Dad. He'd felt, with

Arthur's having made it into his twenties and into a marriage, that his cough and episodes of illness would become less frequent and severe. It was as though Dad had believed turning twenty guaranteed his son exemption from the killer. And so, when Arthur the son fell so desperately ill, Arthur the father could not – indeed, would not – tolerate the inevitable outcome. He'd had to give up. It was as simple as that. There came a point... there... came... a... point...

"What's the use, Harry?" Arthur lay back in the faded maroon armchair, worn threadbare from the impressions of dying souls. "When your firstborn leaves before you... when you've been unable to prevent even that – then it's time to go. There are all the others who've gone before me. And they're waiting, Harry. Now, that doesn't mean you and Charlie should give up! No —I need you and Charlie to stay and face the enemy down. I'm just too tired to stay, Harry," Arthur's hacking cough interrupted and forced him spit blood into his dirty hanky. It took another few seconds to regain his breath. "And too sick. You stay for me... will you, Harry? I've stayed for you this long; you stay for me for the duration, Harry – a true and proper duration." Harry gave up that evening in his futile attempt to understand good and evil. He gave up, knowing evil lurked in the acrid smoke in the air and in the shadows and sparks the fire spewed against the wall and on the sick faces they should have warmed and healed. He gave up his quest in particular because the only good he could find in the world kept dying. Good and evil were co-conspirators, colluders, secret agents, and they could go to hell, as far as he was concerned. He placed his hand on his father's chest as the lacerating cough resumed. Both father and son received some peace from this gesture that had come naturally over the past few weeks to Harry... this connection... this correction. They'd learned that it steadied the father's heaving chest while it gave the son the sense that he could do something to make things different... that he had purpose. Perhaps, even, that there was hope. A modicum of hope, as his Dad had said long ago about Bertie. Once the coughing abated, Harry wiped his father's face with the cloth from the basin Lucretia had left beside the bed.

"Dad," Harry did not want his father to fall asleep before he could tell him the news. "Dad, I've got some very nice news for you... news that will give you some peace."

Arthur looked shocked, "Are you all right, then, Harry? How could there possibly be news in a family dying off – a family with no relatives and no offspring? Are you daft, young man?" He was about to say more when his coughing convulsed him.

Could my father not have been spared – at least my father, Harry challenged. "No, Dad, I'm not daft, and, as much as we don't know what good news is, I have some. It has to do chiefly with you, Dad, but I don't want to excite you... you know... make you worse. Do you want me to tell you? I will; but only if you let me talk and you say nothing for a while. Well?"

"Yes, tell me then. I'll say nothing. Which won't be difficult because what news could you possibly have of nothing?"

"Lie back, then, Dad, and just listen." Harry freshened the cloth with clean water and gently washed his father's face, wiping his auburn hair away from his forehead. "Dad, Lucretia has found Emma."

"Emma? I know only one Emma. And I haven't seen her since just before I married your mother."

"You promised to say nothing, Dad. So, let me talk. And you listen. Lucretia has found your sister Emma. And she lives here in London, not in Little Bardfield. Now, let me tell you how."

Emma – Arthur's long lost sister – had been found in a circuitous way. Lucretia had sent a letter to Little Bardfield, where Arthur had grown up. The letter then found its way to London. All Lucretia had known was that Emma had never married. "It's time," Lucretia had stated, with the logic that only a non-family member could apply to a family situation replete with

hurt and mixed feelings and multiple losses, "for your father to gain some peace with his family, Harry. I don't care what kind of rules your grandfather set for his children and the family property, your father has brothers and sisters who should see him before he dies. After all his years of heartache and hard work, he deserves peace of mind. Reconciliation. God knows how he deserves it. And I intend to help God out." With that, she had sent a letter to Emma Westley, the one sibling who seemed to hold slight promise. The letter had fortuitously found its way from Little Bardfield to London itself, where Emma had recently become Lady's Maid in the home of a Viscount.

Emma, it turned out, had been trying to find her younger brother, finding instead the wrong Westleys. Well, maintained Lucretia, this was as it was meant to be. God's timing was God's timing. The two women met, understood each other and the circumstances, and devised a plan for Arthur's best care. Emma arranged to have Arthur taken into the servants' quarters where she worked and lived... not that there was any difference between the two states for Emma. And Lucretia, Harry and Charlie, moved at seeing the two siblings reunited, formulated the plan for Arthur. He would be in Emma's household until the end. And Harry would remember forever his dear Dad's tears of great gratitude and his lack of objections.

"Harry... Harry." Who was it? The voice was somehow consumed by an organ. Ah... St. Paul's. "Harry... are you all right?"

"Oh Annie, how did you know I'd be here? When did you come?"

Annie laughed quietly. "Harry, you told me you were coming here today. I felt you'd been away on your own long enough. I've been here about an hour, watching you. I didn't want you to be alone on Della's wedding day; you know that. I moved beside you about ten minutes ago. You didn't seem to notice." Annie held Harry's hand.

29. Roll call

*A really fine day. Quite busy today. A box from Iris and a box from
Lolita. A lovely woollen coat and legging – good for Mugsie and
also a Christmas present for the girls, too. Frank and I out to the
Carol Festival. The Chanters and Choir were superb. The church
looked great. It was so fine to go.*
[The Lois Diaries, December 17, 1947]

How does one do this, Harry wondered – how does one celebrate Christmas
as a stranger in a strange land, the land of one's birth, abandoned by
Christmas? This was not the London he knew. And yet, with all the war's
destruction still in a leering gargoyle state, it was his London still. Perhaps
the bombs had destroyed the white plague – the London he knew exposed…
exploded. This was not the Harry he once was, though. If he ever knew who
he really was.

"Confound it, I've always been a stranger in a strange land!" That he'd
spoken aloud shocked him. It also made his thoughts vaguely tangible, the
truth hanging in the air in front of his face, mocking him… *It's your lot in
life, Harry, always was—to be on the periphery of things. Like life and
death. Like love and abandonment. Like weddings. And Christmas. Here
and there. There and here… the Atlantic the Great Divide in your brain.*

It all gave him a great pain in his chest.

And so here he was on Christmas Eve, 1947, in the place of his birth,
desperately missing his family in Canada and desperately wanting to be
with Annie here in England. *You can't have it both ways, Harry, like some
needy little boy. Make up your mind—your feelings will follow. Time to train
them like a puppy—heel!*

Harry sat on the bed and looked at his present for Annie. He'd been happy when he purchased it and had it wrapped and tied with a lovely, wide, red velvet ribbon. From the size of the box, she'd never guess it held a ring. It was something he'd wanted to do for Annie so long ago when life, or was it death, separated them. So, why was it, then, that his heart felt like it would explode from all that he held inside—the huge grief he carried over his shoulder forever. Ha! The ghost of Christmas past! That's who he was.

The bundle of grief spread from his shoulder into his chest and back. Harry lay back on the bed. That served only to make the pain sharper and his breathing shorter. He stood and paced, thinking. And he thought of Lois. She often got pain in her chest... what was it she did? Baking soda—that was it! "A couple of teaspoons in a glass of water—it cures my indigestion every time," she used to say.

Harry went to the kitchen and looked in the pantry to find the baking soda. Once he'd taken Lois's "cure", his panic subsided. There now, his pain was going away with his panic. Such relief!

Home from work, Annie came in the back door, slipping her shoes off and blowing on her hands to warm them. "Oh, it's a cold one out there! Harry, I'm home." She turned toward the kitchen table and stopped. "Harry, what are you doing? You look pale. Harry!"

"Annie, don't be alarmed," he reached out to her and patted his knee. Annie sat there and put her arm around Harry's neck. She kissed his cheek and felt his forehead. "I just had a nasty bout of indigestion, Annie, and remembered how Lois cures hers. So, here I am. And I'm fine."

"But, Harry, you don't get indigestion. I should call the doctor." Annie tried to stand up, but Harry pulled her back to his knee.

"Oh, I do get it, Annie. Very rarely, but when I get it, it's tough. There's no need to think about it any further."

"Perhaps we shouldn't go out tonight. It might be better for you to rest."

Harry laughed. "I want to go to the Evensong. And I'm fine. I got too wrapped up in memories and became my own worst enemy, as Lois would put it. Now, let's put together a nice little repast before we leave."

Annie stood up and placed a big kiss on Harry's forehead. "With one stipulation! I insist you lie down while I put together a little food. If you do that, I'll go out with you."

Harry pulled Annie into his embrace. "You win." He looked into her eyes and smiled, "I love you, my Annie, and I would be most honoured if you would come to lie down with me." He took Annie's hand and led her to the stairs.

Thus were Harry and London's Christmas united.

The twelve days of Christmas had come before Christmas that year… Dad dead December 13th, 1896… eight out of ten family members dead between February 8, 1879 and December 13, 1896. The roll call of the Westley family: come forward as your name is called—Edith, Ellen, Walter, Herbert, Ernest, Sarah, Arthur the younger, Arthur the older. No, Charles and Harry —not you! Your names haven't been called yet. And they will not be called for a long time. And they will not be called in the country of your birth.

Harry ruminated as he swirled his spoon in his second cup of tea. *Who was it who did the calling?* And what was it he had just wondered—*they will not be called in the country of your birth?*

"But I'm back!" Harry sipped his tea.

"Did you say something, Harry?" Annie called to him from the living room.

"No! Just having trouble with a crossword clue." Harry looked back at the puzzle in the centre of the kitchen table. He picked up his pencil. Better to get lost in a crossword puzzle than to conjure up sad memories of Christmases past. Hadn't he just replaced them with his first ever London Merry Christmas? After all, it was now 1948. A new year. A new home.

They will not be called in the country of your birth.

30. Will you be back?

In 1870-72, John Marius Wilson's Imperial Gazetteer of England and Wales described Mile End New Town like this: MILE-END-NEW-TOWN. a quondam hamlet, a chapelry, and a sub-district, in Whitechapel district, Middlesex. The quondam hamlet is now a compact portion of the metropolis; lies N of Whitechapel-road, on the Eastern Counties railway, between Bishopsgate and Mile-End r. stations, contiguous to Whitechapel, Spitalfields, and Bethnal-Green parishes, 1¾ mile ENE of St. Paul's; was once a part of the ancient parish of Stepney, but is now a distinct parish for the relief of the poor; and has a post office under London NE. Pop. in 1851,10,183; in 1861,10,845. Houses, 1,178.—The chapelry is conterminate with the quondam hamlet; was constituted in 1841; and bears the name of All Saints. The living is a p. curacy in the diocese of London. Value, £300. Patron, the Bishop of London. The church stands in Spicer-street, and was built in 1839. There are an Independent chapel in Church-street, rebuilt in 1860; a Roman Catholic of St. Ann, with monastery and nunnery attached; national schools adjoining the church, and built in 1840; ragged schools, called King Edward's schools, in Albert-street; a refuge for destitute girls, called King Edward's refuge, and connected with the ragged schools; and one of the two workhouses of Whitechapel district, occupied, at the census of 1861, by 638 inmates.—The sub-district contains also parts of Whitechapel and Spitalfields parishes; and comprises 64 acres. Pop. in 1851,14,543; in 1861,15,392. Houses, 1,634.

It was – deliberately – 4:30 p.m… deliberately early. He'd asked Annie to meet him at The Blind Beggar. He'd suggested immediately after work, around 5:00 p.m. During that interval, he wanted to have the letter with him and think, away from home, about how to broach everything. Gently. Tentatively.

Harry looked around, taking in the other customers, staff and décor. A splendid pub, actually, where an inn had been built almost three hundred years earlier. *One doesn't get that kind of history in Saskatchewan. Ha – Regina had been called "Pile of Bones" not too long ago!* But what Harry remembered was that this very site was where the seeds of the Salvation Army had been planted when William Booth preached an open-air sermon in the mid-19th century. Booth, the quasi-military, humanitarian ex-Methodist preacher, preaching to the poor sinners of London from a tent. Booth, standing on the ground of beggars and buried Quakers, outlining the road to redemption when most East Londoners were on the road to death. Hell didn't scare them. It wasn't a future destination. It was a current address. *Booth did a lot of good, though,* Harry reassured himself, *feeding the destitute in the streets first and then in the schools… "the heathen," of course.*

Harry took the envelope from his jacket pocket. Frank's beautiful handwriting stared back at him. "Mr. Harry Westley" it said. He took the letter out and re-read it.

Regina, Saskatchewan,

December 25, 1947

Dear Dad,

The four of us have had a lovely Christmas Day, starting, of course, with Santa, then breakfast, followed by Meg and Nell's enactment of the Christmas story. Nell was busy being Mary and the shepherds and angels, while Meg was quite content with being the star of the show, baby Jesus. It was a delightful performance, although, I must confess that it was extremely hard at times not to laugh. There was one priceless moment when Mary told Jesus, "Don't you ever cry like that again or you will have to sleep with the

148

cows."

I'm at the dining room table. Lois is in the living room, reading "Hungry Hill", my gift to her. She loved "Rebecca" and "Frenchman's Creek" so much that I knew I couldn't go wrong with another du Maurier! I'll take her to a movie next week as part of her present. As luck would have it, the movie of "Hungry Hill" will be playing. So, all in all, the du Maurier theme has worked well. And I must say I don't mind seeing Jean Simmons on screen!

The kiddies have a friend each here, so a comparison of Christmas is going on. Nell and Joyce are beginning to get lost together in the Girls' Crystal Annual you sent Nell. Meg loved her dolly from you. She and Annabelle are playing with it at the moment. And Lois and I look forward to using the pudding steamer you gave us. Lois already has a new suet pudding recipe she wants to try.

We do miss you, Dad. Although we're a dispersed family—from us in Saskatchewan, to Della in northern Ontario, to mother in Toronto—we haven't been used to having a family member across the ocean. I suppose you would say to that, "Well, Frankie, my thoughts were always lost in London." But I needed and had your presence with me as a father, and I miss that. I could not imagine a more gentle nor encouraging father than you have always been. Having had you living with us for the few months before you left made the sadness of your journey more intense, I think. And yet, I want you to know that I do understand, Dad, and that my prayers are for your reconciliation with yourself through this return of yours.

I will have to be back and forth to Ottawa in the new year, staying the longest in July. So we've planned that Lois and the girls will go by train at the end of July to meet me and to stay for a few weeks in Toronto and at the farm.

I wonder if you will be back by then?

Well, it's almost time to make the children some cocoa. We all wish you and Annie a very happy New Year.

Love,

Frank, Lois and kidlets

31. Daddy's office

A truth that's told with bad intent
Beats all the Lies you can invent.
It is right it should be so;
Man was made for Joy & Woe…
       [William Blake]

SCENE FIVE—Regina, January 2, 1948

STAGE: a large office in the Art-Deco Dominion Government Building,
with a staff of twenty men in long-sleeved white shirts, some rolled up, with
suspenders and ties. The men are busy at various work activities, some
sitting, some standing. The atmosphere is relatively quiet and energetic.
There is an office within the office, obviously for "the boss." Lois, Nell and
Meg walk into the office.

Lois is wearing her Persian lamb coat, a red hat with a veil, dressy winter
boots and a large "I'm here!" attitude. Her grey gloves are showing from
the top of her red purse. The girls, dressed warmly in winter coats, muffs,
scarves and hats, follow Lois politely. Meg whips her hat off and starts
moving around the room.

LOIS *(pulling her veil up)*: Happy New Year, everyone! Is Frank busy?

MAC *(a wiry, handsome 30 year old, Frank's second in command, coming*
over to talk with Lois, smiles broadly): And the same to you, Lois! *(Meg*
recognizes him, puts down the paperweight she's discovered and toddles
over; Mac bends down to her) Well, little Mugsie, how are you? I still say –
put a moustache on you and you'd be a dead ringer for your Daddy! *(Meg*
giggles and Nell looks slightly disappointed) Frank's just finishing up a
letter with Miss Trelevyn. He'll be out shortly, Lois. I trust you had a good
Christmas?

LOIS: Oh, yes, it was grand, Mac – except that the girls were underfoot too much. You and Rita should never feel badly that you don't have children, especially one like our Mugsie. She's into everything! She pulled the clothes out of the washer last week and dumped a box of starch all over the cement floor. She… *(the inner office door opens and Frank comes out with Miss Trelevyn, thanking her for her work on the letter)*… Oh Frank, dear! *(Lois and Nell walk over to Frank, while Meg goes exploring again)*

MISS TRELEVYN *(a trim 40 year old, conservatively dressed with glasses and black hair severely pulled back)*: Hello, Mrs. Westley – happy New Year!

LOIS *(passing her by quickly, and not looking at the woman, on her way to Frank's office)*: The same to you. Come girls! *(giving Miss Trelevyn what she calls "the brush-off")*

The girls run to Frank – Daddy! Daddy!

The family goes into the office and sits down, except for Meg. Frank gives her paper and pencil to play with.

LOIS: Are you ready for your outing with the girls – it's a lovely day, so you should have fun!

FRANK: I certainly am. Are you ready, girlies? *(Nell and Meg answer enthusiastically)* And you'll have the remainder of the day to yourself.

LOIS: I finished Meg's coat this morning. Do you like it? She doesn't.

FRANK: It's very dashing – and you'll like it, too, won't you, Meg? *(Meg ignores the comment)*

LOIS: Oh yes – a card came today from Iris. It's a picture of Niagara Falls – as if I haven't seen that before! They're having a grand time, and she thanked us for the telegram. She says she'll send a piece of wedding cake when they get home.

FRANK: I wish we could have been at the wedding, but we might as well be at the other end of the world when it's winter here. Well, I'll get my coat on. Girls, do you want to use the bathroom here? *(he takes his coat off the coat rack and slips his arm in the left sleeve)*

LOIS: And... *(she drags the word out and shoos the girls down the hall to the bathroom)* Nell, you make sure Meg is a good girl and she's put together right when she's finished! *(the girls run out of the office, full of pep)* And... there was a letter from Dad.

FRANK: Saying?

LOIS: Well, it wasn't so much what he was saying as it was that it seemed rather sad. Not terribly... but a bit of the old Dad.

FRANK *(doing up his coat, putting on his fedora and picking up his overshoes)*: But no word about changing his mind?

LOIS: Not a peep.

FRANK *(locks his office door and they leave talking)*: Well... the girls and I will have a bit to eat at that little restaurant by the theatre. I know they're going to enjoy "Fun and Fancy Free." That must be what Dad is. I'll put my boots on downstairs. There's the girls. Push the elevator button, Nell!

END OF SCENE

32. Hackneyed phrases

Rather a blowy day. Frank and Nellie out to church. They came in happily about 1:00 and we had dinner. Nell played with her cut-outs and Frank did his music. We were both out to church and he sang beautifully "The Voice in the Wilderness" – also at Knox Church at the Friendly Hour. I played for him. We had a great day.
[The Lois Diaries, January 4, 1948]

"Mr. Westley? My goodness, I don't believe it!"

A vaguely familiar voice. Harry was so startled by it that he dropped the menu. He looked up and then stood, almost reaching to tip his hat until he realized that, of course, he didn't have it on. "Miss Archer – what a surprise! What brings you here, of all places? Please…" Harry moved to the opposite chair, pulled it out and gestured for Miss Archer to sit down. As she sat, he eased the chair in for her and sat down, looking at her. *Pretty woman. She's feeling shy and yet she seems very happy.* "Well, Miss Archer… Angela… what is it that brings you to The Blind Beggar… indeed, even to London?"

Angela smiled broadly, "I had some holiday time to use from last year, and I thought of London. I haven't been here for over ten years. I felt I should visit for two reasons. I wanted to see that it was healing from the war. And, to be completely honest, you are the other reason, Mr. Westley!"

Harry was so taken aback that "I?" became the extent of his response.

Angela laughed, "Oh, I know you must find that statement confusing." She reached over and touched Harry's hand, "May I call you Harry?"

"Please."

"I'll explain. When we parted – dear me, that sounds like the Tosti song that's so popular! Nevertheless, when we parted in Southampton, your disclosure about why you were returning to England and then your honesty about Whitechapel made me want to visit sometime. In a sense, I wanted to see what you had left compared to what I had left. So, I booked the holiday time at Christmas and found my way here. Of course, I've done the traditional sightseeing as well. But, most importantly, Harry, you've been an inspiration to me."

Harry was flummoxed, "An inspiration? Really, I don't see how."

"Oh my goodness, Harry – of course you have been! You left your Canadian home, and, I'm sure, family to return to your homeland. Whatever the story – and I would love to know it – that is a phenomenal thing to do alone. After forty years! And to return to someone you loved. You gave me courage to commit to very personal honesty."

"I must say, Angela, you look well and very happy. And free, yes, very free. How have you done? You mentioned taking time off work."

"Yes, I decided I wanted to be useful to my city. There is still much to do in housing projects because so many people lost their homes in the war. I work for the department that matches people with new homes on the basis of need and time waiting. It's usually very gratifying. But there are times when I have to follow the bureaucracy and make a family wait when their need is so very obvious."

"And your reason for returning home? You and the man you were trying to forget? How has that turned out for you?"

Ever so briefly, a shadow of pain crossed Angela's eyes, and then she smiled, very much in the moment again. "The strangest thing happened. I began to realize I had done what I'd set out to do. I'd forgotten him. I'd forgotten him because he wasn't who I had created in my mind. And once I'd realized that, I had to look at why I had imagined him."

"And what did you discover?"

"That I needed to be free of others' expectations. It's a rather hackneyed phrase, but I do mean this was critical for me."

"It doesn't surprise me, Angela."

"Really? I suppose I shouldn't be surprised that you made observations. You're going to say something about my mother, aren't you?"

Harry looked at Angela's lovely and now very serious face. "Only that your mother spoke for you. I was never so glad to see someone speak up as when you began to challenge me. And now look at you!"

"And you, Harry? How have things turned out for you with the one you had lost?"

"Very well, my dear, very well, indeed." Harry looked at his watch, "In fact, you should be able to meet her any moment now. I made a date to meet her after work today here. Now you must tell me just how you came to be here today!"

"I've been in London for almost a week. I always had the glimmer of hope that I might find you somehow."

Harry interrupted her. "There's Annie now!" Harry waved Annie over and stood up.

Annie draped her coat over the chair beside Harry's, gave him a kiss and sat down. She smiled quizzically at Angela.

"Annie, I'd like you to meet Angela." Annie reached across to shake Angela's hand. "If you remember my story about the mother and daughter I met on the trip home, this is the daughter."

"Angela, I'm very glad to meet you, and I do remember Harry's stories about you and your mother. But how in the world did you find your way to The Blind Beggar?"

Angela laughed, "I was about to tell Harry. When I mentioned I wanted to see Whitechapel, this place was the top choice for almost everyone. 'Best place for a pint and a steak and kidney pie and for some wonderful history,' they'd say. And I must say I can see why, although I'll wait to see if the food passes muster!"

"And, to that end," Harry caught the eye of the waiter, "let's order!"

In this expansion of friendship and validation, Harry did not feel the hole Frank's letter was burning into his breast pocket.

Blast! Two-fifteen and I'm up again. Why is it always the same time? That, at least, is curious... Harry had turned the rocking chair to face the living room window. He looked out, elbows on the arms of the chair, fingertips tapping together. The street lamp had a strong, violet halo. *Must be the fog. Maybe my own personal fog. Same thoughts. Same self-recriminations. Same questions. Same shame. Over and over again at this time of night. But then, why not? I deserve it all... leaving or losing all that I love. Never being definite. Never fully committing.*

"Harry, one never abandons one's children, even in death." Harry felt this was not his own thought. It seemed external, alien. *"Consider the children, Harry. Consider the children. Consider the letter,"* the voice trailed off.

Harry felt oddly comforted. Or was it guided?

The children and the letter? Consider them... examine, scrutinize, perhaps even regard? His thoughts went to his granddaughters and to Frank's letter. And then Della's wedding came to mind. And then that old abdominal drop into grief. But, no, this wasn't his old grief. This was something he had control over. It was also something he had caused – given, if you will – a presentation to the family he had created, an unacceptable legacy.

Harry dropped his hands to his knees and wept. *And there's that blasted tune, whatever it is, going round and round in my head again.*

Harry walked slowly upstairs to bed.

33. For the children, Harry

33 degrees above. Hooray! Frank was at the door when I was just coming downstairs. Brought Nellie and Mugsie a pair of piggy salt and pepper shakers. 2 prs. of nylons for me. Tonight out in one grand blizzard to see and hear Alec Templeton. What a red letter day. He is really magnificent. An awful night but what a good time.
[The Lois Diaries, January 14, 1948]

It was a bright and balmy day again today. Angela and Harry sat in a protected area in Bethnal Green Gardens, across from each other at a small table. Since Angela's agenda for the day was to explore the Bethnal Green Library, she had suggested meeting here.

"It's a lovely spot here, Angela. Museums, libraries... these were never places for the young Harry. I'm glad you thought of it. And, wonderful weather – imagine being able to sit outside at this time of year! In Saskatchewan, we would be bundled up inside, listening to the winds howl and the plumbing groan."

"Surely you had similar winter days when you were young, Harry?" Angela was wearing a rich blue tweed coat and a silk, multi-coloured scarf. The blue of her coat was picked up in her scarf, intensifying the blue of her eyes. Her black leather gloves lay on the table beside her.

"Angela, my childhood was blanketed in fog, stench and death. I apologize for being so blunt; but it is the truth. My truth. London was a city of marked contrasts and I lived in its darkness. I can't recall a sunny day. 'The slums of East London' they called it. And it's still here."

"Hmmm... Dickens... 'There are people in the world so hungry that God cannot appear to them except in the form of bread.' I should have been more thoughtful, Harry," Angela touched his hand. "Is that how it was for you?"

"Indeed." Harry had retreated into himself.

"What is it you remember most from your childhood?"

Harry was silent… removed. Had he worn his visor and dark glasses today to have an escape hatch?

"Harry… Harry," Angela touched his hand again.

"I'm sorry?"

"What do you remember most clearly from your childhood?"

Harry put his fingertips together, tapping them lightly… his way of mulling. "Love. Yes… love."

Angela was stunned. She looked at this unassuming, intelligent man who hid behind his visor and saw his story etched on his face, expressed in his eyes. *I'm seeing him for the first time,* she thought. "Harry, I think I know you and then you take a new angle. How can you tell me about death and stench and then say that love is your main childhood memory?"

"There are things I know beyond a shadow of doubt, Angela. And at the top of that list is that our family loved. My mother and father set the stage with their love for each other and for their children. The word 'love' was spoken and felt. By the time I was born, my siblings had been reduced to four by the deaths of Walter and little Edith and Ellen. But they were remembered, honoured on their birthdays, candles lit on their death dates, names dutifully entered into our family Bible. My parents sacrificed for us, read to us from the Bible, helped us with our schooling and somehow made the scant larder into enough. We could hear the noise of neighbours arguing and hitting children and yet know, unequivocally, we were safe in our own home."

"I've read about Victorian London, Harry. But hearing a firsthand account is entirely different," Angela understood now how this man had been groomed to remain in the background. "Annie said on Tuesday when we met for lunch that your parents were first generation Londoners. How did they come to live there?"

"Mummy... my mother... told me some stories; but I can't remember the details... something about my Dad thinking he would move from Little Bardfield and become successful," Harry was silent for a moment. "He didn't want the rural life, I think."

"Do you know how they met?" Angela spoke softly.

"Somehow my father found my mother in a workhouse. She had left Sheringham to be a governess; but the family turned her out on the London streets. So the workhouse, in Shoreditch, I think, became her only option. I don't know how; but Dad got enough money to buy her way out. And then they got married."

"Workhouses were dreadful, Harry. They were part of a history course I took. I became so fascinated – and horrified – that I read all I could get my hands on. Oliver Twist's workhouse is a glorified view."

How could one not be persuaded by the earnestness and quick mind of this lovely young creature, Harry wondered. "You remind me of my daughter... or a young Annie. And that brings me to why I wanted to meet with you. I don't want to keep you from the day you've planned. And I've talked entirely too much about myself." Harry reached into his pocket and pulled out an envelope. He turned it and pushed it toward her. "Angela, there's something I want to talk to you about. You've become a good friend to Annie and me, and now you know a little of my early life in London. I received this letter from my son last week. I've been troubled about it since. Would you read it over for me? And then we could discuss it... briefly... I don't want to belabour this concern. But I do covet your viewpoint and thoughts for Annie."

Angela picked up the envelope. "All right, Harry. Yes. For Angela... and you." She opened the envelope and took the letter out.

Harry watched the young woman as she read the letter, sometimes reading a phrase or two aloud... *Dear Dad... or you will have to sleep with the cows... I don't mind seeing Jean Simmons on screen... We do miss you, Dad... having a family member across the ocean... I could not imagine a more gentle nor encouraging father than you have always been... I do understand, Dad... reconciliation with yourself... if you will be back by then? We all wish you and Annie a very happy New Year.* As she finished and looked up at him, Harry felt his heart would burst. There were tears in her eyes.

"Harry, I... I don't know what to say. I... could I have a few moments to take this in?" She looked the letter over again, took a deep breath, returned the letter to its envelope. "All right, I'm listening," she managed a faint smile.

"Now you see who and what I am and what I've done. I've painted myself into a corner where, no matter what choice I make, I will inflict more hurt. People are put in jail for less damage than what I've meted out, Angela."

"Self-reproach is a road to nowhere, Harry. You've been thinking this over. What do you need to do about Frank's letter? One of Frank's phrases is the key to it all. He says 'reconciliation with yourself,' Harry, 'reconciliation with yourself.'"

"I'm not sure I'm able to do that. It presupposes a knowledge of one's self," Harry took his glasses off and smiled at Angela, "If you know where I could buy one..."

Angela laughed. "That's better! Enough gloom. Let's see action. What is your plan, Harry, where do you belong?"

"I belong in Canada. As much as I love Annie, I belong in Canada. But I can't bear telling her, hurting her."

Angela held her friend's hand, "Harry, Annie knows."

Harry was shocked, "Annie knows? Whatever do you mean? I haven't said a word."

"We talked intensely last Tuesday. She said you'd received a letter from Frank, but hadn't shared it. She said you always share Frank's letters. And she had the sense you were struggling with it. She said, 'Harry can't stay away from his family forever, but I don't know how to get him to talk about it.' Annie is worried about you, Harry."

"I'm shocked! How could I not have noticed?"

"Because you fell down the rabbit hole, Harry… into that old 'Slough of Despond' thing. When you fall, you no longer see well. Until you take action. Talk to Annie. You will both be relieved."

"I think you're right. Thank you, Angela. Thank you, indeed." Harry felt… *what was it? Focused? Yes, that was it! Focused!*

"Now walk to the library with me. I have an interview for a position there," Angela slipped her arm into Harry's as they walked off.

"Oh! I almost forgot, Angela. You mentioned a song to me when we met at The Blind Beggar," Harry talked softly as they approached the steps to the library. "I couldn't get the tune out of my head for a while. And now I've forgotten it again. Do you remember? I'm sure it is a solo of Frank's. Tosti, I think you said."

The irony wasn't lost on Angela, "I do… 'Parted.' I'll go in here," she began walking up to the main doors, and then turned. "Oh! And Harry!"

Harry turned toward her.

"Remember the letter, Harry. Consider Frank's sage advice… for all the children, Harry."

Angela disappeared into the books of Bethnal Green.

34. *You must go back*

Re-living the wonderful evening last night. He is a marvellous artist. Letter from Iris. Frank taking it easy tonight. He had an asthma attack after work. 24 below.
          [The Lois Diaries, January 15, 1948]

Harry awoke with the song already singing itself in his head. Lovely tune. But what were the words? *Oh stop! The more I think about them, the more I'll forget them.* Harry went about getting ready for the day, sometimes whistling the tune of Frank's Tosti song. In fact, he went downstairs for breakfast with Annie whistling it.

"Well, you're feeling chipper this morning, love. What's that song?" Annie poured a cup of tea for Harry.

Harry kissed Annie on the forehead, sat down and sipped of his tea. "It's a song I'd forgotten until Angela mentioned it when we met at The Blind Beggar. It's plagued me ever since. And I'm getting nowhere with it. I think it bothers me because I should remember it."

"Why is that?" Annie buttered some fresh toast for Harry. "Here's some new black current jam and cream."

"It's just that it was a solo of Frank's," Harry dressed his toast. "Lois accompanied Frank, of course – with such perfection and sensitivity. They were such an invincible unit when it came to music."

"You must miss that," Annie stared into her teacup. "Harry, I've been meaning to ask you about Frank. I know…"

Harry interrupted her, "I know what you're going to say; at least, I think I do. Were you going to ask why I didn't share Frank's last letter with you?"

"I was. You don't have to tell me anything. It's just that you've been rather quiet since it came. And his letters usually make you happy."

Taking her hands, Harry reached over to kiss Annie, "I'm sorry, Annie. Once I'd gone into myself, I couldn't seem to work my way out. Hence, the little visit with Angela yesterday. What I'd like to do is give you the letter this morning. You can read it during lunch at work and then we can have a good chat this evening. How does that sound?"

Annie beamed, "Much better!"

"Well, then, you get yourself ready for work and I'll go upstairs and get the letter for you." Harry seemed not to notice he was again whistling the elusive song.

SCENE SIX—Regina, January 15, 1948

Frank comes in from outside, the whistle of his breathing seeming like part of the weather. The winter prairie wind is howling; snow blows in through the door as Frank steps into the front porch. The snow is swirling so violently that the outdoors cannot be seen through the frosty porch windows. He is covered with snow and turns to close the door with both hands. Propped against the door, he stays there, with his head bent, wheezing for a few minutes while his breath settles slightly. With great effort, he takes off his boots and puts them neatly against the wall.

Frank opens the inside door and steps into the hallway. His breathing is quite audible, with a whistle. Nell runs into the hallway from the living room. She is holding a book. Lois, coming down the stairs from stage left, looks scared. Meg, a doll in hand, comes out from the living room.

NELL *(eagerly, happily)*: Daddy, Daddy! Can you read to Meg now, please? She wants Tippity John and she doesn't like the way I read it! *(She looks at her Daddy and stops talking.)*

LOIS *(loud, fearful)*: Can't you see that your father can't breathe? *(Nell shrinks, as Lois turns her attention to Frank)* What do you want to do, Frank? Do you want your chair? *(She helps him out of his coat)*

FRANK *(wheezing, barely able to talk)*: Yes… I need to… get room in my lungs…

Lois goes into the living room, followed by Frank and then the girls. Lois pulls a straight-backed armchair into the centre of the living room. Frank leans over it, his hands gripping the arms of the chair. He tries to breathe more deeply. Every breath comes out in a frightening wheeze. Lois gets Meg to sit and play with her doll and comes back to Frank.

LOIS *(agitated)*: What do you want me to do, Frank? Oh, I hate this! Why can't it just stop. What should I do?

FRANK *(firmly, quietly)*: Just… leave me be… I need… air…

LOIS: But it's not right!

Frank continues to attempt to bring his breathing under his own control. Nell slips out into the hall and comes back with Frank's slippers. She kneels down and taps her father's left ankle. Frank slips his foot into that slipper. Nell repeats the ritual with the other slipper.

Frank's breathing becomes deeper. Still supporting himself with his arms on the chair, he is able to raise his head and look around. The whistle from his constricted lungs abates.

FRANK: There… it's much better now. I just need a few more minutes.

NELL *(still kneeling):* Why does the cold weather make you breathe with a whistle, Daddy?

Frank looks at Lois.

LOIS *(looking at Frank)*: The shovelling makes it worse for your Daddy… Frank, why do you insist on shovelling when it always brings on an asthma attack?

FRANK *(standing up now, mildly irritated)*: Who else is going to do it? *(He relaxes.)* And the girlies and I have to get out tomorrow. If I didn't start the digging tonight, I'd never be able to tackle it in the morning. *(He takes a deep breath.)* Ahhh, that's better. A cup of tea would go well now! Nelly, you go over and look after your sister. Your mother and I are going to have some tea. *(He smiles at Lois.)* And there will be a little spot of tea for you, too, Nelly.

Lois goes to the kitchen. Nell, a light skip in her step, goes to read more to Meg. Frank, heaving a huge sigh of relief, picks up his book.

END OF SCENE

35. The stuff of legends

Quite clear and cold. Hurried off to church. Came home to a roast
chicken dinner. It was nice to have a lazy evening after those noisy
kiddies have been around all day. Frank out to church. Quite cold
when he came home – 18 below.
          [The Lois Diaries, January 18, 1948]

"I'm home," Annie called to Harry as she came in from work that afternoon.
She came up behind him as he fussed at the stove. "What are you up to,
love?"

"Oh, just a little of this and little of that," Harry turned to her and embraced
her. Did his hold on her feel desperate, he wondered. "Sit down, my sweet.
I've made some nice tea – picked it up at Lyon's with some biscuits this
afternoon after I assisted at the hospital. They still have such a long way to
go before their documentation is up to snuff again. Back to the tea – it's new
in from India."

Annie sat at the table Harry had prepared with a lovely white rose in her
favourite red vase, their favourite Noritake teacups and three plates, one
already holding the tea biscuits. "Very nice!"

Harry fixed the tea and sat down. "Have a biscuit, my Annie. Do you know
that in Whitechapel alone, from October, 'forty, to June, 'forty-one, the
Germans dropped seventy-two bombs. And here's the hospital still trying to
be headquarters for health and home."

"I didn't know that, Harry. Good lord, what must it have been for the
duration of the war?"

"I should take you to see the maps Guy's has with all the bombs plotted on
them," Harry saw Annie's expression change. "If I'm here... I'm sorry,"

Harry became quiet and looked into his teacup. "Has London always been a place for casualties, war veterans, of one shape or another? Annie, I do not want us to be casualties again," Harry's voice, while quiet, was decidedly determined. "Did you read the letter?"

"I did, Harry, and it broke my heart… for you, for Frank, for me, for Della… and for May. She's a casualty, too, don't you think?"

"She is," Harry paused for a moment. "How can anyone not from London understand a Londoner? Even, I suppose, how can anyone – anyone – not a Cockney understand a Cockney? I made my way in the world solo and May saw that quietness of mine as weakness. She has a brusque, competent personality, not at all philosophical. You'd think we could have complemented each other; but, no, quite the opposite was true. I think what we did was to intensify each other's extremities. Poles apart we were."

"Did she understand your childhood? You explained it to her, didn't you?"

"I tried. But how does one explain filth and illness to someone who knows nothing outside of cleanliness and good health?" Harry sat back in his mulling pose, fingertips together. "I did show her the family records in my Bible to explain myself better."

"Did that help?" Annie's heart ached for Harry. Surely the record of the persistently dying family would be enough for May's heart to open up. "Harry… did she understand?"

Harry looked at Annie, "She said, 'Well, that's a sad story. But you couldn't have been all that poor if your family could afford a Bible like that.' I let it go. And I must say I was so proud when Aunt Emma sent Frankie a gift along with Della's baby gift, a rather cultured thing to do. I don't know how many times I had to read that story to him – <u>Teddy Tall of the Daily Mail in Historyland</u>. He still has it. I had three London connections after I left – you and Aunt Emma in London and Charlie in Lethbridge."

Annie reached over to hold Harry's hand, "I never thought to tell you,

Harry; I don't know why. But Emma and I maintained contact for a while after you left. I heard she was quite ill during the Great Flu."

"Hmm, perhaps that was it. I wrote her to thank her for the kiddies' presents and didn't hear back. So I wrote again at least twice and then heard nothing. I could only assume." Harry poured them each another cup of tea. "Well, Annie, let's talk about the letter. How did it break your heart?"

Annie reached for her purse and took the letter out, carefully placing it to the left of her plate. "I believe I have it memorized," she looked at Harry, wondering how they could possibly find their way through this difficult territory, "and I feel, Harry, that Frank is now who I was – the person waiting for you across the Atlantic. Only, this time... this time, this person has true claim to you." Her eyes glistened with her own truth and its connection to the son she had always wished had been hers. "Do you see?"

"I believe I do."

"Look at him, Harry!" Annie pointed to the letter. "Can you see him writing? I can. Not only writing, but painting a picture. I see this family, all absorbed in the intimate mechanisms of Christmas Day, under the loving hand of their father... husband... neighbour. Do you see the colours and postures and textures? Can you feel the mood? Can you?"

"Yes." Harry's voice was barely audible.

"No, Harry, I don't think you do. You don't see who the artist is – you don't!" Harry looked perplexed. "Harry, the artist is you! You created this picture. And you created it out of every ounce you could muster to hold your life together and get your solitary self to Canada." Harry was about to talk. "Don't you dare try to deny that, Harry Westley; don't you dare! You and May may have been the North and South Poles; but you met her, dared to ask her to marry you and together you created Frank's family and Della's. Own it, Harry – own it, every smile and tear of the whole process."

"Annie, I... I... I don't know what to say. Why does every decision I make end in loss?"

"No – no – I don't see it that way," Annie remained firm and clear. "What I see is a man – a dear, dear man whom I love very much – who has made… no… resurrected… his original family. Listen… listen," Annie picked the letter up. "'I needed and had your presence with me as a father, and I miss that. I could not imagine a more gentle nor encouraging father than you have always been.' That is an adult son who loves… no… cherishes… his father greatly."

"Annie, what are you saying? Do you want me to leave you?"

"No, I do not want that. But what I want isn't relevant at the moment."

"Annie, that simply isn't true," Harry felt angry now. "You are more relevant than anyone in this discussion."

"No! For once in your life, let this be about you," Annie's knew her frustration would make her cry if she weren't careful. "Harry, let's step back and not let this turn into an argument. It's too important! How can we get back on track?"

Harry stood up, walked over to Annie and pulled her into his arms. She crumpled. "Oh my Annie, my Annie," he kissed her head and stroked her hair. "Let's go upstairs and lie down. Look at me," he pulled his handkerchief from his pocket and wiped her eyes.

"Oh, Harry, whatever are we going to do?"

"Well, if you don't know, my little mudlark, I do!"

Annie giggled and held Harry's hand as they walked upstairs.

"I love this cuddling as much as the sex, Harry… well… almost as much," Annie kissed Harry's chest. And all was well now.

Harry laughed, "Legendary old-timers making up for lost time, that's what we are, my Annie… legendary!" Harry turned on his side, "Annie, turn and let's just look at each other as I say a few things, pertinent to the infamous letter." Annie turned toward him. "I don't want to discuss it any further for the moment. But I also don't want to leave important things unsaid. I think these are the options we'll need to talk about. Do I stay in London? Do I visit Canada and return to London? Do I return to Canada? Do I ask you to return to Canada with me? What do you think?"

"I think," Annie said as she raised herself to look into his eyes, "that you are right, sir, and that it is time to have more of what we had – dinner can wait." She kissed him with such renewed passion that Harry had no choice but to succumb.

"Well, I'm more than a legendary old-timer now, my love."

36. Joyless duties

Blustery and miserable out but much milder. Tonight Frank and I enjoyed an army Party from Toronto for one hour. Napier Moore was master of ceremony. Percy Faith's orchestra and members of the airforce took part. It was great. Frank is off to the armories. I suppose I'll wait up for him.
[The Lois Diaries, January 19, 1940]

"That was our home – the main floor. Two rooms – the kitchen and the bedroom." Harry and Annie sat on the Buxton Street curb across from the tenement of his young years. "Thank you for coming, Annie. It means a great deal to have you here… for me to think out loud, as it were," Harry grasped Annie's hand and held tightly.

Annie kissed his fingers, "You never really said much about Buxton Street, did you? By the time I met you, you were so independent and living with Lucretia. For me, your life was Commercial Street and west." Annie felt an old sorrow seeping out of the brown-bricked, dismal row houses. "It's as though the bricks have sopped up the tears of all those families and turned their backs on the outsiders."

"And the sickness, Annie – the thick green sputum and the dark red blood of it all. And the damned resignation of the parents – etched into their steely eyes and granite faces. They all looked the same… harsh sculptures built around and over their once innocent spirits." Harry's voice had become hard and strongly Cockney. "Mummy's face was still very pretty, because she died young. But my Dad's face was thin, tough, angry… and by the end bitter. He did love us, though, he did. And he never lost the ability to laugh – 'Larf wiv me, then 'arry, that's better'n crying cabbages in Covent Garden, ain't it?' And we'd laugh. I often see my Dad in Frank – always, no matter what, the ability to laugh and to set people's spirits straight."

"There had to have been great love in your family, Harry, or you wouldn't be who you are," Annie mused and then smiled, "even though I don't know this strong Cockney Harry!" Harry chuckled with her. "Harry, you've never said much about your mother's death. And yet you remember her so well, so lovingly."

"There's not much to tell about her dying," Harry's voice returned to its usual softness. "Like the rest of us, you know."

"Ah, but once, Harry, once," Annie turned Harry's face to look into hers, "once a very long time ago, you said, 'She died by accident.' And I asked what you meant and you said you'd explain sometime. Perhaps now?"

Harry turned away and looked at the unforgiving, ungiving brown bricks, "I'm not sure. I was so young. But I do remember a neighbour carrying her home and seeing her neck bleeding... bleeding awfully. And then so much commotion. And waiting on the other side of the curtain while the doctor came. And everyone talking in hushed voices. She said to me how sorry she was – 'I'm so sorry, my little Harry.' She died that night. From then on, I pictured her framed in blood, calling to me, 'my little Harry, my little Harry.' She even visited me on the boat over – 'give me my babies, little Harry, my babies.'" Harry wept.

Annie wept, too. "Harry, do you think... have you ever wondered that perhaps...?"

"I have. But I stop myself, Annie. What good would it do to let myself wonder? I could never know. If someone could tell me with certainty, I shouldn't be surprised. He was beginning his diabolical career then, wasn't he?" Harry wiped his eyes and smiled. "It takes me back to what my Dad said – 'I'd believe in God, I would... if there was one speck of evidence of him intervening in my life.' And yet I always knew Dad believed."

"Well, for what it's worth, I do think your mother could have been one of his early victims. Women had to do what they had to do. And, whatever your mother did, she did because she had to, for the family."

"Look at this street," Harry pointed, "and around to the other streets – Spital Street at the corner and just down it is Hanbury. Hanbury, Annie, Hanbury! His second victim was found behind a house there. Whitechapel keeps the most outrageous secrets London ever knew. Horse dung and human waste covered the roads. One never forgets that smell, Annie. I looked through records the other day to learn that Whitechapel, little Whitechapel, was seething with seventy-six thousand people in the late 1880's. All I knew when I was little was that there was no such thing as being alone, and yet I was safe only with my family. I remember Mummy saying to me one day when someone pushed me into the slop in the street, 'Harry, you're all right, you're all right. I can take you home. Some people don't have a home. There are some people who pay a penny a night to sleep standing up in a room. A rope holds them up. We always have enough money to pay for our two rooms, Harry. We keep you safe. So don't worry, Harry, and don't let a tyrant take away your confidence.' And she took me home and washed me off with rainwater she caught in a barrel outside at the back door."

"I had no idea. Life on Ellen Street was tame in comparison," Annie looked over to the corner of Spital Street and shivered. "What does all of this mean, then, Harry? Have you found what you needed here?"

"Much closer, I'm much closer than I was last night. I see now why I've always felt on the outside of life. Protection, I suppose. And habituation." Harry stood and offered Annie his hand, "I had a sister, Ellen, Annie – born and died in the year before I was born. Come, love; let's walk. Let me show you my posh neighbourhood."

The two walked in silence until they reached Spitalfields' Market. Harry stopped outside the London Fruit Exchange, "I remember seeing a picture in the Leader Post of the King and Queen here. They were honouring Mickey's Market – it's in the basement – for the shelter they provided during the Blitz. Extraordinary, isn't it? This is the area of horrendous slaughters… poverty, Jack the Ripper, the Blitz… all of them murderers."

"And it's over for you, dear Harry," Annie slipped her arm again in Harry's and they began walking west. "You know that, don't you?"

"I do."

"London's over, isn't it?"

"It is."

Silence prevailed again for about ten minutes. "But we're not over, Annie."

"No, we're not, Harry; but we must go back to our parted state."

And in his mind – or was it his heart? – Harry heard Sarah… *Harry, one never abandons one's children, even in death. Consider the children, Harry. Consider the children. Consider the letter.* There was some consolation in having done what his mother asked.

Around 3:00, Harry woke up. The tune started up in his head – again! But no – it was more that the tune had wakened him. And then Harry realized that it was not the tune so much as it was the words… the words to Frank's solo… the Tosti song… yes, that was it! "Parted."

Harry turned toward Annie, put his arm around her and whispered in her ear, "Annie… Annie… wake up just a little, not all the way, just enough to listen."

Annie stirred, "Mmm… Harry, what is it? All right. I'm mostly awake."

"May I sing to you, Annie? It's that solo of Frank's I couldn't remember. Would it be all right?"

"Yes… go ahead… but you'll put me back to sleep."

In his clear, quiet tenor voice, Harry began…

> *Dearest, the day is over,*
> *Ended the dream divine,*
> *You must go back to your life,*
> *I must go back to mine.*

Back to the joyless duties,
Back to the fruitless tears,
Loving and yet divided,
All through the empty years.

How can I live without you?
How can I let you go?
I that you love so well, dear,
You that I worship so!
You that I worship so!

Annie turned toward Harry and kissed him. "Oh Harry…"

"Our love knows no bounds, Annie… no bounds."

"How can I let you go, Harry?"

"How can I let you go? I'm not sure that I can. Come, my Annie."

37. Toronto the faithful

Not nearly so blizzardy but colder. Ironing a bit. Frank came home tonight to a nice warm house. Changed into his Tuxedo and out to choir practice and on to the Shrine Convention. He was home in good time. What a time they had. Letter from Dad.
[*the Lois Diaries, January 23, 1948*]

The late afternoon had drawn in, making the house on Spadina cozy. Flames crackled gently in the fireplace, the only heat needed on this not unusual Toronto February day that had been nicely above the freezing mark. Ada had maintained the original gentility of this handsome mahogany-trimmed home, adding to it her own refinement in her sense of style and colour. May sat comfortably in a plush armchair, reading a letter. Ada knocked and entered the room with a tray of tea and biscuits. "Oh, that's lovely, Ada. Just what I need."

Ada set the tray on the tea trolley. "Well, I could sense in your voice there was something wrong when you called downstairs to me… you know, that slight high-pitched edge you've had since we were children?"

May chuckled. "Usually, it was because you had teased me and made me angry!"

"And it might have been your annoyed voice when you called; but you look sad, May," Ada handed her sister a biscuit and tea. "What is it? Has it got something to do with that letter on your lap? From Harry, I would think?"

May handed the letter to Ada, "Would you read it, please? Out loud. That way, I can take it in without the initial element of shock.

 Ada sat down and read:

January 15, 1948

Dear May,

Thank you for at least letting me know you received my last letter.

Rather than couching my message in cautious words, I'm going to give it to you as it is.

May, I am returning to Canada. My hope is that it can be to you. I would be happy to live in Toronto. I could perhaps stay in a small room in Ada's house while you and I look for an apartment nearby. I don't believe it would difficult for us to return to our former relationship as married friends. And I believe it would be good for us to be grandparents together.

I understand that you may want to have nothing to do with me. I do understand how very angry you must be with me, even though we were separated before I left for England. If this is the case and there is no hope of reasonable reconciliation, I will understand. I would then return to Regina.

Regardless of where you might prefer I live, I shall come to Toronto to learn where my future lies!

I will arrive at Union (interesting word) Station at 2:47 p.m. on February 29. I've arranged to go to Edgar's house and will call you from there to hear your decision.

You know I've agonized over my choices in life – you've seen me do that so many times. And so many times, I've never been sure about my hesitant decisions. However, this time I know. I had a dream wherein I heard, "Consider the children, Harry." And a day or so later, a friend pointed out to me that I've "resurrected" my original family in Canada and that "London is over". For the first time in my life, I had a true sense of belonging... and "home". And it wasn't London, and it wasn't Canada. It was within me.

I do look forward to seeing you again, May. Whatever your decision, I hope that you can find it in your heart to forgive this distant husband of yours. I thank you for tolerating my discomfort in life all these years.

With love,

Harry

"Well, that's a different Harry!" Ada blurted out the words without thinking.

"What do you mean?"

"Give me a moment to think, May," Ada looked down at the letter. "Well, it's a Harry who's clear about what he wants and what he's done. He's apologetic for his choices but not for himself, and…." Ada stopped.

"And?"

"And that's a good thing, I think. Don't you? Who would have thought this would be the purpose of the whole escapade?"

"What in the world do you mean, Ada – the purpose? The purpose? I doubt there is one."

"Perhaps it was for Harry to have peace and to stop living in two worlds. And in two eras, for that matter. You must know what I mean."

"I do," May's voice broke.

"I know you have to think this over; but what's your first inclination?" Ada gave May her hankie.

"A half hour ago, I would have said he should be shot. And Annie with him." May blew her nose. "But now… well, now I want to talk over the option I see for his return… with you."

"You already know you want him to return? And you mean, of course, to Toronto?" Ada couldn't have been more surprised.

"Oh yes, but I want your opinion before I make up my mind for good. It's a counter offer, actually," May took a deep breath. "If you'd be willing to rent your small apartment on the third floor to him, I'd offer that Harry would come back, live there, and I'd cook suppers for him. He could come down at 4:00 and go back to his place at 8:00. That way, we could spend time figuring how we could live together in my apartment," May looked down for a moment. "Well, what do you think? For me… for both of us, I think…

it would be returning to life as we knew it eight months ago." She chuckled, "It's funny, you know. It's like starting over the way we started when we first met. Only, this time, Annie is explicit in our interactions, whatever they turn out to be."

Ada had to force herself to stop being thunderstruck; she needed to offer something… some encouragement… in response to May. It was her turn to take a deep breath, "Well, I must say, first of all, that I'm surprised, May. I didn't think you and Harry would ever be together again. I've been a while now without Suzy, and I will never stop missing her. She can't come back. Harry can. And Suzy and I always had to keep our life to ourselves. You and Harry don't have to; you can have your relationship however you want it. You are husband and wife… socially acceptable."

May looked at her dear sister, the one who had supported and understood her more than anyone. She reached over and touched Ada's hand. So this was what sisterhood could turn out to be… this sharing, the non-judgment, this honesty, and indeed, this love. "And you're all right about renting Harry the third floor?"

"Absolutely! Let's go up and have a look at what might need to be done."

May followed her sister up and past her second floor apartment, with its lovely sitting room, fireplace, kitchen, bedroom and bathroom… up to the third floor. And there was what might become Harry's apartment – a sitting room, a tiny kitchen with a table for two, a hot plate and an ice box, a small bedroom, and, across the hall, a bathroom. They wandered separately, assessing what small changes might be made. "It's a little dark, don't you think, Ada? Lighter curtains would make a difference."

"Yes… and a fresh coat of paint. A good scrub, of course. That might be all. It's darling, actually. I've always liked it that the table and chairs match the red and white kitchen. And the red settee against the white walls ties it all in well, without making it seem heavy." Ada turned and looked at her sister, "May, I'm very happy at the thought that you and Harry might live together in my house! And Iris and Frank will be so relieved. And Lois will have her "Dad" back."

For the first time that evening, May relaxed. "This might be the final formation of our marriage; but we'll be under the same roof again. Now let's go down and finish our tea and biscuits. Appearances, you know, Ada… and I've missed having him nearby." May locked the door and followed Ada downstairs. "And I shall try not to hold the whole thing over his head," she spoke quietly to herself.

38. The Blind Beggar

Cold. Tried to get the house warmer. Darn it. Baked a cake and
cookies. Trudy, Geordie, Muriel, Winn, Judy and Mrs. Giles were in
for a cup of tea. We had a nice time. Frank out to Women's Musical
Club practice. Waited up for him. Wrote Carrie. Book for Nell from
Dad. 19 below at 11 PM.
[The Lois Diaries, February 10, 1948]

The time following their decision passed ponderously for Harry and Annie.
Silence added more and more weight to the process. And yet, what was
there to say? Useless, sometimes silly, thoughts came to mind and added
dull mass to the silence. Rituals, once comforting, were now painful.

It had been so difficult, that discussion about details, at The Blind Beggar
last week. They both knew what had already been decided and what was
going to be said and felt. They knew they would return to family, Harry to
Toronto, Annie to her sister in Leigh-on-Sea.

This morning, Harry set the tea in the centre of the table and poured a cup
for each of them. He felt so stifled in the muteness... the thick, sticky
miasma dimming all their senses and feeling like the Buxton Street air that
had killed his childhood. He would try again. "Annie, we must talk. How
can we leave it like this? We love each other; we have for so long. We can't
let this end with regrets, or worse, bitterness. Annie," he urged her chin up
with his index finger, and leaned down to kiss her. And there were her tears
again, this time with a vain attempt to smile through them. Harry kissed her
and sat across from her. "What do we need to do, my Annie?"

The scene at The Blind Beggar flashed across his mind. All their feelings
had clustered around them that evening, caging them, so that they were in a
distorted world. Words were useless. Thoughts hung in the air, in so many
colours, all of them dying from lack of breath. "I must go back... don't you

see?... Frank and Della... the grandchildren." "What about me? What will I have left? I don't mean to upset you. I do understand. But..." Inept phrases in the same vein travelled in tiny circles, as though repetition would help. Instead, more grief was created. Annie and Harry occasionally sipped their tea and nibbled on their biscuits in a futile attempt to look ordinary. And perhaps occasionally they did, via their abilities to compress everything – volume, tone, feelings. At last they were able to compress size, so that they and their now smaller mass of insoluble questions could trundle on home. Silently. They made love that night. It was all they had left – it was who they were as one. And yet there had been traces of resignation and desperation woven into their unity.

"Well, Harry," Annie took his hand and kissed it, "I think that within the next day or two, we should get over ourselves. I hate this feeling of sadness. I don't want to waste anymore time that's ours. No more rationalizing..."

"And no more wishing," Harry interrupted. "But I will never stop wishing you could be with me. Never."

"You said you understood why I can't go to Canada with you!" Annie seemed upset again. "Harry, who would I be in a strange land?"

"I know, I know," Harry spoke very softly, "but that doesn't mean I won't always wish you were with me."

"Yes," she touched his hand. "If we don't do this, Harry, if we don't get over ourselves, we will reject all of what we've had together here – the places we love, the movies and books we enjoy, cooking, coming home to each other... we'll stop remembering because it will be too painful. However we feel now would be the way we would feel about us forever. Harry!" Annie was almost herself again, "Why don't we each pick our favourite things and do them so we'll have this as the icing on our... our own peculiar wedding cake?" She paused. "Or, unwedding cake."

"Don't do that," Harry was firm. "Don't do that to yourself, Annie. I understand, but stop."

"But we have been married! Longer than we thought the other night at the pub. We've been married since we first met at Memorial Hall. I saw you and I knew, I knew..."

"As did I," Harry interrupted. "As did I. And we will continue to be married. We've done it apart before, Annie." And he laughed.

"What *are* you laughing at?"

"I couldn't help it! I suddenly thought that we'll have been 'married apart' for a much shorter period this time. I don't know about you; but I don't have another forty years in me!"

"You're incorrigible, Harry," Annie didn't want to give in to her urge to smile. "Now let's plan what we want to collect in our memories... for however long they might last."

Harry's heart sank when he realized how quickly these days would disappear. He put his hands behind his head and stretched back. "You know, when we waved good-bye at Victoria when I left... a lifetime ago... I panicked. I was so afraid of losing you. And I did. And here I go again."

"No, we're going back to a state we've honed into an art. We can do it, Harry. We know what it's like to be married now. I'm sure others have done the same thing; but it's not common... it's not common to stay committed as we've done. That won't change... ever!" Annie got up and pulled paper and pen from a drawer. "Perhaps if we each thought of three things..." She stopped talking and looked away, lost in thought.

"A penny for your thoughts, my dear," Harry's voice brought her back.

"Harry, do you think there really is a reunion in heaven? Whatever heaven is. Or is religion all just something – that opiate – to keep us from knowing life as one prolonged state of uncertainty?"

"My little semi-Marxian," Harry loved the continuing sharpness of Annie, "with a touch of Sartre thrown in. Well, I just go back to my distinction between religion and personal faith. I remember Frankie as a young boy challenging me – 'Mother says she loves me, Dad. She says Christianity is about love; but she never shows it. To me.' He was about twelve then and I understood him. I'd tried for years to get her to ease up on Frank. And here was Frank challenging his parents' beliefs. I knew he was wondering how May's faith fit with her actions."

"What did you say to Frank's question?"

"He's always had such a gentle, spiritual nature. I told him to stay close to me and that I would try harder to spare him her reactions. He said, so clearly, so intentionally, 'Never mind, Dad, I can do that for myself from now on.' Two years later, he did… stop her. I heard a commotion between the two of them and got to the kitchen in time to see Frank holding the broom and, in his quiet, rational fierceness telling his mother, "You will never hit me with this – or anything – again, Mother. I'll leave home before you do."

"My goodness, Harry! How could she? And yet, he's very attentive to her, isn't he? And what are you saying about heaven then, Harry?"

"Well, I believe. I suppose it's somewhat like believing in air travel. I would think that's the biggest exercise in faith we can use as a comparison. We buy a one-way ticket – that's believing in and belonging to the faith. Then we take the journey, trusting there's a skilled pilot or captain and that there's a strange and exotic destination… one of rest and re-creation and perhaps healing and some kind of reunion. That's putting my faith into action… because it's a one-way journey. We have no way of checking the validity of the other side until we go there."

"Except for the fact that most cultures have a belief in something better after death," Annie looked happier. "Let's not even tackle eternal life! Instead, I'm going to believe that heaven *is* a place of reunions."

"And I am, too. Who knows? It's been said strong belief can make things happen. We've got that!" Harry was silent for a few moments. "Perhaps reunions prepare us… maybe they're a form of forgiveness."

"Hmmm… perhaps. I'm thinking of our reunion… we forgave… forgave each other for misunderstandings and assumptions?"

"That's what I mean, Annie! Reunion… forgiveness… reunion… that cycle gives light to the soul and helps us know how to take the final journey. Perhaps that's why I need to go back to Frank and every Westley who is now Canadian… Perhaps there's a larger picture than we can imagine. Perhaps it's my most important task, bringing both sides of the pond together."

"Harry, let's stop now in trying to make sense. If the moment is indeed all that we have," she stood. "And, let's stay in the moment. We don't have many left. Let's forget about planning. Come now," she offered her hand, "a quick game of cribbage before bed."

SCENE SEVEN—Regina, February 11, 1948

It's 9:00 p.m. on a bitter, windy, extremely cold night. The night has the howling, malevolent nature only prairie people can apprehend. An anxious Lois, wearing a flannel nightgown, a sweater, a red tartan bathrobe and big, white slippers is in the kitchen, holding the door to the basement open. The sound of coal being shovelled into the furnace plays percussion to the wild wind music. The shovelling stops.

LOIS *(calling downstairs)*: Can you find anything wrong, Frank? I'm so cold! Is the furnace okay?

FRANK *(calling back)*: I'm coming up – give me a moment.

The slam of the furnace door is heard and Frank comes up to the kitchen.

LOIS: Here, I've got tea ready.

They sit at the green enamel table and Lois pours the steaming tea.

FRANK *(sipping his tea)*: Ah, that feels good. *(Frank puts his hand over Lois's.)* Don't worry – the furnace seems fine. What I think happened is that it's so viciously cold, the furnace devoured the coal in record time. I'll stoke it before bedtime and then set the alarm for every two or three hours.

LOIS *(still very anxious)*: I was so scared for the kiddies. I mean, they both have colds. And then I panicked and wondered why house fires happen so often in winter. And then I worried about you…

FRANK *(interrupting Lois with a chuckle)*: My apologies, My Lady, but all is well in our world. Would you like me to change all that?

LOIS *(laughs and relaxes)*: Don't you dare! *(She cradles her teacup with her hands.)* Oh, tea does help warm me up.

FRANK: One of your oatmeal cookies would make me even warmer!

LOIS: *(She gets up to fetch the cookie tin; notices a letter on the counter near it and takes the tin and the letter with her to the table… she opens the cookie tin and Frank takes two cookies.)* We haven't had a chance to talk about Dad's letter. I thought we'd talk at supper. I tried to bring it up with you.

FRANK: I didn't want to get into it with Nell around and get her hopes up until we'd talked alone.

LOIS *(somewhat miffed)*: Oh, you give her too much credit. She wouldn't have been bothered. She wouldn't even have been sure what we were talking about!

FRANK *(takes a deep, exasperated breath)*: Lois – let's not turn this into an argument. I'd like to hear your thoughts. And I'd like to tell you mine. But I'm tired and I don't want to waste time on an irrelevant argument. Nell would catch on and then make her own assumptions. And that's how children collect worries. Now – what did you think about Dad's letter?

LOIS *(pouting)*: That's not true! *(She finishes her tea.)* I suppose I was surprised that Dad paid attention to your letter. I really didn't think he would change his mind. Did you?

FRANK: I know I said I wasn't sure. But, deep down, I knew Dad wanted... needed... to come home. I know my father. I know how much, and how quietly, he loves. Heavens, that's what took him back to London – his constant love for Annie. And yet, it's that very love, that constancy, that's bringing him back home.

LOIS: What do you mean? It seems like sadness upon sadness to me. Poor Dad.

FRANK: You see – now you're understanding life through his eyes. And I want that sadness to be understood by Dad, not just accepted. Godammit, he's a hero, Lois! And I think that's what Nell sees in him. There's a great similarity in the two of them.

LOIS *(genuinely shocked)*: A hero? Dad?

FRANK: Yes! Biblical, even... yes... Biblical. As much as you say your father laid down his life for others, so has my father, over and over, from the time he was very young. There is no greater love. I was never so convinced of that as when I wrote him that last letter. Something compelled me to give him a challenge... a wake-up call... a call. Yes, that's it – a call to completion!

LOIS: All right – I get it! I do, Frank. Are you all right with his returning to Toronto, though?

FRANK: No, but I understand. I think he belongs here with us. I'm that selfish.

LOIS: And protective. Let's go to bed. It's warming up nicely.

(The couple gets up from the table, Frank switches off the light and they leave the kitchen. A few moments later, the light is switched on again.)

FRANK: Consarned furnace!

(Frank, flashlight in hand, exits down the basement stairs. The furnace door creaks and clangs open, and the shovelling begins. FADE…)

39. I must go down to Leigh-on-Sea

It is starting to be a cold old month. Letter from Della. Dad is well on his way across the ocean now, or even home by now, I suppose. Poor Dad. The kiddies are pretty good altho' they need to get out more. Frank is out to Chanters tonight. Then he'll have a quick meeting with Ian, Tom and Bill. They want to start a quartet. Frank thought of the name "The Strollers". With the theme song, "I was strolling through the park one day... in the merry, merry month of May..." They want me to be their accompanist. I like the idea. I think.

[The Lois Diaries, February 18, 1948]

Harry and Annie sat on a little wooden bench outside Allen Gardens, across from 22 Buxton Street, Harry with his arm around Annie while she leaned against his chest. A little bouquet of white and red carnations lay across his lap. This was as they had planned the morning. This was their leave-taking. No "until we meet again" promises this time. No, this time there was only the implicit acknowledgement of finality. The finality of their physical time together... with the acknowledgement that their love remained, stronger than it had ever been.

"I see them all... the brothers I knew, my parents. Although, I always felt the sadness of the deaths of 'the little ones,' as my Dad called them. Edith, Ellen, Walter. Sorrow seemed to dwell in the dank air. The air itself killed us, Annie." He was quiet for a moment, simply staring at Number 22... *lost in the number, the birth number, the birth order, the order of poverty's death knoll.* "Coloured, stinking air, a mixture of black coal and muck. My mother tried to keep us clean; but every ounce of water was filthy. We played in these streets, in the sewage... we had to play somewhere, didn't we?"

Annie wiped her eyes. "It's different now, though, isn't it? There's still so much repair and rebuilding to do from the bombing; but the streets are relatively clean. And people are caring for some kind of garden, like this one. I know it's not much; but people care, Harry. They really do. And you must remember that. Remember the green places, Harry. And leave your grief behind here this time. It's safe with me. And it's safe in this curious garden."

"Yes, Frank would like your thoughts, Annie. I've felt his and my mother's spirits lately. I can still remember everything about her – her gentleness, her beauty, her curly auburn hair like Della's, her eyes… ah yes, her eyes. She spoke with them. She didn't need words to convey love and understanding. The windows to her soul, they were, and they gave the first clue to her razor-sharp intelligence. How very tired she must have been"… *bone-weary, heart-heavy, breath-gone, Harry, consider the children, my Harry, my little man, I'm so sorry, Harry, so sorry about… so sorry you had to see… so sorry about the blood, Harry, so much dying, so little breath, it's my repentance you carry, let it go, let it go…* "there are times I can't shake the images of her covered in blood… and the screaming, the screaming," he kissed Annie's head and ran his fingers through her hair. "Ah, Annie, when I'm gone… when I've left you… again… I may be nothing but haunted, haunted by the intangibility of you, of Sarah. Do you ever wonder what the purpose of life is? In the end, it's a solitary journey, mostly walked on the knees." Harry was silent for a moment. "We're all monks, nuns… Annie, you must know… you must never forget that I have never been so happy… so free… as I have been in this London interlude… in this Annie interlude."

"And I ask the same of you, Harry. Our pact is never to forget. And when we do slip away, to come back… to come back to us – that is especially true when any haunting happens. If… when… that happens, think back to this very moment. Us as one on Buxton Street," Annie sank further into Harry's embrace. "Harry, what if, just what if Sarah has been so present with you for the past while because you have done what she needed you to do?"

"Whatever do you mean?"

"Well, what if she couldn't rest completely until someone had put the whole family to rest?"

Harry turned to face Annie. He put his hands on her shoulders, "Are you saying that I've brought rest… peace… to my family? How? I mean, here we are leaving each other, and you want me to believe this has all been about my family? My dead family?"

"No… about Sarah, " Annie scrutinized his face. "Listen to me. Just for a moment, let our story go and go back to your mother's. Never have I heard you say you doubted her love. Did anyone doubt her love?"

"Not a one."

"Then, Harry, you have brought her soul peace. And, in that sense, you've finished her story. Perhaps I should say 'completed.' There were too many threads left dangling in Sarah's story… too many threads for a mother to let them go," Annie put her arms around Harry's neck, "in the same way that you could never let them go. In the same way that you could never stay away from your children, Harry." Annie's eyes filled with tears.

"I understand. Come, let's leave our flowers for Sarah Pegg." Harry took Annie's hand. They crossed the street and looked up at the reddish brown brick wall facing them. "There's precious little space for flowers here. We were all in there somewhere."

"Just set them against the wall, Harry. Sarah sees them."

Harry knelt and placed the carnations against the rusty brick. Annie knelt beside him, her arm around him. "Well, the time has come, my dear," Harry stood and helped Annie up. "Annie, I…"

Annie placed her index finger over his lips, "Harry, we promised… we promised not to second guess ourselves."

Harry enfolded Annie in his arms, pulling his overcoat around her. "My Annie. I love you. This is a cloak I'm putting around you, my cloak of love and protection… always around you. Always." He held her tightly.

Annie sobbed. Harry soothed, "It's all right, my sweet. Take your time; take your time."

When her weeping lessened, Harry cupped Annie's face in his hands. "Annie, look at me. I'm taking a picture of you in my mind. I have a whole album of pictures of you. I love you," he kissed her with the full anguish of his love. And Annie reciprocated. "Annie," he whispered in her ear, "when you go home, look in the bedroom closet. I left my tweed jacket there beside your red dress. Take it out and wear it once in a while, would you?"

"Harry, I'll wear it to bed. Oh, Harry," she kissed him and wiped his tears with her scarf. "Good-bye, my Harry."

"Good-bye, my Annie."

They turned from each other. As they had promised, neither Harry nor Annie turned to look back.

Annie walked east toward Spital Street, toward the apartment, their home. She would soon return to her childhood home in Leigh-on-Sea. London was over. How could she bear it? Only by leaving… only by leaving.

Harry, suitcase in hand, turned west toward Brick Lane, toward the tube… *toward the train and the sea and my London trunk, already on the ship, with my gifts for everyone… so that everyone will know, "He bought this for me, he thought about me, in London"… toward New York and the train to Toronto. And then the phone call… the phone call… "Hello May… hello… did you know, May, did you know life is a series of reunions and partings?… are you interested in a reunion of sorts… for the family?… are you interested, May?… for the family, May, if not for us? How would you like that to be? I'll understand if you want me to live elsewhere in Toronto… in the world… however, I'm back to stay in Toronto… for the family… our family, May… for the Westleys and the little ones… and for someone, someday to understand… to understand like my Annie… like my Annie.*

The train stopped. Harry pushed on with the others. St. Paul's station would be next and then on to Victoria. Yes, St. Paul's. *Do I know you, Guv? Where's our Mum? Bertie needs her. Where's our Mum?* "It's all right, son, I found her," Harry whispered aloud to the newspaper boy, "you can leave St. Paul's now. Go home, son."

Harry cared not an iota what the staring man next to him thought. In fact, there was nothing more that could ever affect him… he had his picture album in his head. And his love in his heart.

"Good-bye, my Annie."

40. A spoonful of curry

SCENE SEVEN—Regina, Saskatchewan, March 22, 1948

A still life study: Set in the Regina kitchen on York Street. Nell is at the enamel table across from the sink (this house is one of the few in the area to have running water). The large, complicated wood stove is pumping out heat, ready for the afternoon of baking and cooking. The mother closes the icebox door and goes to the table, where ingredients are laid out.

LOIS *[Begins cooking with genius, eagerly trying something new, while Nell pulls over a chair to watch]*: "I love trying a new recipe. Your grandfather brought me this!" *[She holds up a mustard yellow tin with a red crown and beautiful black lettering on it.]*

NELL *[examining the label, able to figure out many words now. She rests her index finger on the label's elephant]*: "Did he go to India, too? What's c-u-rr-y p-ow-d-er?"

LOIS *[smiling, energized, and mixing a few spoonfuls of curry into the bowl of ingredients]*: "No, no! He got the curry in England. For me! He knew I'd love it! India is a colony, so it comes from there to England. Doesn't it smell wonderful?!"

NELL *[screwing up her nose, looks pensive. She is putting two and two together, wondering why Grandfather Westley came back to Toronto.]* "Why did Grandfather Westley come back? Why will he and Grandma Westley live on two different floors in Auntie Ada's house?"

LOIS *[too involved in her new recipe to answer carefully]*: "He came back because it was right. And your Grandma Westley moved to Toronto because she wanted to live with Auntie Ada, her sister. We had to move to Grammie's—my mother's—in Ontario because of your Daddy's work…

only it became eight months instead of a lifetime. You remember! You loved it at the farm. *[Lois disappears into her thoughts.]*

NELL *[anxious not to lose her story]*: "I will always remember living there! But why will Grandma Westley and Grandpa live in separate rooms now and not in a house like they used to? I wish Grandpa would stay here with us."

LOIS *[mildly irritated]*: You and your big ears, Nell! Because things change. Like with us—we're back here in Regina, and I miss Ontario. Actually, your Grandpa lived with us for quite a while before Mrs. W. and Dad left for Toronto and London. Living apart in Auntie Ada's house will be because your Grandmother will never forgive him for going away. [She licks her left baby finger, dips it in the concoction and puts her finger in her mouth for a few savouring seconds, looking up. She looks back down at the brown and green mixing bowl.] They were never good for each other, so who cares if they're happy. Now I need just a touch more curry and a dash of sugar. Your Daddy and Grandpa are going to love this recipe! I found it in this English mag." [She picks the magazine up for one more look at the recipe, lays it down and plunges back into the task at hand.]

The light fades to feature Lois as creative chef and Nell as questioning child, mulling over the desirability of curry, what a colony is and the things that she noted while her family was "down east" for half the time Harry was away.

NELL *[to herself, because her mother is lost in her cooking the way she becomes lost in her music]*: "Did Grandfather Westley have a good time with Annie?"

FREEZE at the exact moment that Nell has figured out the sum of two plus two.

FADE TO BLACK...

END OF SCENE.

Father and son sat across from each other in the Hotel Saskatchewan's dining room. Nell sat comfortably on Harry's lap. When the waiter arrived with their fish and chips, Nell jumped down and sat on her chair between the two men. "This is fun, Daddy and Grandpa!" Both men placed small portions of their meals on Nell's plate, and the trio relaxed into the coziness of a pleasing, familiar setting.

"Almost as good as in London," Harry gave Frank a knowing glance. "I'm pleased we could get together for a good chat before I leave, Frank."

"Would you take me to London sometime, Grandpa... please? I'd like to meet the King and the Princesses!"

"I'm not certain I'll get back to London, love. I'm getting older, you know." Harry looked over at his son, "I hope Lois does well at the doctor with Mugsie."

Nell looked rather crestfallen and went back to sprinkling vinegar on her chips.

"Lois will likely get sulpha for her. It's worked miracles for Mugsie's kidney problems." Frank reached across the table and touched Harry's hand. "I've taken a longer lunchtime, Dad. There are some things I want to talk with you about, too," Frank smiled warmly. "It's been so good to be with you. I don't want you to leave unless it's right for *you*."

Before you leave? I don't want you to leave? Nell's five-year-old mind formed question after question. She could feel her heart pounding, "I don't want you to leave, Grandpa. You were gone so long before, and I missed you very much." Her eyes glistened.

Frank swept Nell's flaxen hair aside and kissed her on the forehead. He took his handkerchief from his breast pocket and dabbed her tears. "Remember, Nell, I told you that Grandpa and I would be talking big people words... because it's all 'stuff' that big people talk about. 'Stuff!' Big, boring stuff!"

Nell giggled, "Stuff!"

"Your Daddy is right, Nelly. Whatever decision is made – whether I stay here or move to Toronto with your Grandma – we'll see each other often," Harry gave Nell his special wink, and she giggled again.

"Okay, I'll read the books I brought," Nell smiled, "when I finish my fish and chips!"

"Good girl." Frank made his hankie into two babies in a cradle. He placed it beside Nell's books and looked at his father, "She loves trying to figure out how I do that trick."

"Did you know I taught it to your Daddy?"

Nelly smiled, "Yes, Daddy told me. He said you would do it for him if he was sick or sad. And you would make him kettle broth."

The two men laughed and left Nell to her own world.

"Well, Dad, how are you feeling about this decision to return to Toronto? Is that where you truly belong? You deserve to know. And to be wherever that place where you belong is. I think you know from my last letter that I want nothing more than to see you certain … and happy… in your choice now. You came to terms with so much in London. Then your choice was to leave. So, it's very important that you're certain about choosing Toronto over Regina."

Nell looked up from her book, "I'll tell you who you really are, Grandpa. You are the best Grandpa in the world." She went back to her book.

"From the mouths of babes," Frank spoke softly. He felt oddly proud of Nell.

"I am as I always am, Frankie… happy to be with you and Lois and the kiddies… happy that Della will visit your mother in the fall."

"Well, that's really about everyone else but you, isn't it? But never mind…

are you glad you returned?"

"I'd change the wording… I know it's right for me to be back." Harry was ill at ease.

Frank leaned forward, elbows on the table, his chin resting on his fists. "Look at me directly, Dad. Are you sure you should be in Toronto and not in Regina with us?"

Harry closed his eyes tiredly for a moment. When he opened them, he looked out the window at the busy foot traffic on Victoria Avenue. He felt immensely sad and couldn't look at his son. "The operative word being 'should' – yes, I should be in Toronto. Your mother and I decided this would be best. She said in her note that Spadina Road would be 'headquarters,' a place where the family would visualize us together, as parents and grandparents."

"And so 'The Great Divide' continues. I thought perhaps Mother might be very happy that you'd chosen to return. I thought perhaps you'd share her apartment. After all, it's commodious and has two bedrooms. And you and I kept her up to date over these many months. Why does she keep shutting you out?"

Nell could sense anger in her Daddy's voice. He never got angry at his Daddy. "Why are you mad at Grandpa, Daddy? Don't be mad at Grandpa!"

"Oh no, Nelly, no – I'm not mad at him."

"You sounded mad. Being mad hurts people's feelings," Nell was very sad.

"I'm so sorry, Nelly," Frank leaned over and kissed her cheek. "I can see how it seemed like that to you. My feelings are strong because I love Grandpa, and I felt frustrated about him understanding that I want the very best for him. I won't make you feel that way again, Nelly. I'm sorry."

"It's all right, love. And I'm going to try harder to see what your Daddy wants me to see. You go back to your books… without a worry in the world." *Consider the children, Harry, bring me my babies, Harry.* He turned to Frank and smiled, "Let's try this again, Frank. Your mother and I haven't talked about the living arrangement you asked about. We've exchanged one very brief note each. She felt it best for us to leave any discussion until we're together in Toronto. I've arranged to stay in a nice room on Ossington until we've discussed what we'd like to do. The more things change, the more they stay the same, Frankie. She knows I'll arrive April first and that I'll call her the next day. Quite honestly, I'll be satisfied with any arrangement." Harry sighed and leaned back in his chair. It was all so confusing, so hard to make anyone understand... except Annie.

"Dad," Frank spoke quietly, "you're tired. And I think you're sad... still. I wanted your grief..." he hesitated... "well... gone... not gone, I suppose, but to have been transmuted into some kind of contentment. You deserve it, Dad." Frank realized his own sadness. "Please don't simply give in... not this time. You haven't done all this travel and insane recovery to end up where you started."

Harry sat forward and patted Frank's hand, "Frankie, you remind me of Ernest. He..."

"Are you finished here, gentlemen... and lady?" The waiter intruded into the discussion. "And would anyone like anything more?"

Both men were relieved to look at their dessert menus. Each ordered tea and pie, lemon meringue pie, of course. After all, the hotel was famous for its pies.

Nell piped up, "Remember I don't like pastry, Daddy." She looked up at the waiter, "I'll have a chocolate sundae with no cherry, please."

The three men chuckled. The relief that Nell's innocence provided for father and son was palpable. "Indeed, your Highness!" The waiter gave a short bow.

Frank didn't want to lose the focus of the discussion. And yet he feared pushing his father further into his grief. "Dad… Dad, I feel we must finish this conversation, even though I'd say we're both finding it difficult."

"I agree… to both things – the need to finish and the struggle involved in it all. Crikey, it's an old struggle, Frank!"

"I know, I know – let's just dive back in, shall we?" Frank noticed that Nell was sleepy. "Nell, when you've finished your ice cream, you could lie down on the booth seat. And if you're chilly, put my vest over you," he slipped it off, gave it to Nell and took a deep breath. "Well, then, Dad, are you feeling all right that you've said good-bye to Annie?" He couldn't believe he'd finally said it. What relief!

Nell peered over the top of her book. There was that name again… the one everybody whispered.

"It's wording again, Frank." The waiter served the tea and desserts. "I'm not feeling 'all right' or 'good' or 'happy.' I have done what I knew I must do," he tucked his napkin in above his tie and savoured his first bite of pie. "That hits the spot! You mentioned the word 'contentment' a few minutes ago. It's not a word I would use. I would say that I've achieved a sense of… not resignation… a sense of acceptance. I've done what I had to do. I found Annie, and we will never be apart in the old way again." Harry's voice was breaking. He took a moment to wipe away some crumbs. "I have done what needed to be done."

Frank sensed the very air they were breathing was sad. "Dammit, Dad," his blue, long-lashed eyes were fierce; his voice quietly resolute. "Stop dodging every effort I make to keep this about you. How do you see returning to Toronto as what you have to do, Dad? I mean, we all hoped you would choose to stay with us. I, for one, will continue to miss you, and you know how much Lois and the kiddies love you," Frank's eyes welled up. His whisper became very soft. "Lois relates to you in a way that is unusual for her. You know that. You're her 'Dad'. Perhaps more than anyone, she needs you in her life. And you're more than a Dad to me… actually, you've been my mother, too… we… give me a minute," Frank felt as though tears would overcome him. He took a few sips of tea, "Dad, the dearest hope of the four of us was that you would return to live with us." He put his hand over his father's, "No… you know our dearest hope was for happiness for you."

"Ah, that elusive entity!" Harry paused, "Frank, I'm not dodging your questions. Truly. At least, I haven't meant to. It's easy to slip into old habits. And I don't know another way… with your mother. I don't." Harry sighed. "Oh, this is hard. Anyway, how could I stay in the city that had systematically killed my family… except for Charlie and me? So, if Charlie could take drastic steps to end the poverty of the Westleys and not turn back, I could… I must, too. Annie and I even thought she might come with me. But we realized it was too late. It wouldn't work." Harry suddenly looked surprised, "Lord! If I don't really fit anywhere, what would Annie do here? Now I completely understand her reasoning!"

Frank looked at Nell. Yes, she was sleeping nicely now. "Of course, I see it, too. Back to you, Dad – I'm asking about you!"

"Give me a moment, Frank. I need to say this clearly – for myself as much as for you. I have found happiness for myself. I have," he was silent for a moment. "One might think I abandoned it, coming back as I've done. But, that's not the case. What I found, Frank, was vast… vast on the emotional plane. I found the young boy and the young man I'd left behind. In a sense, they were the lost parts of me. And I found what Annie and I had had together. And we simply breathed new life into it… like some child that we'd lost." He was afraid his tears overcome him… he couldn't have others, not even Frank, see him like this. Nevertheless, Harry wept.

"Take your time, Dad." Frank was shaken to see his father cry.

Harry regained his voice. "Son, I don't want to add anyone's worries. If I remain here – as father and grandfather, and, yes, husband – I've secured a place for us on some kind of Canadian genealogy map. The London placement never happened, you see," Harry wiped his eyes, "I put my two parents and my six siblings to rest, Frankie… laid them to rest, I suppose. Someone needed to do it, to finish their story. My God, Frank – they don't even have markers of any kind to prove they existed!"

"Dad," Frank's eye glistened, "Dad, I love you. Please don't…"

"The certainty I came back with," Harry interrupted, "is that what Annie and I have can never be destroyed, Frank. Indeed, it has never been absent. If you're ever feeling sorry for me, please don't forget what I've just said. Annie is the love of my life. And how much does she love me? Enough to have followed your lives through my writing. Enough to have prevailed despite traps that were set on our path. Enough to know, within herself, that she could say it was time for me to return to you all."

"Ah, now I feel as though I know Annie a little, Dad. I've wanted to, you know… to understand a woman who truly loved you."

"I wish you could meet her, Frank. We wrote all through the years, you know, so we were never out-of-date with each other. When I saw her again last September, she was the same. It was as though we'd aged together. There was a comfort level immediately. Her personality and depth were still there and fuller… and her strawberry curls were the same as ever, just faded a little. You would love her, Frank," talking about Annie acted like a potion for Harry, "and that would be because you couldn't resist her intellect and her strong ability to find amusement in any situation."

"Now you look happy, Dad! I'll have to talk more with you about Annie." Frank was relieved – this was his father happy as he wished him to be. "You're happy – and you can return to this at will. Switching topics again; but I have one more question. You probably don't know this, but I recall Mother being unhappy because she claimed you had married her 'on the rebound.' And I used to wonder what that meant. Did you… marry Mother on the rebound?"

"Definitely not! I was feeling very alone and sad that Annie couldn't come to Canada. I'd returned to Theosophy because Annie and I had become involved in our youth. I thought perhaps I could find some friends… at least at an intellectual level. But it didn't work this side of the Atlantic. I decided I'd branch out to other lectures and church services. Your mother – you know the story about our meeting through the Salvation Army – began showering attention on me. And we started building a relationship on what we thought were shared beliefs and mutual ideas about family. But we each had different understandings of relationships. I was never good at them, Frank."

"Except for the relationships with your own family and then your children and grandchildren. And Annie. And Lois. Dad, no more self-denigration… please."

Harry stood up. "I stand corrected." He saluted and grinned.

Frank laughed, "Stand at ease, mate."

Their old ritual did its job – as a medium of lightening intensity. Harry sat down. Emotions settled. Comfort increased. Frank poured another cup of tea.

Harry put his hand up to decline. "Son, I believe… I know… that all is as it should be. When you said 'no more self-denigration,' my insides snapped to attention. I decided to put my mild morass aside. And it dawned on me that I'm moving to Toronto for May's sake. I am! It's the least – and perhaps the last – I can do for her. Do you understand?"

"I do, Dad. I do. I respect you for how you've worked this through. And I respect Mother, actually, for the way she has handled this whole journey of yours." Frank took his last swig of tea and put his napkin on the table. "You know, Dad, I've always respected Mother. I simply always wished she loved me. Sons and mothers… complicated, don't you think?"

"I do. And, Frank, there are many modes of abandonment. It had nothing to do with you." He smiled his loving smile, "Thank you for everything. I love you, son. And sons and fathers… complicated, too, don't you think?"

Frank leaned forward, "Not for us, Dad. Not for us." He looked at his watch. "It's almost time for me to go, Dad. I want you to know that the four of us will come for a vacation in early August. I'll phone Mother and let her know tonight. In the meantime, mum's the word."

Frank caught the waiter's eye and picked Nell up to wake her. "It's time to go home with Grandpa, little Nelly. Daddy's got to go back to work." The waiter placed the bill on the table. Frank reacted more quickly than his father, "It's mine, Dad."

Bill paid and needs taken care of, the trio left the restaurant and walked along Victoria Street. "Let's say good-bye to Daddy, Nell. And we'll just walk over to the bus stop now." Frank bounced up the Dominion Building stairs, turned, took his hat off, waved and disappeared through the elegant doorway.

Harry and Nell held hands as they walked toward the bus stop. "I wish I could have gone into Daddy's building, Grandpa. I love the elevator in there. Except for one thing." She was quiet.

"What's that one thing, Nell? I hope it's not a bad thing," Harry looked concerned.

"It's the elevator operator."

"What is it that he does, Nell? You're always with your mother and Mugsie, aren't you?"

"Oh yes, and that's why I don't like it! The elevator man always says to Mugsie, 'If you had a moustache, you'd look exactly like your father.' And he never says anything to me. And Mummy laughs and likes it."

"And you feel left out, don't you? Oh those big blue eyes need to go to their laughing state again." Harry wanted Nell to forget her problem. "Think about it this way, love. Think about how funny Mugsie would look with a moustache! And then think about how funny you'd look, too!"

Nell loved the idea, "We're not boys! What a silly thing the elevator man said. Did you know I want to be an elevator operator when I grow up?"

"You'll be an operator of some kind, my little Nelly," Harry affirmed. He took Nell's hand and they skipped to the corner of 13th Avenue and Scarth Street.

41. The Ossington magnet

It got quite cold last night after we'd been to hear Dr. Kinnaman. Fascinating. So it's very cold again today. Below zero. There surely is a lot of snow. What a country! Poor Frank wants to use his bike so badly. There was a letter today from Dad. He says he and Mrs. W. will be living together again; but on separate floors at Auntie Ada's. Poor Dad. I wish Frank could see his Dad. I played the piano on CKCK radio today.
[The Lois Diaries, April 7, 1948]

Harry's mind travelled back across the Atlantic as he trudged, suitcase in hand, toward Ossington, Toronto Central for him, and yet his latest home. *Crossing the ocean is like travelling from one side of the brain to the other*, he mused. *The ocean's a hulk sitting there forever, separating two oppositional hemispheres, like some priest whose sole job it is to take confession. Inert. Neutral. Unknowable. And my part? My part is to submit to absolution. From the Priest of the Unknowable. If only I could believe in the God I've created.* Harry stopped at Bloor and Ossington and looked around. Much the same as ever. He turned south. Not far now… 687… ah, here it is. The owner said the key would be in an envelope on the table in the common hallway.

Harry walked up the stairs, crossed the typical Toronto porch – wooden, columns needing repair and some gingerbread features below the eavestroughing – and opened the door. And there it was – the key to the rest of his life. He stopped for a moment and looked at the door. "My God, what have I done?" Seized with anxiety, he plodded up the stairs to number three, the door on the left and opened it. "Not bad, not bad at all," he spoke aloud, "little hotplate, daybed, nice chair and chesterfield… not bad at all. Certainly very clean." He opened the door to his room and peered down the narrow hall. There were the shared bathroom and telephone. "All very good," he pronounced and closed the door. He would call May in the late afternoon. For now, he needed to shake this sense of doom and tiredness. Harry opened a window, removed his shoes and stretched out on the bed, his ankles crossed, his hands behind his head. Ah, the gentle breeze felt soothing. It wasn't long before Harry slept.

Her telephone was ringing. Harry wanted to hang up. He dreaded this conversation with this woman he had so greatly hurt and angered. But so much depended on this conversation – the rest of his life and all of his relationships. What if…?

"Hello."

Same voice. Sharp. Brusque. Strangely, though, it was good to hear her… to know she was there… to know life was real and not a dream. "Hello, May. I'm in town now and settled in my new place." *Now what, for heaven's sake?* May would see this conversation as solely his responsibility. He spoke strongly, "How are you?"

"Well, Harry, I truly thought we would never speak again." There it was – that cold precision, like that of a scalpel. "You know I don't like talking on the phone. I'd rather speak in person. Wouldn't you?"

"It might be good if we'd talk a little over the phone," Harry extended the warmth May refused to give, "you know… smooth the waters a little, catch up on the family. In other words, prepare a little for seeing each other again. It's been a long time, May."

"No, Harry, that would be a waste of time. Phone conversation is too disorganized. And we'd have to go over everything again. It's a waste of time, too."

"All right, have it your way," Harry was irritated beyond words. But, what was the use? "What would you like?"

"Well then, I knew you would arrive today," May took back the reins, "so I have a stew on. Let's see… it's almost half past four. Why not come over now? It's probably a twenty to thirty minute walk."

Not even an iota of warmth, Harry thought. "All right. I'll leave in about five minutes. Is Ada home?"

"Well… yes, but I don't want her to be part of this…"

"Yes, of course, May," Harry had to interrupt – to short circuit this palpable need for power. "It's just that I have a little present for her, and I'd like to give it to her in person."

"Then I'll see you around five, Harry. Try not to be late. Good-bye." May needed this conversation to stop. She simply could not let Harry know she was so rattled by knowing he was indeed here and life was going to take a detour yet again.

"Good-bye, May. I will not be late," how Harry disliked her parental tone. "I look forward to having a good chat with you." Harry realized he was talking to the dial tone.

Harry tidied up, put on his coat and hat and locked the apartment door. He walked outside and stood on the porch, looking up and down the street. Yes, this was our Toronto. Frankie would walk down to Bloor and over to Harbord Collegiate. And Della loved to visit her best friend down the road. Such lovely little children they were. With these memories, why did he feel so anxious? Harry took a deep breath. He steeled himself against his longstanding fears of May's anger and walked briskly up to Dupont.

He had not felt this nervous for ages. "Well, I'm trapped into seeing this through now," he spoke aloud and the intensity of his own voice startled him. He approached the corner to turn east onto Dupont.

May opened the door to Harry's rather tentative knock. "Well, you look fine," May smoothed her skirt and wondered why she felt suddenly nervous. "Come in," she stepped aside to allow Harry to enter. "You remember – your coat can hang here and we'll go up to my apartment," she gestured toward the stairs.

Harry followed her up the stairs. He felt tight somehow, as though he were constricted by something. Lightheartedness might help, he thought. "You're still wearing Shalimar, May?" But the effort fell flat. "I've always liked that fragrance." May did not respond.

"Here we are," May opened the door and ushered Harry in. "Do have a seat, Harry." May did not look directly at Harry and was obviously uncomfortable. She continued to stand.

"Ah, the stew smells good. Would it be all right if I looked around first, May?" Without waiting for permission, he walked slowly around the living room. "I must say you've a lovely place here. There's much good light from your front and side windows." He picked up a framed picture from the end table, "Ah, yes, us as a young family in Swift Current." A sudden sadness threatened to overtake him. He turned around. "And, there's the kitchen. Quite sufficient! Quite sufficient, indeed!" Everything was ultra-tidy and efficient. Of course, that was May's way. "Oh, and I see you have a bathroom of your own. And two bedrooms?"

"Yes – so that Della will have her own when she comes." Now May stared at Harry. She was a woman who would take no challenge to what she had said.

"I see," said Harry. And he did. "Then the matter of our being together here has been ruled out? I just thought with the good size and two bedrooms…"

"It has indeed, Harry. I'm surprised you ask." May looked more annoyed than surprised.

"Do you want to chat before dinner or during?" Irritation met irritation. Harry sat down in the red velvet armchair that had travelled with them from

Regina to Toronto… back to Regina and now to Toronto again with May. Curling his hands around the mahogany arms, Harry felt comforted… there was a calming familiarity in this chair that could tell many family stories.

"During," May's directive snapped Harry to attention, "the meal is ready and we don't want to spend too much time on details. As I see it, you simply step into the picture, on the third floor. The way we talked about it. Since I have a well-established routine here, there's no need for you to feel you have to do anything," May headed back toward the kitchen. She looked back, "Have a seat at the table, Harry, and I'll finish things off in the kitchen." Her manner was clipped, business-like.

Harry sat at the table for two beside the side window at the end of the living room. He looked around the room. Nicely decorated. So very orderly, so clearly designed by May with absolutely "everything in its place, Harry." And with no place – nor need – for Harry. He felt a sudden pang for his London home.

"Here you are – stew and biscuits," May placed Harry's dish (how well he knew the dinnerware) and sat opposite him. The savory aroma of the stew was in sharp contrast to the awkward emotional atmosphere of suppression. Napkins on laps, they bowed their heads in some form of obeisance to a life long dead.

"Well," Harry had perhaps never felt so awkward, "Let's dig in and chat." He took a bite of his stew, "Very good! What would you like to talk about, May?"

May dabbed lightly at the sides of her lips with her napkin. "It's – or it was – your favourite recipe." She spread her napkin carefully over her lap and gave it a pat. For a moment, May seemed softer. She quickly recovered, straightened her back and pursed her lips. It would be to no one's benefit for her to relent. This must not be seen as a conversation so much as being a reiteration of the items of an agreement. "Your accent is certainly stronger than it used to be. I suppose my letter was clear enough that we don't need to talk much. How did you understand my proposal?"

"Well," Harry put his fork down and smiled. There had to be some way, however tentative, to reconnect. "Having spent the better part of a year in London, of course my accent was revived." May looked very uncomfortable. Was it jealousy, Harry wondered? He smiled warmly again, "I believe the understanding, were I to accept your offer, would be for me to rent the small apartment. You'd cook supper and we'd spend from 4:00 until 8:00 here. Am I correct?"

"You are. I actually thought... or rather, I shared an idea with Ada."

"And?" Harry prompted. May had become silent. "May?"

"Oh! I remembered that I talked with Ada about seeing if the two of us could work toward living together in my apartment." Here was the softer May again. But May didn't see or feel it in herself. Incorporation was therefore impossible. She became firmly, intentionally silent again.

"You didn't mention that to me. I'm surprised! And you decided...?" Harry was startled by the need to be patient with May, startled that she had become lost in thought.

"Oh," May flicked her fingers in the air, "it would never work! There isn't enough space here. It's best for each of us each to have our own apartment."

"Indeed." Harry knew when paying attention to May's signals was important. She had allowed a vulnerability to surface and would work hard now to flick it away to another world. Sad, but not surprised, Harry began clearing the table.

"Just put the dishes beside the sink." May's command was clear. She picked up the whisk and tray and began brushing crumbs from the tablecloth. Harry interpreted her edict about the dishes as a command to put his questions by the sink, too. May walked to the sink and shook the few crumbs into it, washing them away with tap water. "I'll wash the dishes later."

"No, I'll do them, May." While he was sincere in words and gesture, Harry knew he was back on the treadmill of request and rejection. He must learn in this new life not to offer.

"Not tonight. You just sit down; you must be tired from all your journeying," May's smile was sincere; her voice kind. Disarmed, Harry sat and relaxed into the armchair. "I've got rice pudding for dessert. And we can finish off what needs to be understood about our life in Toronto."

"Ah… rice pudding. How lovely, May. Thank you. I am tired. It's a long trip across the Atlantic." Harry was ready to converse.

May brought two bowls of rice pudding to the table. The reluctant couple sat at the table again. "I know you're not used to having dessert at our meals, Harry; but I remembered how you especially like the Johnny's Jacket, so here you are – a treat!" They both began enjoying the pudding when May put her spoon down and looked steadily into Harry's eyes. Her voice was firm, "I hasten to point out Harry that this is an exception. You know I am a person who needs to keep expectations realistic." She returned to her rice pudding, took a deep breath, and stated, "There… that needed saying. Just so the lines are clear."

Harry looked at this woman he'd married almost forty years ago. He hardly knew her. They hardly knew each other. And yet, here they were again, trying to make a go of it. The problem was "it" had never been fully described and decided upon. The best he could do with a description, a goal to aim for, remained "peaceful cohabitation." And yet now, cohabitation had been further truncated. "Peaceful proximity" might clarify the living arrangement.

"Delicious prox…" Harry cleared his throat. "Delicious pudding – just as I remember it!" Harry folded his napkin, placed it on the table, sat back and crossed his knees. He refused to convey any sense of acquiescence. "I brought you some lovely tea from London, May. I'll make some when we've finished our chat." He waited for a response from May. None was offered. Harry sat forward and spoke strongly, "I believe I have a clear understanding of the resumption of... shall we call it 'our life together'?"

"Let's not. We've never had a life together... you would say, since Della was born."

Harry supposed that the mention of London had brought out the severe and perhaps jealous May again.

May continued, "And, as for your gift of tea, thank you, and I'll thank you also not to mention London or anything to do with your time in London in my presence ever again, Harry. Do I make myself clear?" May regarded Harry stonily, "Do I?"

"Perfectly. As you always have, May. And, as I always have, I'll play it my way, which is simply to do it your way when we're together." Harry was angry. And he was tired of being angry at this woman. "And, in the vein of keeping the lines clear, I'll pay for groceries and your rent... as usual. Is there anything we haven't discussed yet about my being in Toronto?"

"I suppose whether or not you're going to go along with the plans. And, if yes, when you would want to move in." May's demeanour was aloof.

"Of course, I'll go along with the plans. And let me just reiterate what I told you in my letter. I am doing this for the family, so Della and Frank and families will have us together in our roles as grandparents. They all live far enough away that they won't be bothered about what our daily routines or feelings are." Harry's voice was firm. And yet there was kindness in his bearing toward his wife. "I foolishly thought, May, that we might, after so many years of missing the mark with each other, enjoy aging together. I came back, May. I came back."

"All right. And I agree," May was disarmed by Harry's quiet intensity. "We're home base, so to speak. They can even visit together here. There's so much unused space in this house. Would you move in soon?" Was there a hint of wistfulness in that question?

"I've paid for my new digs until the end of the month. I think I should stay there until then. It would be a little tight financially to pay for two places for me and one for you... with the cost of the ship back from... or, back home."

"I hope Ada will be fine with that." May seemed thoughtful, genuinely wondering about her sister's response.

"She is. I checked with her, of course. It's more about her and my finances, and I felt it was only fair."

"Of course," May stood, "would you like to see your apartment? I mean, I'm not sure what you want. And I don't want to force you. I..."

Harry was touched by her uneasiness. She seemed almost confused. And that was an odd state for May. "I'll wait until I move in. But thank you for your work in settling this for me, May." He touched her arm gently and waited for a moment. "Now – how about that cup of tea?"

"To be honest, I'm suddenly quite tired now. I don't know why. We'll have tea together when you move in... if not before."

"I understand. I think we've both found this reconnection stressful." Harry picked up his bag from the floor, "Again, May, I am so sorry for what I've put you through. I am... truly. Perhaps over the next while, before I move in, we could talk more about... about the past year? I hope you'll find it in your heart to be able to do so." He reached into his bag and pulled out a beautifully wrapped gift box. He offered it to May, "Your tea and another gift for you."

May, becoming mildly agitated, stepped back and clasped her hands together. "I'd prefer not to, Harry. I really do not want anything from England. Send it to Lois, why don't you?"

"All right. But I'll leave Ada's gift here, on the table." Although he could see that her distress was not anger, Harry felt defeated. "I'll see myself out. Good-night, May." Harry mustered a smile and turned toward the stairs. And then he stopped. He put down his bag, walked over to May and embraced her. May was thunderstruck. "I am not going to force anything, May." Harry was as surprised at his behavior as May was. "In fact, neither of us should in this tough stage of re-adjustment; but I want you to know I am back for good. I will not leave you again, May." He felt her physical resistance melt and kissed the top of her head.

As Harry gathered his bag and walked down the stairs, he realized he was quite sad. His vision was blurry. *What have I done? Never hurt another person's soul, Harry, my little Harry. Consider the children, Harry. We're all children, my love, my Harry. All children.*

"Harry!" He stopped and looked up from the middle of the stairs. May was dabbing her tears with a hanky. "Good-night, Harry. It's good we were able to settle all this. I feel fine about it. I hope you do."

"I do, May. And we'll talk more." Feeling more optimistic, Harry turned and went briskly down the stairs, collected his coat and hat and stepped out into the lilac-laden air. *Every single choice I have made in life has led me to this place. And this place is final. And perhaps it will be bearable.* He breathed deeply and walked up to Dupont.

May continued to lean against the door she had just closed. Her body shuddered with her deep suppressed sobs. "Dear God, how could all this happen? Why?" She expected no resolution to what was unanswerable. She had done so well with less and less of Harry over the years… the children making it easy, as they grew up, to have a clean separation. And now this? Why could Harry not have stayed in London? It was so much easier having a clear reason… justification… for life in Toronto.

May walked to the sofa and sat down. Her grief consumed her once again. Why had Harry been affectionate? She wiped her eyes and cleared her throat. And then it dawned on her. How dare he? How dare he treat her with affection?

May picked up the phone and dialed. "Hello, Ada. Harry's just left. Why not come up for a cup of tea? There's a little gift from him here for you."

42. Tea and apple pie

And when this we rightly know
Thro' the World we safely go.
Joy & Woe are woven fine,
A Clothing for the Soul divine;
Under every grief & pine
Runs a joy with silken twine.
        [William Blake]

Harry turned his hot plate off and sat down to a breakfast of an egg, sausage and toast and a lengthy read of the Daily Star. The Arab-Israeli War was certainly the most alarming topic. How could a country be born one day and go to war the next? Ah, well... it was all about the diaspora and the lost tribes, anyway, and certainly a significant marker in history. Harry finished his tepid tea and took his dishes to the sink. Ten o'clock – enough time to wash the dishes and put things away. And then shave and call on May at eleven. His mind wandered. He was nicely settled in and the apartment was comfortable... but so small. And sometimes the walk up to the third floor was almost too much. But the worst was the loneliness – the utter loneliness. Here he was in a small, but certainly adequate, apartment, in the thriving centre of a huge city – and he was lonely, lonely in the second month of his return. *Ah, Annie, I miss our chats, your presence, our enjoyment of each other.* Harry rinsed the sink and went *to the bathroom* to shave. Then, hat and tinted glasses in his hand, he walked down to the second floor and knocked sharply on May's door. Why was it always locked when she knew he was coming?

May opened the door, stepped out and turned quickly to lock the door behind her. "You look lovely, May. Is that a new dress?" Harry was intent on initiating a positive mood and maintaining it. Always utilitarian, May was, nevertheless a striking woman. Her brown dress had three-quarter length sleeves with short white stripes in the linen and a tiny, white ruffle running alongside the dark brown buttons in the bodice. The belt matched, as did her small hat. Her look was finished off with white gloves and purse and brown, sturdy pumps.

"Yes, I actually bought the outfit because you were coming home. I knew I would get a lot of use out of it. Where would you like to go for lunch, Harry?" May, while still terse, nevertheless seemed prepared to be more leisurely than was her usual style.

"I thought we might take the streetcar up to St. Clair and try Fran's Restaurant. What do you think?" Harry had thought that this would be a good choice for May. And he needed to branch out further than he had to date.

"Yes – let's go there. I've been before." She took Harry's arm.

Seeing the continuing ease in May's attitude, Harry was grateful that he had suggested this outing. *Such a curious couple we are,* he thought as they left to catch the streetcar, *mismatched with a familiar discomfort... and that's us at the best of times.*

Dinner had moved along quite easily with discussion focused on May's friends in Toronto, her church and her sister-in-law's quilting. And now the waitress had returned, wondering about dessert. "Well, the banquet burgers were certainly delicious. What about dessert, May? What would you like?"

"I'll have apple pie and tea, please. Harry, have some yourself – Fran is famous for her apple pie."

"Well, if you recommend it... make that order double then," Harry smiled at the pretty young woman waiting on them. "And, there's no rush." In saying this, Harry hoped to underscore for May that this was indeed an outing and not an excuse to tally up how they were or were not doing together, in particular, how he might be perceived as missing the mark. If there were any possibility of that happening, Harry wanted to thwart it before it arose.

"You said there were a few things you wanted to discuss, May. Have at it, then," Harry grinned impishly. He was now secure in having shaped a light and reasonable atmosphere for chatting about May's agenda items.

"Oh yes, just a minute," May turned to open her purse. She retrieved a piece of paper and put it on the table. "I've made a list." She fastidiously smoothed out the paper.

Harry's heart sank at the return of this old pattern. May and her notes... nails set aside for the elements of detachment and order and then driven into the wall of separation.

May looked down at her list. "Let's see," she looked over at Harry. "You're all right about this, aren't you, Harry? You look bothered." May was genuinely surprised at the change in Harry's expression. "I'm only trying to keep our communication clear."

Was she being sarcastic or merely oblivious to his needs... indeed, to him. "Yes, May, I'm accustomed to your notes."

Impervious to meanings behind words, May looked down at her list. "Let's see. Three major categories: Our seeing each other. Frank and Della. Being social. I do want to be sure we're as clear as we always were, Harry, before you left me."

And there it was. May's anger couched in four little words. Harry made no attempt to hide any expression of vexation on his face. He took a deep breath. "The first category, then – our seeing each other. Do you mean like this?"

May looked uncomfortable. "No... no, I don't mean planned times like this," she looked at her list once again, as though to consult it for her reasons. She looked up at Harry, "No, what I mean, Harry, is spending time together every day. I find it rather much. Don't you?"

The stifling presence of control and rejection began to infuse the air. Why had he bothered to try to engage her as two aging adults who would want the best for their duration together? "I hadn't thought, May. It has been comfy for me, and I suppose I assumed it was for you, too. Why is it uncomfortable for you? If you're not happy cooking all the suppers, I'm more than happy to share. You know that." *He and Annie enjoyed cooking together.*

The waitress served the tea and apple pie. As they prepared their tea, May looked at her note again and then at Harry, "No, it's not the cooking, Harry. I'd have to do that, regardless. It's… it's actually that I find we're together too often. This current arrangement is more time than we've ever had together. I find it a little… a little…"

Harry waited briefly. "The amount of time we spend in each other's company? You find it…?" Harry wanted to move the discussion along and get home. *Home? Where was that?*

"Yes… I find it a little… somewhat… overwhelming. I'm just very used to being on my own. And I like that way."

"All right," Harry was succinct, "what would suit you, May? Far be it from me to cause you any further grief. I'll go along with whatever you wish."

"Good," May's smile looked for all the world like self-satisfaction to Harry. "I think if we had supper together Monday and Thursday and one weekend day every week. Wha…"

Harry interrupted her, "Fine. That's one category down. What's next? Frank and Della, isn't it?"

"Now, now, Harry, don't get testy. I haven't seen that part of you for quite a while," May's laugh was somehow condescending. "Well, this one is very straightforward. I just wanted to clarify, given that you were in London, that our roles will remain the same with our children and grandchildren. This isn't new. Just a clarification."

"I imagine the clarification is simply a reiterative prompt, so to speak, of the fact that you see Della as yours and Frank as mine."

"My goodness, Harry, you don't have to be rude!" May was offended. "That is merely the way life turned out for the best in our family." She suddenly looked stern, and Harry could see that her pragmatism and authority were fast closing ranks against him.

Leave it be, Gov. "That's fine," Harry did not care to recall how the male and female camps had been formed so early in their family life. "And now on to your final category. Social. What do you mean by this?" Harry wanted no more of his pie. It didn't digest well with anger.

May folded her note and slipped it into her purse. "Social. Yes. I wanted to point this out before there's a problem. Do you remember last week you and Norman went out to a lecture? I would prefer that you cultivate your own social circle and keep my brother within the larger family circle. The same applies to the people Ada and I invite in for Canasta." She reached across table to put her hand over Harry's, "I'm sure you understand."

Harry recoiled. "Yes, I understand. Indeed."

"Good," May seemed quite satisfied. "It makes it so much easier. For everyone. Did you enjoy the pie?" May took her lipstick from her purse to freshen up her lips.

"Crikey, May, I'm shocked! I would have thought that, at our age, there wouldn't be so much necessity for control, so many lines drawn in the sand. It's all very sad," Harry crumpled his napkin and placed it firmly on the table, "and galling. The one good thing is that there is full clarity now. I shall abide by these edicts."

"Well then, Harry," May stood up, pulled her gloves on with great attention to the straightness of each finger seam, and picked up her purse. "This wasn't meant to make you angry or sad. It's just that it had to be explained before more time passed. I've got some shopping to do, so I'll see you for supper tomorrow."

Before she could further dismiss him, Harry stood. "May, I'm going to say this only once. And may it suffice for the rest of our lives. Remember this moment." Harry's English voice was firm and deliberate. "I did not leave you, May. You left me. You wanted me to live with Frank and Lois while you made up your mind about moving to Toronto. Although, I had the sense you had made up your mind about Toronto before you asked me to move out. I did not leave you, May. You left me."

May turned on her heel and left, her footsteps resonating off the tile floor.

The waitress had hurried to the table, "Oh sir, I'm so sorry. I didn't know you were ready to leave. I'll do the bill quickly and…"

Harry sat. "No, I think I'll have more tea, please. I'm in no rush… no rush at all."

He closed his eyes – *Make for thyself a bed on high – And I will sing a lullaby. All here; all there; all low; all high – And I will sing a lullaby… Harry… Harry…* "Sir… sir."

Harry felt a hand on his shoulder and looked up.

"Sir, I've brought your tea. But are you all right?"

"Yes, yes, I'm fine. Just very tired. I must have drifted off. Thank you."

"Good, sir." She began to leave when Harry touched her arm.

"I'm very sorry if I alarmed you."

"Better safe than sorry, sir." She smiled so warmly that Harry felt *touched by… by… yes… by love… how odd!* He would definitely come to Fran's Restaurant once a week for dinner. "I don't feel so alone here now," he whispered to himself, "if only…"

Harry arrived home at almost three o'clock. The house was quiet as usual – it was a true serenity created by Ada. He walked to the mock Jacobean desk – so beautifully cared for… "I'm leaving this to Frank, Harry," Ada had told him. Harry checked for the mail. How fitting – there was a letter to May from Della and a letter to him from Frank! Harry took his letter and climbed to the third floor.

Breathless, Harry took his jacket off and placed it carefully over the back of a chair. Loosening his tie and undoing the top buttons of his shirt, he looked at Frank's handwriting. Just what he needed. Harry took a deep breath and sank into the sofa. Hoping for affirmation that there would be a visit this summer, Harry scanned the letter. There it was!

We're all very much looking forward to seeing you during our holiday east this summer. We'll arrive at Union Station August 2 and will then take the train to Welland. We'll visit Lois's family until the 14th at which time, Gordon says, he'll drive us directly to Spadina to save us the confusion of Union. We'll return home from Toronto on August 19th to ensure my return to my office on August 23. Would you let Mother and Aunt Ada know, please, that our estimated times are now actual?

Dad, I do want to have a good block of time with you!

Love from your

Chip off the Old Block!

Harry lay down on the sofa, placed the open letter over his heart and fell asleep.

43. Rise to any occasion

Every Tear from Every Eye
Becomes a Babe in Eternity.
This is caught by Females bright
And return'd to its own delight.
The Bleat, the Bark, Bellow & Roar
Are Waves that Beat on Heaven's Shore.
        [William Blake]

SCENE SIX – August 1949, 176 Spadina Road, Toronto

Nell comes skipping into the kitchen from the dining room of Auntie Ada's house in Toronto. It's a large, well-equipped, immaculate Edwardian kitchen in a white and sea-green theme. Nell is wearing a red dress and has two white bows in her hair. Fred Bowman, who had been the chauffeur of the previous owner, is in the kitchen tidying up. Fred is a tall, dapper, sixty-five year old, casually but well-dressed, even first thing in the morning. As usual, he wears a bow tie, black pants and a white shirt, and his shoes gleam. He has white hair, cropped in a brush cut. He is his usual extroverted, loquacious self.

FRED *(happy to see Nell)*: Nell! How are you this morning! Have you had breakfast?

NELL *(smiling and secure in this man's presence)*: Yes, Mr. Bowman, thank you. Mummy made us some oatmeal and toast in our room. She says it's fun using that little stove!

FRED: It's called a hotplate, sweetheart. All of our suites come with enough equipment for our guests to make easy meals. But you know how much our guests love to have evening dinner together when Ada and I cook.

NELL: Oh, yes! I thought that man was so funny last night! Daddy and

Mummy did, too. *(She makes a face, with her eyes crossed.)*

FRED: Mr. Carbury... yes, funny. But he is a bit extreme at times. Well, Ada and I thought that this was the best way to use the house – having guests. It earns us enough money for food and to pay the taxes. We live simply. Now then - how about a little drink of chocolate milk? Sit down at the table. *(He goes to the fridge for the milk and then to a cupboard to get a fancy glass. He then moves to the table to pour the chocolate milk, setting the bottle on the table by Nell's glass.)*

NELL *(sitting down at the table and pulling her skirt out neatly to the sides of the chair; she feels quite grown up)*: Mr. Bowman, have you lived here for a long time?

FRED *(sits down across the table from Nell)*: Oh yes, sweetheart, I was the chauffeur here for many years. That's why I still do some chauffeuring for people in the area when their chauffeurs are away. I'm the best chauffeur around! Yes, yes, a long time. I love Toronto! Do you?

NELL: Oh, I really, really love Toronto. It's so... it's so... it's not like Regina at all! Last night, when I couldn't sleep because it was so hot, Daddy took me downstairs and outside. Nobody could hear us on that red carpet. We could see Casa Loma outside! It was so, so beautiful, and all the lights showed up in the dark. I'd love to live in a castle like that when I get older – but not as old as you.

FRED *(laughing heartily)*: Well, if you do, then I'll live long enough and old enough to be your chauffeur!

NELL: Mr. Bowman, you said that one day you would show me that staircase. *(She points beyond Fred to the second staircase that goes upstairs from the kitchen.)* That secret staircase.

FRED *(turns around to look at the stairs)*: I did, didn't I? Well, let's show it to you today, then. It was called the servants' staircase, and it goes to an apartment for Ada and me. We have our own rooms. That keeps the rest of the house for our guests.

NELL: Grandpa and Grandma Westley are guests, aren't they? They live here, don't they? *(Fred nods.)* Why do they live on different floors? Why does Grandpa live all the way up on the top floor - and Grandma Westley, why does she live on the middle floor?

FRED *(ill-at-ease)*: Well, sweetheart, that's for your mother and father to explain to you.

NELL *(somewhat crestfallen, looks down)*: I wish they lived on the same floor. Grandpa is sad, I think. Except when he's with me! Grandma might be sad, too, but she talks more and does more things with people.

FRED *(stands and reaches over to pat Nell on the head)*: Here now - they're adults. They've made some decisions, and this must be best for them. Don't feel sad for big people. Big people are around to take care of you! And you're here for a vacation! Do you want to watch me shave again? And then I can take you with me for my first drive today. We'll climb the secret staircase when we get back. Let me wipe your moustache off, first. *(He picks up a tea towel from the rack and wipes the chocolate milk off Nell's face.)*

NELL *(brightly, as she tilts her head back so Fred can do his job)*: Oh yes, Mr. Bowman! I love driving in your big shiny black car! We don't have our own car in Regina; but Daddy says he'd like to get one. I'd like him to get one like yours. Mickie has one. Back in Regina. She's my only friend who has a car. Her Mum said she had to get one after Mr. Olson died so that she could find a job. But I like your car better.

The task over, Fred leaves the towel on the counter, and he and Nell head for the door, Nell tagging along after Fred and chattering: I like the way you talk, Mr. Bowman. Your New York talk. Would you take me to New York, too? Are you going to sharpen your razor on that big black strap? May I have some soap again, too, please? How long…?

FADE TO BLACK while the chattering becomes distant and disappears. All the while, Fred has been whistling "Zip-A-Dee-Doo-Dah."

END OF SCENE

Frank slipped his jacket on, looked in the mirror and turned to Lois. "Do you like this tie with the jacket?"

"I do. And it doesn't look too dressed-up. It's just right for your little outing with Dad," Lois slipped a millefiori necklace over her head. "Now for some lipstick." Lois was quite striking in her light blue dress with red accents. "Your mother and I are going to leave shortly. What about you and Dad?"

We'll leave soon, too. You know that nice little tea house we noticed the other day? I hope you weren't planning to go there. Were you?"

"Heaven's no!" Lois laughed. "Can you imagine your mother and I not shopping for some new clothes?"

"And stopping for ice cream," Frank chuckled. "I want to talk to Dad about joining a group or a choir. He needs somewhere to use his talents… to be free. It's tough seeing him so left out here."

"Have you ever thought of taking your mother out for tea sometime? I wonder if she expects you to do that sometime."

"Absolutely not!" Frank was unequivocal. "We've never spent conversational time together since the sleigh ride incident. Neither of us would have a clue what to say to the other. There's far too much that's never been said for far too long."

"I just thought I'd check. So, good – I'm glad you're going to talk to Dad about getting involved in some different activities! He needs that. I hope you can convince him. He seems sad. But he and Fred seem closer now that Tom's gone." Lois put her gloves on and examined herself in the mirror.

Satisfied, she gave Frank a peck on the cheek and left.

Frank looked in the mirror. Sure enough – there was the red mark left on his cheek. He pulled his extra hanky from his pocket, wiped the kiss away and walked up to his father's apartment. As he was about to knock, the door opened. And there was Harry, ready to go out. "I heard you coming, son."

The eagerness to go out together was evident in Harry's whole demeanor. While it might have made Frank happy, it broke his heart. It was so evident his Dad was lonely. *Do you miss Annie, Dad? Did we all pull you back here for our own reasons when your place was with her in London? I'm sorry, dear Dad.* "Dad, I…."

"Yes, Frank?"

"I… Lois and I found a new little tea shop, not all that far from here. I thought you might like it there. It's at Dundas and Ossington… the Lakeview. We can walk or take the streetcar."

"Let's go then, son… and I'd like to walk… stepping out like we used to do when you were young!"

Frank smiled. He felt very proud of his Dad… "You can rise to any occasion, can't you, Dad?"… *with such grace and forgiveness.*

As father and son headed south, Frank stopped, perturbed. He looked back. "What is it, Frankie?"

"Strange," Frank was actually talking to himself. "All right, Dad, let's move along. I had the strangest feeling that a woman was right behind us… almost on our heels."

As they had done many times before, the men enjoyed roast beef sandwiches and tea. "This place rather reminds me of a place Annie and I always enjoyed in London… The Blind Beggar. It's not in such a rough area as Whitechapel, though."

"Do you miss, Annie, Dad?" Frank spoke gently.

Harry looked down, "I do, Frank, I do." He looked up at his son and smiled, "But not as much as I did in the years before I saw her again." His eyes glistened. "I'm grateful for that London reconnection... I am." He sipped his tea. "And I'm deeply grateful to be back as a father and grandfather. This really is a gift from Annie. She loved me enough to know what was critically important for my soul." Harry's eyes twinkled, "Although I would prefer that Mabel and I were back in Regina."

Frank laughed, "How we would all love that, Dad! And it wouldn't be any greater distance for Della and her family. Have you ever asked Mother about returning?"

"Just once. She says she will never leave her family and friends here in Toronto. And I understand that."

"Hmmm... so do I," Frank topped up their teacups.

"Frank, you're so like Annie really... the way I can talk to you... the way you make me think... hah... even the way your pour your tea. Did I tell you Annie followed your life through our letters?"

"No! Why would she be interested in me?" Frank stirred his tea aimlessly.

"Because you are part of me, Frank. By the way, I'm sure your tea is well-stirred now! And because your name was the name we wanted for our first child."

Frank was shocked. "Well, I suppose there are many things you kept to yourself through the years. I just don't know why she didn't try to fully explain things to you, Dad. Why did she fall off the map for so long?"

"Star-crossed lovers, you know, Frank," Harry winked. "Now to something even more important. You mentioned earlier you thought there had been a woman behind us."

"I did. It was quite unsettling. I knew there was someone behind us and I had the strong sense it was a woman. But when I looked back, I'd been wrong. It was mildly disconcerting; that's all. And then I felt silly for having thought so."

"Sometimes that's more intuition than silliness," Harry spoke quietly. "Sometimes we need to look past the here and now."

"I'm not sure I know what you mean, Dad."

"Just before my mother died, she said to me, 'I'll always be at your side, Harry.' I've had many experiences of that promise, so perhaps you've had a sense of your grandmother, son."

"Perhaps," Frank mused. He pushed his chair back, "I'll square up for our lunch and let's walk back."

As the two men headed east toward Spadina, Frank asked, "How did she die, Dad?"

"Well, the doctor wrote down 'phthisis' – the 'white plague' that killed so many... killed everyone else... except for Charlie and me. But I overheard, as young as I was... I learned she had actually received a terrible knife wound to her neck. She was a beautiful, loving woman, Frank. I'm glad you've met her."

Father and son were lost in their own thoughts for the rest of the walk. Frank had never thought of himself as having an English grandmother, a Sarah... a Sarahmother who was still loved by his Dad. A special mother who was killed... murdered... Who? Why?

At three o'clock the next morning, Frank sat bolt upright in bed. "Lois," he nudged her shoulder until she woke.

"What is it, Frank?"

"Did you hear that woman crying and asking for her babies?"

"No, Frank. For heaven's sake, you've had a dream, that's all. Go back to sleep." She turned her back to Frank and fell asleep.

Frank couldn't shake the dream. He got up to look out the window… perhaps he would see the distraught woman or hear her again. But it was utterly quiet, and all he could see was an opaque pool of creamy light at the corner of Dupont.

44. Shades and sizes of angels

I walk to school on an old buffalo trail. Sometimes I find Indian arrowheads on the trail. It goes through the Government Grounds. Mummy says I'm never supposed to take candy from the old men who live in the big government building there, even though a lot of them fought in the war for us. "You just never know," she says. My Daddy explained to me that both Regina and Saskatchewan are very young and before any settlers came, Regina was called "Pile of Bones." This is because the Cree hunters killed the buffalo for food and to make their teepees and clothing. So, all that was left was the pile of bones – a huge pile! This was actually very holy to them, Daddy said, because they believed the herds would return. They wouldn't return to stay, just to visit. The name "Pile of Bones" comes from the Cree language, where it is "Oskana-Ka-asateki." My Daddy knows an Indian Chief named Chief Abel Watech, another chief and a Cree princess. When I go downtown with Daddy on some Saturdays, we see them and we always talk. They wear their own Cree clothing and head-dresses. They are very kind to me. I love finding the arrowheads and I have a nice collection from my walks to school and in the Qu'Appelle Valley. My Mummy's father was a minister in Regina and he would go to the Qu'Appelle Valley to meet with the Cree people there. He had a very long name – George Frederick Charles Welsman. So people called him Charles. He died before I was born. I have a picture of him shaking hands with chiefs on horses. Everyone says I look like him, which is fine; but sometimes I wish people would say I look like my Daddy – without a moustache!

[from Nell's Grade 4 'Why I Like Local History,' a Benson School project, November, 1951]

SCENE TWELVE—December 21, 1952

Nell, nine years old, and her father, forty-one, are in the kitchen of their Regina home. The east window looks out to the Giles' house. Nell is at the

232

big wood stove, against the east wall, stirring candy syrup. After all, it's Sunday, and this is her ritual on a late winter afternoon. She is wearing a white apron over a tartan skirt and green sweater. Frank, in a brown vest and trousers, with the sleeves of his white shirt rolled up, is sitting at the kitchen table beside the east window, working on some kind of writing, pen in hand. If you move closer, you'll see that he is copying out the music and words to a part of Stainer's "Crucifixion" on a piece of manuscript.

NELL *(holding the spoon up and letting some syrup drop into a glass of cold water)*: No, it won't be ready for a while. *(She returns to her stirring.)* Why are you staring at that music, Daddy, and tapping out the time? I'd rather just hear you sing.

FRANK *(slipping his pen into his vest pocket)*: Well, on Christmas Day, the choir is singing the chorus "And suddenly there was with the angel" and Mr. Moore wants me to sing the opening recit, the opening line, instead of a soprano. Then the choir comes in with the chorus. So I was singing it in my head and making sure my tempo was right. *(He looks down at the music and sings.)* "And suddenly there was with the angel, a multitude of the heavenly host, praising God and saying."

NELL *(stirring)*: What's heavenly host?

FRANK: A whole flock of angels.

NELL *(giggles)*: You're silly – angels aren't birds! Do you believe in angels? The other day, Gail laughed at me when I said I did. She said that I probably still believe in Santa, too.

FRANK *(clasping his hands behind his head and leaning back in the wooden chair and tipping it onto its back legs)*: Well, first of all, Santa and angels are quite different! Secondly, one must have some kind of faith. And, finally, one probably has to have an experience. And, I suppose, firstly, if you'll pardon the jump to the essential, there must be openness. A receptiveness. I'm not saying one has to believe; I'm saying one has to be open to believing.

NELL: Like you did at the train station in Toronto?

FRANK: Precisely. You'll learn all along in life that the world is full of sceptics – people who try to make fun of what you believe. So, you need to figure out carefully what you believe in and stay strong. And, of course, always be willing to learn. You see, Gail judged you and in doing so, closed herself off from entertaining the miraculous.

NELL: Hmmm… entertaining? Did you see that angel at the train station?

FRANK: I think I did. I think he was the man who was walking away from us.

NELL *(picking up her glass of water, still stirring)*: But that was a man! Angels have wings and fly and have robes!

FRANK *(letting his chair rest on its four legs)*: Ah, but I believe angels can come in any shape necessary. I learned that from my father. We certainly needed a strong person to pick my mother up from that stampede. And he disappeared more quickly than really was possible.

NELL *(dropping another string of syrup into the water)*: Oh good! About 2 more minutes! I'm going to try beating it myself this time; but it's so hard. *(Returns to her stirring.)* I might have to get Mum to help me. Did Grandpa talk to you about angels? What did he say?

FRANK: Well, he believed that his mother was an angel because he had visits from her in dreams and talked to her a number of times after she died. He said she was still sad about her babies. He was only six when she died; but he always seemed so attached to her. And then, even though for a long time he questioned if there were a God, he became very certain about God.

NELL *(stirring more forcefully now, her face flushed and matching the glow of the stovepipe, pushes a stray curl up off her forehead with the back of her left hand)*: And he wrote out your songs from school. And some of them were about God.

FRANK *(moving to stand beside Nell)*: Let me know if you want me to help... You know, now that I think of it, Dad came to believe that being spared was God's plan for his life. He always wondered why he was spared from death as a child, when so many weren't, and why he was spared from the Great Flu Epidemic, when so many weren't.

NELL *(puffing from stirring so hard)*: Ooh, that's a big thing to figure out. I'm glad Grandpa was spared. I still wish he lived with us. But Grandpa made sure you knew about good things like God and ... *(looking over to the table)* and... music, didn't he? Daddy, did you take music lessons when you were growing up? I hate my lessons. Miss Mont isn't very nice to me.

FRANK *(sitting down again by his music)*: Well, I told you I'll talk to her whenever you want. *(Somewhat wistfully...)* No, except for a brief time when we rented a piano in Swift Current, I didn't take lessons; but Della did. I learned to play by ear... just the way I heard things.

NELL *(taking the pot off the stove, putting it on a cutting board at opposite end of the table from her father and beginning to beat the mixture)*: Why didn't Grandpa and Grandma let you take piano lessons?

FRANK *(running his fingers through his thick black hair)*: I'm sure they had a good reason, and I'm sure it was about spending the money on the child with the gift. Perhaps they felt I wasn't as gifted as Della. Anyway... that's why my father kept that song book for me and taught me tonic solfa. *(Looking out the window...)* He knew how much I loved music. He'd say, 'Come into my parlour, Frankie' - that meant his lap - 'and sing me your newest songs and we'll record them'... *(Looking back at Nell and smiling...)* You're having a hard time with the candy now, aren't you? Do you want me to try beating it?

NELL *(nodding enthusiastically, places the pot flat on the board)*: Yes, please! You have to tilt the pot toward you, just a bit and stir very, very hard. *(Frank follows the orders.)* But why didn't they let you take lessons if they let Auntie Della?

Lois comes into the kitchen through the dining room door. She has her Sunday jewellery on - large matching earrings, necklace and brooch - and a crimson dress with navy trim at the neck and navy, three-quarter length cuffs. As always, her lipstick is fresh. Her navy high heeled shoes are well-polished. She has carried her knitting with her from the living room. She places it on the kitchen counter and puts a floral yellow apron on.

LOIS *(cheerfully)*: I heard you talking. Here, let me do that, Frank; it takes a special knack at this stage. *(She sets in to the beating of the candy with a snapping motion, born of musical strength and culinary expertise.)* Your grandfather did teach your Dad enough music so that he could read it and play the piano by ear. And your Dad bought a clarinet when he was a teenager and learned to play it… very well. I helped him with it.

NELL: But you never played the clarinet!

LOIS *(slightly breathless from beating the candy)*: Nell, bring me the pan, and you can scoop candy into it. *(Looking at the pan…)* Good! - you've buttered it well. All right, you get the candy out while I hold the pan. *(The process begins.)* It didn't matter that I didn't play the clarinet. Once you're a music teacher, you can help with many instruments.

FRANK *(standing up, dipping his finger into the candy and licking it off)*: I've finished my memorizing, so I'd say I'm done with work for the day! And it looks as though you have. *(He kisses Nell on the forehead.)* Yes, Nelly, we all miss your grandfather. *(Frank walks out of the room, humming "and suddenly, there was with the Lord…")*

LOIS *(smoothing the candy in the pan)*: Nell, all we have to do is score the candy and then you can put it on the back porch table to cool off. Mugsie will be home from Annabelle's around 4:00. Give Mr. Carlson a piece when he comes to the door. And then we can all have a little treat!

END OF SCENE. Spotlight on Nell, licking candy from the wooden spoon.

FADE TO BLACK.

45. The final chorus

He who mocks the Infant's Faith
Shall be mock'd in Age & Death.
He who shall teach the Child to Doubt
The rotting Grave shall ne'er get out.
He who respects the Infant's faith
Triumph's over Hell & Death.
            [William Blake]

Much to Harry's surprise, May was waiting for him as he descended the stairs. "You look lovely, May. Is that a new dress?" They lingered to chat outside her door.

May smiled, "It is. I bought it last week just for tonight. I love Ada's Christmas parties," she primped slightly for Harry as she smoothed the green taffeta of the waist and skirt. "I thought the red design in the green of the bodice was a nice touch for Christmas. You'll enjoy the party, Harry."

"All right, I shall." *Why did those words feel like a command? It wasn't May's fault. No, it was his because his mind had been with Annie for the past few hours. Heavens, all he needed was to set his mind to enjoy himself. Maybe he should have bought that Peale book that came out this year. All right – think positively!*

Harry gestured to the stairs. "Shall we go down? It sounds happy downstairs."

And happy it was. Ada... Fred... Susie – everything had been prepared by them from the Christmas decorations, appetizers and mulled cider to the scent of ham and creamed onions. And, best of all, over near the piano, there it was - the table May had talked about. She'd been allowed to contribute to this part of the meal – the table of treats. May had explained Ada's tradition "the Eve of Christmas Eve" dessert – shortbread by May, fudge by Ada, and minced meat pie by Fred. Now Harry was convinced he could forget his earlier feelings.

"Harry, you haven't had any dessert at all. Are you all right?" Ada and Harry sat beside each other, near the piano.

"Perhaps I'll take some to my room after the carol sing. I'm very tempted, Ada; but I ate too much at dinner, I think. Indigestion, you know."

Ada laughed. "I do know!" She patted Harry on the shoulder. "Well, it's time to sing." She got up, sat at the piano and began playing a cheery "White Christmas." At the embellished end of the song, Ada improvised her way into "We Three Kings" and called out for everyone to join in.

"Now it's your turn, Harry," Ada beamed at him, hoping to give him the courage to say yes.

Harry stood and bowed to Ada. He turned to address the group of friends, "My so-called repertoire is small when it comes to Christmas. And don't forget I play by ear."

"Let's start with 'Hark the Herald Angels'," May called out, "I always liked hearing you play that."

"Most certainly, then, May," Harry played, beautifully for a self-taught pianist, and people began to join in.

After two more carols, Harry stood and smiled. "Now I must tip my hat to old traditions. I must say that it would be ever so much fun if Frank and Dora were here to recite 'If Santa Claus should stumble when he climbs the chimney tall, There's always ice up on it - I'm afraid he'd have a fall.' Do you remember how they loved reciting that poem, May?"

May beamed, "'Dear me, what sorrow that would bring to all the girls and boys!' I do, Harry. We had fun."

"Indeed." Harry was deeply touched that, for a moment, all four of them had, in a sense, been together. "Now, Ada, it's your turn again."

During the next few carols, Harry's mind drifted again… Annie, Frank, Dora… Regina, Toronto, London… Mummy, Bertie, Ernest, Arthur, Dad… he seemed to see or feel their faces floating by… and the babies… *save the babies, Harry, oh please don't let them die, save my babies, save… the weight of it all.* Harry pulled himself back to the present moment and joined in the final chorus of "Joy to the World." But the moment was gone for him. All that was left were the ghosts of Christmases past. And indigestion. He really must excuse himself.

Harry reached for one of May's shortbread cookies and a Christmas napkin. Turning to the group, he gave a slight bow. "I must say 'good night' now, folks. It's past my bedtime," he smiled weakly. "Enjoy the rest of the evening. I've had a lovely time. And I shall be going off with a treat!" He held the cookie up to make his point.

"Are you all right, Harry?"

"I am, Fred, thank you. Just a little squiffy, you know. Good night all."

As everyone said good night to him, Harry left the party, happy to be thinking of the comfort of his own room and the prospect of sleep.

46. Halvah and Mandarins

Little Lamb who made thee
Dost thou know who made thee

Little Lamb I'll tell thee,
Little Lamb I'll tell thee!
He is called by thy name,
For he calls himself a Lamb:
He is meek & he is mild,
He became a little child:
I a child & thou a lamb,
We are called by his name.
Little Lamb God bless thee.
Little Lamb God bless thee.

[William Blake]

"Put away your game and come to the table, girls," Lois called into the dining room from the kitchen.

"Aw, I want to keep playing," six year old Margaret complained. "Please!"

"Could we just finish this part of the game so that Margaret can learn more about subtraction? She has to try to get past that ladder so she doesn't lose points." Nell felt quite pleased with herself for thinking of a good excuse to keep the game going.

Lois wasn't as impressed as Nell had hoped. "No, I want you both at the table now. You've had a nice, lazy morning, and it's already ten o'clock. I've made a special Christmas Eve breakfast."

Frank folded his newspaper and stood up, "Leave the card table as is and the game will stay as you've left it. Waiting for you." Frank took Margaret's hand, "Come on, let's see what your mother has prepared."

Father and daughters sat at their places at the table, watching Lois reveal their traditional Christmas Eve treats.

"Ah, crumpets. And Welsh rarebit." Frank rubbed his hands together. "My mouth is watering!"

"And look!" It was Nell's turn to be gleeful, "A whole big plate of figs and mandarin oranges. I hope Santa's going to put a mandarin orange in my stocking tonight!"

"Has he ever forgotten?" Lois laughed, "Don't worry, Mugsie, he won't leave one for you. He'll remember you don't like them."

Margaret's eyes brightened, "I love those cinnamon buns you baked. And that's the cheese I like, too! Could I have a bun now, please?"

"I know how you feel, Mugsie, but grace first. Shall we?" Frank bowed his head, "For what we are about to receive, dear Lord, we are truly thankful. And we are especially thankful at this time of year when we celebrate your human birth. Amen." Frank paused briefly. "Now – dig in!"

Little Margaret belted out, "Sturly thankful!" because it always made Mummy and Daddy laugh for some reason.

There was a great clattering of plates and silverware to the accompaniment of the happy noises of the small family. As the momentum slowed down, Nell asked, "Mummy, do you have that special dessert... that... funny name. Oh, I love it! You know, you slice it. Are we having it?"

The other three laughed. "Nell, you can remember," Frank encouraged her.

"Sure you can, Nell. Think hard!" Margaret was Nell's biggest fan.

"It starts with 'h' and it ends with..."

"'H'!" Nell interrupted her Daddy. "Halvah! Are we having some? Are we?"

"I'll get it now." Lois stacked the plates and took them to the kitchen. And, like magic (because she had prepared the plates ahead of time), she returned with Halvah for everyone!

"Oh, there's the 'phone! I'll get it – it's probably someone from the church about tomorrow's solo," Frank went into the hall to take the call, while Lois and the girls carried on with the exotic (for Regina) dessert.

"My goodness, your Daddy is taking a long time on the phone. Frank!" Lois left the table and went into the hall. "Frank!"

And there he was, sitting on the chair under the phone, his head between his hands. He looked up and put his finger to his lips, "Shh... come and let's sit on the steps. I have something to tell you."

Alarmed, Lois whispered, "Who called, Frank? What's the matter?"

Frank put his hand over hers to steady her. "It was Mother," he took a deep breath and held Lois's hand strongly. "Dad... Dad died a few hours ago." He broke down.

Lois stroked his back, "Oh, Frank, you've lost your most special friend in the world." And she, too, cried, "And I've lost my second father. Whatever happened?"

Frank pulled his hanky from his pocket, wiped Lois's tears away, and then his. "Mother wondered why he hadn't gone down for breakfast, so she eventually went up to his room and knocked. When there was no answer, she thought he must have been asleep. In another hour, both she and Ada were concerned, so Mother went upstairs again. She tried the door, and it was open, so she walked in. And there Dad on the floor. She called to Ada to phone the operator for an ambulance." Frank stood up and began pacing the hallway, "My goodness, what are we going to tell the girls? Nell and Mugsie," Frank called, "come here for a moment, please."

The noise in the dining room ended abruptly. "Coming, Daddy." The giggling sisters came through the living room into the hall. Both girls stopped and became silent when they looked at their parents. "What's the matter, Daddy?" Nell was alarmed.

"How would you two like to return to your game while Mummy and I do the dishes. We need to talk over some Christmas plans. And then, when we've made some decisions, we'll tell you about them. How would that be? There's nothing for you to worry about."

"Okay, Daddy!" Nell whispered to Mugsie, as they went back to their game, "I bet they're planning another secret for us, and that's why they looked so surprised!"

Frank and Lois went into the dining room to clear the last of the food and take it to the kitchen. "You wash and I'll dry." The ritual began to be soothing as the backdrop to his racing mind. "My head is starting to clear, although I still can't believe it," Frank picked up another cup to dry. "This is how I see it. Pack. Take the next train to Toronto. Explain things to the kiddies. What am I forgetting?"

"Nothing really; but do your packing after you've phoned for your ticket," Lois took the tea towel out of Frank's hands. "Go on, dear, make your call and put your clothes out on the bed. Doing the dishes will take my mind off things."

Within an hour, Frank was back in the kitchen. "It's done. The train leaves at 7:35 tonight. I called Mother to let her know, and she said Della will book for the same train and get on at Vermilion Lake. And I've laid out my clothes and toiletries on the bed. Oh, and I found the luggage I need. It's a good thing I'm used to travelling. I'm trying to think of it all as business. Otherwise, I'd be overcome by wanting desperately to be in two places at once."

"It's all right, Frank. The girls and I will do well. I promise."

"I've phoned Mac and Ian and asked them to let people know. That will cover business and music. Mrs. Giles and Trudy know to check in on you.

And Car knows. Oh… and the Gileses want you and the girls to have Christmas dinner with them." Frank took a big breath, "Phew!"

"Oh, thank you, Frank! I was trying hard not to get panicky; but I've never had to do Christmas alone. I was getting so worried that I'd be edgy the whole time." Lois looked much relieved. "Let's sit at the table and relax a bit. Do you want some tea?"

"Yes, tea would go well now. Here," Frank stood. "I'll put the dishes away while you make the tea. In fact, why don't we include the girls in the tea? That would be the best way to explain the turn their Christmas is about to take."

"Frank," Lois pondered, "did your mother say how Dad died? I hate to think about him all alone in his room, needing help."

"She said the doctor was certain it was a heart attack. He also felt Dad wouldn't have been in pain for much time at all. How in the world would he know that? Mother said they'd had a lovely evening last night of carol singing and Christmas treats and that Dad seemed especially happy. He even played the piano for a few of the carols."

"Well, that's a lovely memory for us to have." Lois looked at Frank. He suddenly seemed so far away. "Isn't it? What's the matter, Frank?"

"Lois, Mother also said Dad excused himself early from the festivities, saying he was slightly tired and thanking everyone for the evening. What if… what if Dad actually died last night? What if he was alone for that long?"

"Frank, we can't let that thought take hold in our minds!"

"I know, but I couldn't help it from crossing my mind, Lois," Frank felt oddly impatient. And then he felt a strong anxiety – the companion of loss. "And, you're right – Dad knew London wasn't his last destination." Frank's irritation disappeared, "Now, come and we'll tell the girls. I think they'll be happy that you and they can drive me to the train station."

Frank had never missed his father so profoundly. What would he do without the compass of his life?

47. Purification

Dear Daddy,

I hope you are feeling well. I like my watch very much. I like the walkie talkie too. Mummy has to call me to keep me from reading the Book of Treasures when company is here. Margaret is always sleeping with her teddy bear. Margaret and I sleep on the chesterfield. We are lonesome for you. We went to church yesterday morning and on the way home we picked up three orders of fish & chips. I hope you come home soon. We put on a program for Mummy and will put it on for you when you come home.

I love you,
Ellyn

December 27, 1952

May was flanked by Della and Frank. She stood unflinchingly, a handkerchief in her hand. Ada and Fred stood beside Frank. Other family members filled in the first two rows of the chapel. "Blessed Assurance" droned to its end and everyone sat down.

The minister, gowned in black and genial in affect, delivered a warm welcome and prayed for Harry's... and everyone's... souls. Uncle Norman then went to the pulpit to read the twenty-third psalm.

"And now," the Reverend Simpson announced, "Harry's son, Frank, will sing a favourite hymn of Mr. Westley's, 'And did those feet in ancient times?' And accompanying Mr. Westley's son will be his daughter, Della."

Frank's voice soared, it seemed to England's shores, with Harry's yearning for England to be one of the lost tribes of Israel. And, though they hadn't been a duo for years, the brother and sister seemed as though they made beautiful music together on a regular basis. It wasn't until he sat down that Frank felt almost overcome with emotion. He looked over at Della to see that she, too, had tears... so much music, Dad. You kept records of everything we learned...

"We are gathered here in this quiet morning hour to honour the memory of Harry Westley who passed away very suddenly on December 24 at his home here in Toronto in his 71st year," the Reverend spoke quietly to the sixty or so people who had come out in this Christmas holiday season. "Mr. Westley was born in London, England, and came to Canada early in this century. He married his life companion in 1910 and two children blessed this union: his daughter, Della, and his son, Frank. The family home was established in Regina across many years, where Mr. Westley was employed in the auditing office of the Government. He retired six years ago."

Frank's mind wandered... it was all so neat and tidy... all so barebones... if only a smidgeon of his Dad's beautiful truth could be told... if anyone really knew...

"Mr. Westley was keenly interested in music and literature and much of his spare time in life was devoted to the pursuit of these avocations. He was a church chorister for many years, and an ardent student of British Israelism, and a collector of poetry and philosophic writings."

... a philosopher himself and a fine musician... say that!... say that he understood everything in tonic solfa with the mind of Bach and tell how he could quote Bertrand Russell for hours if you wanted him to...

"We are here especially as friends that our very presence and the message of this time might comfort those who were nearest and dearest to him – Mrs. Westley, their daughter and their son, both of whom have made long journeys in haste to be present today." A rustle of affirmation moved toward the family. "I never stand in the presence of this mystery of this closing of life and say, 'There is no death.' For it is the common experience of all mankind – the young and the aged, the rich and the poor, the prepared and the unprepared…

… and what was my father, then – to you, Mr. Simpson? Young or aged? Rich or poor? Prepared or unprepared? And what do you mean when you say prepared… or unprepared?

It makes humanity one under God, for no matter to what continent or clime the experience comes, it leaves grief, bitterness and pain. But it also opens the door to a new revelation of God's love. For there is purification in suffering. There is healing for the open wounds. There is comfort for the broken hearts. There is hope in despair. There discipline in sorrow. There is God in the midst.

… Purification in suffering… do you hear that Dad? Do you? Purification? Suffering revealing God's love in a new way? What do you say, Dad? Dad? Frank felt an inexplicable anger take hold in his chest. He took a deep breath and considered compassion.

"This breath of life has returned to the Giver," the reverend droned generically on. "But it continues to breathe through influence in the lives of those to whom it brought love and an appreciation of God. Its passing opens the door for God's Holy Spirit of comfort and power to rebuild if we yield our lives anew to Him."

… oh why didn't you just leave it at Dad's breath being with God and yet living in us? … why take the focus off Dad – just like everyone did for his whole life – and tell people to 'yield our live anew to Him'? … why?

"Frank… Frank," Ada whispered and nudged Frank's shoulder, "it's time for the last hymn." She handed him his hymn book opened to the hymn.

"Thank you, Aunt Ada." Frank acquiesced to the dreary, "Fast falls the eventide…"

The minister spread his arms, ready to pronounce a benediction. "The family invites you to visit and enjoy light refreshments in the guest room downstairs." He bent his head, "The grace of the Lord Jesus Christ and the love of God and the fellowship of the Holy Spirit be with you all. Amen."

As the family stood to leave the chapel first, Frank took his mother's arm. "Are you all right, mother?"

"Yes, yes. Of course, but keep me steady, Frank. I don't really relish meeting with people this way."

"Nor do I. But Della and I will help get you through this."

"You're good children. You know, the strangest thing happened when you sang 'And did those feet in ancient time?' I felt there was a woman with an English accent – not unlike Harry's – singing. But no one there was English."

"That's all right Mother,' Frank smiled. "It was Sarah."

Before May had time to question her son, cousins and nieces and nephews and friends came to offer comfort, talk about memories, sip on tea and coffee, and eat watercress and ham sandwiches.

48. The Bible

The Child's Toys & the Old Man's Reasons
Are the Fruits of the Two seasons.
The Questioner, who sits so sly,
Shall never know how to Reply.
He who replies to words of Doubt
Doth put the Light of Knowledge out.
[William Blake]

Back at Spadina Road, a small gathering of immediate family relaxed in Ada's comfortable living room and ate from luncheon plates of tired leftover sandwiches and dainty desserts. Conversation burbled in soft continuity. Some had taken their shoes off. The deep red upholstery and burgundy woodwork provided a warm comfort.

The theme, if anyone were truly honest, was one of attempts to come to terms with who Harry was. If anyone were even more honest, there was an underlying unease with a sub-theme of "Who was I to Harry?"

"Did he ever go to a doctor, May?" "Did he ever complain of pain?" "Was he happy?" The answer was always, "No."

Frank and Della shared a few childhood anecdotes, Frank's being funny and Della's being sweet. But, of course, no one had known Harry, if he were to be known, until they moved briefly to Toronto when Frank was a teenager. A brother of Ada and May's laughed, "Perhaps we scared him off and that's why you moved back to Regina, May!"

"Mother, did anything you saw give you concerns about Dad's health? Or did he say anything about it?" Della seemed so sad.

Going back to the central theme response, May answered, "No. He had his heartburn problems more often. But, of course, we were all," she looked at

Ada and Fred and smiled, "used to that problem." She looked at Frank, "And he always used Lois's concoction for it. He would have done anything she recommended."

In a habitual gesture, Frank sat quietly for a moment - head down, eyes closed, thumb resting on his cheek and fingers placed between his eyebrows. He looked up and spoke quietly to his mother. "What I noticed, more than anything, when we were here last summer, was his lack of energy, his inability to exert himself. It wasn't a mood. He was almost incapable of walking up those stairs," Frank looked out into the hall. He clapped his hands on his knees and stood up quickly, needing to close the topic quickly. It raised too many feelings and this was not his singular grief. Or was it? "And what could have been done, anyway? Well, folks, I'll say good night and good-bye for now. I must climb those stairs myself." Frank shook hands with the men and planted kisses on the cheeks of the women. "I have a room to clean and a suitcase to pack, and 'miles to go before I sleep.' I'll see you early tomorrow morning, Della." He turned from the door, gave an exaggerated bow and shone his handsome smile on the group.

"Good night and good-bye, Frankie," they all called out to him in a dishevelled sort of antiphonal response.

Frank smiled at the curious group of relatives he had just left. He loved them all.

As he reached the second floor, he looked at the narrow, steep staircase to the third floor. "It's hard enough for me. I see now how hard it was for you, Dad." As he climbed that last staircase, he was suddenly consumed with an anguish he hadn't felt before, far deeper and much older than he could identify. He succumbed to weeping as he entered his Dad's room, the room he had shared on visits and the room that had become his for this ashes to ashes, dust to dust visit. He took his hankie from his pocket, wiped his eyes and scanned the room. Ah, yes, the wardrobe. That was all that was left to clean out for Mother.

Frank opened the wardrobe door and was reminded how easy it had been to store his own clothes with his father's. *"Remember that all worlds draw to an end,"* Frankie, *"and that noble death is a treasure which no one is too poor to buy."* It was his Dad's voice. Where in the world had that thought come from? Ah, yes, from the new C. S. Lewis book he had been able to get for Nell - the wardrobe had reminded him! Just the thought of reading more with Nell encouraged Frank. He laid the suits on the bed. Of course, they were all in perfectly acceptable shape for the "donations box". The ties and shirts could go there, too. As Frank folded the last shirt, he was compelled to hold it up to his face. *Yes, that was the fragrance, 'whence is that goodly fragrance', the fragrance of comfort, of Dad.* Another wave… tidal… of grief. Frank moved the shirt, a tie he remembered as his Dad's favourite and a Harris tweed jacket to his own suitcase. His mother had insisted both he and Della should take whatever they wanted of their father's. Della had taken her favourite books, sheet music, a watch and some ties and handkerchiefs for Mark. Frank had forgotten until now. He collapsed onto the bed, enervated and yet somehow consoled that the sorting of Salvation Army and trash was complete in this room. Perhaps…

Perhaps this is the way in which souls are released… fully released… unfettered… free from time and pain… "find it, Frankie, find it." Find what? 'Narnia! It's all in the wardrobe just like I told you!' More Lewis! The wardrobe? The wardrobe? Is that Dad's voice?

Frank glanced over at the wardrobe. *Find it…* Was that a shelf he'd missed at the side above the hangers? *And then he saw it. At the top of the wardrobe. There was something there.* Frank went to the wardrobe. Yes! There was something on the shelf… a huge book, fine brown embossed leather, decorative metal hinges, the spine looking somewhat sad. There it was as Dad had said…

Harry had written a letter in the fall. *There's a very important Bible I want you to have, Frank. It's yours. I want you to see the truth – to be a carrier and guardian of my family's truth. It's all in the Westley family Bible – the London Bible. It was beside my mother when she died. It was the richest, in the richest sense of the word, belonging we had. I hope it lasts forever in our family somehow. I hope each generation discovers it. It was with Annie all these years. She was going to bring it when she was to come over for our marriage. And she had kept it so carefully through the years. I want you, as the elder child, to have the Bible.*

Had he known his health was so fragile?

Frank lifted the Bible carefully from the shelf and placed it on the bedside table. *It all seems to fit ... the box for clothing Dad said they had - and now the boxes I have here, the picture of Jesus he always kept on the table, now the big Bible gleaming under the light. Yes, it was all the same. Frank felt a sense of fear, almost like a little boy would feel. Oh Dad, I understand... I'm beginning to.*

What was that? Frank noticed an envelope peeping out from midway in the Bible. He opened the exquisite clasps with great care and opened the Bible to where the envelope was. The Bible opened at the family history. There it was – all the names, the birth dates, the marriage dates, the death dates. Some notations were in his father's perfect penmanship.

That's so typical of Dad... leaving a marker in the place he wanted me to see before anything else. Frank picked up the envelope to replace it. *There's something in it. Oh, and it says, 'For Frank' on the front.* He opened the envelope.

My dear son,

You will be reading this because I've disappeared from this world... something some people accused me always of trying to do!

Please know that there is nothing I have loved in this world more than my family.

And Annie. This "news" about me will be a shock to her because I had not told her I wasn't feeling well. Would you please call her as soon as possible to let her know of my death. She, as I told you, loved you like a son. You were her Frankie. That's why I know, as hard as it will be for you, you must be the one to tell her. She has family and friends in Leigh-on-Sea, where she moved after I left her. Her telephone number is in my diary, which I know you, being a diarist of sort, too, will have kept.

My love will always surround you, son.

Your Dad.

Frank organized the boxes neatly for his mother, closed the wardrobe to his own Narnia, and finished his packing. Before he closed his suitcase, he fetched his Dad's diary from a pocket and put it on the bedside table. Frank sat on the bed and threw himself on the pillows. He was so tired. And yet he felt somehow very content.

Frank woke at six o'clock the next morning. He was shocked. He hadn't changed into his pyjamas. And he hadn't ruffled the bed or himself much. It had been such a deep, restorative sleep. He'd even had a brief, lovely dream of meeting Aslan – big and glorious, his mane flowing, his eyes so kind and voice deep and resonant. Very God-like, really. But, my goodness, he needed to freshen up and get ready for the trip home.

Something nagged at him... something he mustn't forget. He turned the bedside light on. Ah... he must phone Annie for his Dad. Oh dear...

Frank sat on the bed and picked the receiver. He talked to the Operator, giving her Annie's phone number. He took a deep breath. The Operator came on the line, "The number for your party is ringing now, sir."

"Thank you," the phone in Leigh-on-Sea rang. And Frank's heart began to speed up.

"Yes, hello, am I speaking to Annie? … No, Annie - may I call you Annie? … no, it's not Harry, it's Frank… Yes, Annie, your Frank… Annie… Annie… it's all right… well, no, it's not all right from our point of view, Annie. Harry died… but you've sensed that already, haven't you, Annie. When? On Christmas Eve… I'm so sorry, Annie; I know how much you loved him, how much you loved each other…" Frank broke down. He needed a moment to control himself… "No, Annie, he didn't suffer. It was a heart attack… Annie… no, I won't give up the telephone. I'll stay with you as long as you want. I'm so sorry, Annie… Just sit for a moment. I won't leave you until you're ready, Annie…"

About the Author

Ellyn Peirson packed up her prairie childhood and moved to Ontario at eighteen. Her career moved from child welfare to a private counselling practice. While Ellyn enjoys designing websites, she is passionate about writing and photography. She perceives writing as the energetic combination of attention, eccentricity, music, perception and solitude. For her, writing is physical and metaphysical. Ellyn is a creativia.org author. Her first novel was *Antonia of Venice*, a historical novel about Anna Giraud and Antonio Vivaldi and *cancerwords*, a collection of poetry emanating from her warfare as a mother in her son's battle with a rare cancer. She has also edited her son's writings, which are published in the book *I am Keats as you are* by Glenn Peirson. Along with Andrew Ruhl, Ellyn has published *After the Interlude: a Dialogue about Death and Beyond*. She has also had a short story published in *The Danforth Review*, a poem published in *Jones Av* and another poem published for *The Red Priest*, an English early music group.

Made in United States
North Haven, CT
01 May 2022

18755471R00157